Kingdom of Monsters
Sister Worlds Book 3

TIFFANY NICOLE TERRY

DEDICATION

Whether you are born sisters, or choose them later in life, there is no stronger and no more difficult of a relationship.

We are not meant to be the same. We are not meant to agree. Being a sister means being fiercely loyal to a woman that you support, even if you disagree, even if you fight, and even if you could not be more different.

She is the mirror that shows you the truth of who you are and of who you could be.

This book is dedicated to my sister, Whitney. We are equal parts opposite and the same. But I owe my life to the fierce nature of her love, her support of my dreams, and her belief in who I am and who I will be.

Her love is the kind of love that only a sister is capable of giving. I love you and thank you, sissa.

CONTENTS

ACKNOWLEDGMENTS

Thanks to my little girls for their patience.

There were many nights, after I finished a long day of corporate work, where they asked me to not write so I could spend time with them.

It is never easy to love more than one thing, but I will always love them the most. I hope I do enough to prove that to them.

GLOSSARY AND MAPS

Places	Pronunciation	Description
Naldash	Nahl-dash	The planet where the story takes place
Denlerack	Den-ler-ahk	The sister planet, thought to be dead, that can be seen from Naldash.
Belarone	Bel-la-rohn	One of the three kingdoms. Surrounded by mountains and forests.
Extelli	Ex-tell-ee	One of the three kingdoms. On the cliffs over the coastline.
Lisodanya	Lis-oh-day-nyuh	One of the three kingdoms. In the plains, lots of farmland.
Erion	Err-ee-on	Village in Belarone Kingdom.

People	Pronunciation	Description
KaLeah Trapper	Kuh-lee-uh	Brown-haired girl from Erion village.
Clegg Trapper	Kleg	KaLeah's father.
Princess Amirra	Ah-meer-rah	Blonde-haired princess, daughter of King Erazus.
Prince Bylex	By-lex	Son of King Erazus.
Prince Nikolat	Nik-o-lot	Son of King Erazus

King Erazus	Err-ay-zuss	Belarone King
King Mikroth	Mik-roth	Lisodanyan King
King Sarzoe	Sahr-zoh	Extellan King
General Zoseff Array	Zoh-sef Ay-ray	A general of the Belarone army.
General Hilip Daven	Hil-lip Day-ven	A general of the Belarone army.
Elektra Dean	Ee-lek-trə	Black-haired rebel from Sarda
Colt	Kolt	Rebel leader
Keldon Keldon	Dayn Kel-don	Dictator of Denlerack and KaLeah's biological father
Ash	Ash	Brown-haired orphan child
Huntra	Hun-trə	KaLeah's mother
Lina	Lee-nə	Rebel twin
Lainie	Lay-nee	Rebel twin
Rustin	Rus-tin	Rebel
Alister	Al-is-tewr	Rebel
Von	Von	Rebel
Zuri	Zewr-ee	Rebel
Felisha	Fə-lee-shə	Rebel

Animals	Pronunciation	Description
Dirlin	Durr-lin	Dear-like.
Draggot	Dra-guht	Horse-like, covered in scales and fur, main, talons and hooves.
Doquer	Doh-kər	Wolf-like.
Juliebee	Joo-lee-bee	Bird-like, scales and

		feathers. Long talons.
Wuvat	Woo-vat	Cow-like but has dragon scales.

Dragons	Pronunciation	Description
Klackire	Klak-ire	Mythical dragon.
Anissa La Alani	An-ih-sah Lah Ah-lah-an-ee	Mythical dragon's real name.
Nala	Nah-lah	Race of flying dragons, extinct.
Dynack	Dy-nak	Race of land dragons, extinct.

Extelli Kingdom
ruled by King Sarzoe

Orion Village
Belarone Kindom
ruled by King Erazus
Lisodanya Kingdom
ruled by King Mikroth

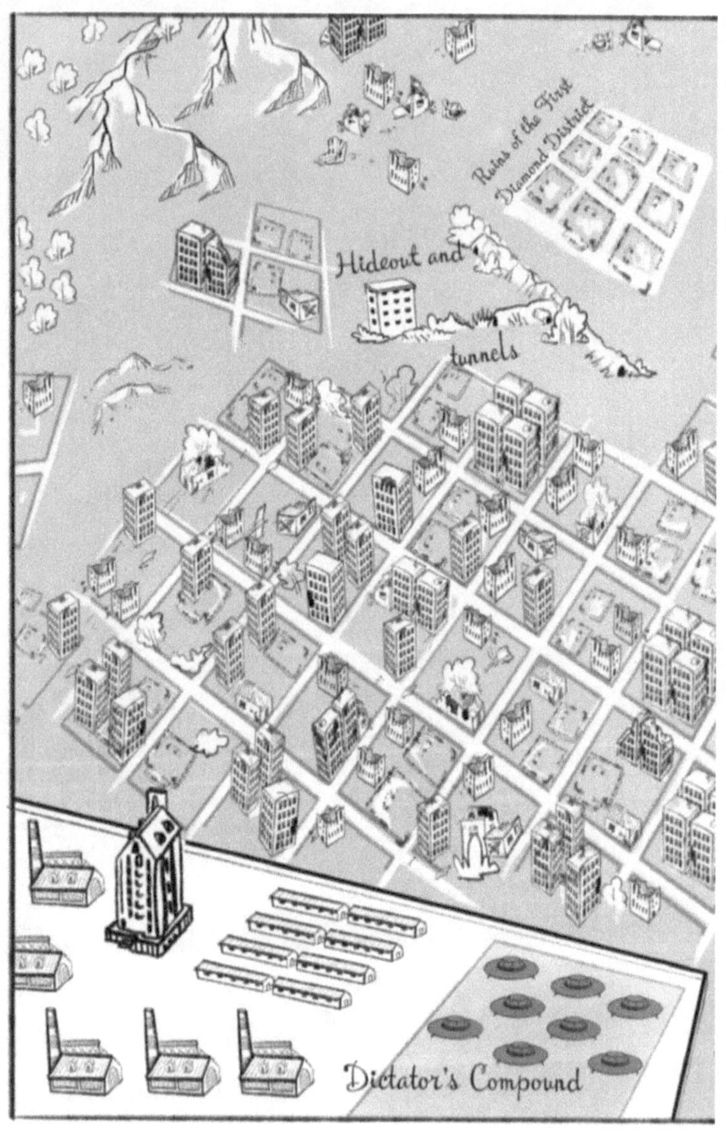
Ruins of the First Diamond District
Hideout and tunnels
Dictator's Compound

Prof. Wheelwright
Morbel Diamond District
Sarda
The Mud Lands

PROLOGUE: ANISSA LA ALANI

Her mother flew so fast into the cave, that she skidded as she tried to stop, her massive black wings spread out wide, her scales shimmering violet in the faint moonlight.

Baby Ash, I am so sorry, she said, telepathically pushing the thoughts into Ash's mind. *They have found us.*

Ash's translucent white wings, a stark contrast to her mother's, slumped heavily down her back. The young dragon shrunk away from the cave entrance in fear.

Can we fly away? Ash asked, sending a small, squeaky growl out through the cave.

You won't be able to fly fast enough, said her mother.

Ash's wings were larger than the land dragons but smaller than the cliff dragons. She could fly, but nowhere near as fast as others like her mother.

The enormous dragon stepped closer to her baby and Ash saw bloody claw marks in her scales.

You are hurt, mother, Ash said.

Ash, baby, I am going to fly away and leave you here to hide. If you fly with me, they will surely catch you. But maybe if they see me fly away, they will chase me thinking that you are with me. Once they follow me away, you must try to find another cave to hide in. Lightly cover your wings in mud and travel by night. A moonless or cloudy night would be safest. Your wings are too easily seen in the darkness.

No other dragon had wings like Ash's. The cliff dragons were born with translucent wings, but they all darkened to a violet, sapphire, or midnight black coloring within their first year. Ash's had never changed. But it wasn't just the wings that were the problem. Her scales were emerald, matching those of the land dragons.

The land and sky dragons were mortal enemies, and Ash could easily be mistaken for either. In the wrong setting, that could mean death.

She realized that her mother was saying goodbye and her throat clenched tight, suddenly too dry to swallow.

They had been on the run and hiding for her entire short life of a few years. She couldn't play with other dragons, and she'd not been allowed any freedom to test her wings for great distances.

Ash was different and her existence was forbidden. Her mother had tried to explain why. There was a fear, a superstition among the dragons, that if the two species were to breed, a new species would grow up stronger than both.

You were either a Nala or a Dynack. You either flew and lived in the treetops and in cliffside caves, or you burrowed beneath the dirt and hunted in the tall grasslands.

Whenever the two species met, they battled to the death.

But when her mother met her father, they didn't battle. They had fallen in love and produced a forbidden offspring: Anissa La Alani.

Her mother called her Ash both as a nickname, and a way to keep her real name secret, in case she did manage to survive past her youth.

Her mother nuzzled her nose against Ash's cheeks, and Ash closed her eyes, feeling the wet, warm tears falling from her mother's eyes onto her emerald-green scales.

I do not want to leave you, but I must, my love, she said. *Stay hidden in the shadows of the cave until you hear nothing, then sneak out and find a new place to hide. Keep your wings and your scales hidden. Otherwise, they will all know you are different.*

Her mother stepped back, and the cold cave air washed over her.

Mother?

I love you, sweet Anissa La Alani.

The dragon bounded out of the cave, her footfalls causing rocks to crumble down from the walls. She spread her black wings open and flew out of the cave entrance.

Ash heard roars carrying across the wind outside.

There were hoots and guttural signals coordinating an attack.

Ash did as her mother said and stepped as deeply into the cave as possible. She was much smaller than any of the dragons hunting her, so they would have difficulty checking the narrow tunnels.

Ash tried to breath as quietly as possible, straining to hear her mother's voice in her head.

Instead, she heard multiple thuds as dragons landed in the cave.

We've gotten your mother, young one!

A deep voice entered her mind and a growl carried throughout the cave, sounding as if it were right next to her. She closed her eyes tight and pressed herself into the wall, blocking her own thoughts from the intruders.

Where is that little abomination?

It has to be in here. This is where she flew off from and it wasn't with her.

Maybe she hid it somewhere else and came here to distract us.

She isn't that clever.

Don't you want to see your mother one last time before she dies?

What kind of a child are you to leave your mother to die on her own? Don't you love her?

Rumbles and snarls seemed to come from all directions. Most were deeply male, but one seemed to be female. They were scouring the cave and she listened to each heavy step.

They shuffled, scratched, moved boulders and bones, and each sound sent a new shiver down Ash's spine.

They will not find me, she thought to herself. *I am tucked beside the rock. I feel the rock. I smell the rock. I am the rock. They cannot find me because I smell like the rock. I look like the rock. I do not breathe. I am no longer a dragon. I am a part of this cave, and the cave is a part of me. We are the same.*

A dragon came close. It was the female one. She was smaller than the others and able to stick her head into the entrance of the small crevice Ash was hiding in.

The dragon sniffed deeply, looking intensely around and in her direction.

But Ash could no longer see her own paws or talons. She couldn't bend her neck and she realized that she had actually become stone.

The female dragon pulled her head back from the nook and kept searching other areas of the cave. No one else came to explore that area.

Finally, she heard them leave. She tried to pivot her eyes around.

Did I really turn to stone?

She tried to move but couldn't. She couldn't even wiggle a talon.

My leg is free of the stone. I am no longer a rock. I am a dragon.

As she thought it, she saw the flesh return and her green scales upon her leg as she stretched it outwards.

My other leg is free of the stone. My arms are free of the stone.

Again, she watched as she moved. The stone that covered her transformed back into her emerald-green scales before her eyes.

How can this be? Are all dragons magical? Why didn't my mother tell me this?

She had heard the word "abomination" and recalled how her mother had said the two species feared a combination of the two… they feared her.

Is this why? What am I? Can the others do this?

࣪ৎ⚬৩

Days later, hunger drove Ash out of the cave. She had

spent those days turning herself into all manner of things: a tree, the wall of the cave, a bush, and many creatures. Her heart hoped that her mother would fly into the cave and be impressed with this newfound gift.

Ash imagined herself talking to her mother, showing her how easily she could think of a thing and then become it, no matter if the thing was a pebble or a bolder. Her mother would be so proud, blowing puffs of smoke in celebration. Ash could disguise herself and they could go out hunting together.

Her stomach growled, bringing her back to the cold reality of the empty cave.

If I had only discovered this magic sooner, then she wouldn't have had to hide me from the world. I could have saved my mother.

Deep in her chest was an aching pain that moved tears out of her eyes.

My mother is dead. She isn't coming back.

Ash curled up into a ball on a nest of dried grass and cried, trying to inhale the last remnants of her mother's smells so as to remember her forever.

She cried through the loss of her mother's touch, her voice, her lessons, and gentle encouragement. Ash let the crippling guilt ripple through her as she bellowed into the darkness.

She doesn't know how long she cried, but her hunger eventually overcame her grief enough to motivate her to stand up on her wobbly legs.

I will leave as a juliebee, the small flying creatures with red scales and black wings.

Ash pictured the creature and then saw herself change into one.

I wonder if I eat bugs as a juliebee if I will be full?

Ash hunted the skies for the first time, zipping and diving, clumsily trying to catch small flies until instinct took over and she started to eat.

The green scaled dragon went out into the world in disguise, changing from creature, to tree, to bush, and to stone as she traversed the land. She was able to hunt on the ground, and when she flew, she became a juliebee.

It was exhilarating being out in the sunlight, flying like a normal Nala dragon, or running as a rodent through the grass like a Dynack, completely unseen.

She saw other dragons, but she dared not try to take their likeness. She was afraid they would ask too many questions and wonder why they didn't know her or her family.

Ash knew that she was safer on her own, watching the other dragons from a distance.

Over the years, she watched them feuding. She watched them start wars, battle for days, and kill each other over minor things. It broke her heart.

She wanted to find a way to unite them all. She wished they could see how happy and peaceful she was, as a combination of both species.

One day, she watched as a baby Nala accidentally fell into Dynack grasslands. He was chasing some small creature, giggling happily while his mother called out for him, frantic.

Ash blended in with the cliff she stood on. Blending into her surroundings had become as natural as breathing. She could vanish with a thought.

She watched the mother search and could hear the baby dragon playfully drifting through the grass.

I have to get him out. I can get him out faster than she can. If I find him, I can scoop him up and back to the skies.

She hesitated.

It wasn't just the Dynack dragons who feared her. The Nala's, even this mother looking for her young, would ostracize and perhaps try to kill her.

Her claws dug into the side of the cliff as she held herself back from helping.

She heard the Dynacks running toward him—hunting him in the tall grass. They were upon him quickly. He squealed in pain as they dug in their teeth, tearing him apart, and his mother howled in grief from the sky.

It was too much for Ash. She felt as if her own heart was being ripped from her body, and she heard the memory of her mother's own screams when the dragons had hunted them both that fateful night.

The sky was a beautiful light blue. The temperature was perfect. Puffy white clouds drifted gently on a warm breeze. A bright orb cast peaceful light upon the planet while one species of dragon murdered the child of another.

There was a tingle at the base of Ash's spine that moved up into her head. Sounds of a million spirits filled her mind as they all cried out in a mix of anger and pain.

Separate them all. Protect them from each other.

The words were so simple, so clear, and began a chain of events that she didn't expect.

The ground started shaking. She and other Nala dragons took to the sky, but the Dynacks just ran wild throughout the tall grass as the world shifted around them.

She watched the planet began to split apart. Dragons screamed, flew, dove, and clung to trees as they fell into crevices.

It took her a few moments to realize she had done something. As the planet began to split apart, each planetary half pulled dragons back to it. The side with the cliffs and mountains began pulling in the Nalas, even as they tried to fly away.

The side with the flatlands and grasses, sucked the Dynacks out of their burrows from beneath the cliffs.

Ash floated between the two as the halves drifted further and further apart, reforming back into two spherical wholes. She watched the lands hold onto the dragons as she drifted out into the starry space between them.

They both began their own journeys around the sun, but apart. One planet became two.

What have I done?

ॐ

In the first year of life without her mother, Ash learned she didn't have to eat or drink to stay alive. She had either been born immortal or had become so over the use and expansion of her powers.

After five years, she learned the full limits of those powers. She could become any element and manipulate elements. When she blew red flames, she could set things on fire like regular dragons. But when she breathed out blue flames, she transported rocks, trees, and even animals from one place to another.

To entertain herself during long days, she would zap creatures from one side of Naldash to another. After years of doing that, she decided to try zapping animals clear across to the sister world, Denlerack.

She spent most of her time on Naldash, since it reminded her most of her mother who had loved flying across the mountain ranges. Denlerack was much flatter and reminded her of the baby dragon who was killed in the grasslands.

Of course, splitting the races apart did not save them. She watched the dragons turn on their own, fighting and feuding until they died off completely. That was when fleshy creatures started to show up more and more, walking on two legs and hunting animals with tools.

These humans, as they called themselves, spoke from their mouths and by hiding among them, unseen, she learned their language. She watched them plant and grow food. She watched them hunt. She watched them build homes, fall in love, and have children. She watched them die.

Why am I still here? she wondered, as she drifted among the humans living and dying on the sister worlds.

What is my purpose? Is it my punishment to live forever alone on the worlds that I broke apart? Am I even alive any longer, or am I just a phantom?

Over the years, people found and pieced together dragon skeletons. They painted murals and carved depictions of Ash's ancestors, molding the discoveries into their own origin stories.

The stories bothered Ash.

There were always human warriors rising up to conquer and tame or even kill the dragons. They made themselves out to be smarter and stronger than the fierce creatures, claiming that their own ancestors had ridden dragons into battles. The people had everything wrong, and so she began to push the correct stories into the minds of the artists, wood carvers, and storytellers.

Every once in a while, for good measure, she'd appear before one of them immediately after giving them a story. And then she'd vanish.

People began to fear her and called her Klackire. They begged for her to save them, heal them, or make them rich.

People would pray to the dragon spirits. She heard them asking for help when they were desperate or cursing them when things didn't go their way.

Ash influenced their stories and their prayers, telling them how a great dragon had split the sister worlds to stop the feuding. She would answer some farmer's prayer for rain or transport a lost child back to its home safely. But when they asked to bring back their dead or heal their sick, she knew that was beyond her magic.

They would weep and beg, and her heart would ache for them, but she was powerless to help.

Over the years, she watched the people fight more and more. Great leaders would start wars. Thousands of their own kind would die. It was all very confusing and disheartening for her.

There was a family rising to power on Denlerack who were not only killing their own people, but the entire planet. Ash saw the rivers running dry, the air growing thick with smoke, and the planet's ability to grow food dwindling.

Denlerack had embraced something they called technology. Its people discovered electricity and created many inventions, where Naldashians had not.

Denlerack had enriched its people but starved its landscape.

Is this my fault? she wondered.

Had she divided the worlds in such a way to keep all the good resources for Naldash? Did the people of Denlerack have to create the technology in order to survive in a more challenged land?

She started paying closer attention to a member of the wealthy family who had elevated himself to world leader. She wondered if she could somehow get the planet back on a healthier course.

One night, drifting out among the stars, she saw a woman crying at her window from inside the Denlerack dictator's mansion.

The dragon flew closer, straining to see through the window, wanting to hear the reason for the woman's cries.

The woman had long, wavy brown hair with a red tint in the dim light of her room. Her belly was big and rounded, carrying a child.

Ash became so engrossed in the woman's sadness that she completely forgot to focus on being as still and clear as the air.

The woman saw her and gasped. "Spirits," she exclaimed.

Ash immediately shot upwards, disappearing into the cloudy night sky.

Days later, something drew her back to that window. She couldn't explain it to herself. Maybe it was loneliness. Maybe it was the sadness in the woman's eyes.

She floated outside the window, and after a few moments, the woman noticed her and walked to the glass. Without hesitation, she unlatched it and swung the window outward.

"Are you really there or am I dreaming?" the woman asked. "Are you Klackire?"

That is what your kind call me. My name is Anissa La Alani. I must know why you are crying.

"I heard your words in my head." The woman touched her forehead, as if the words had drifted in through her skin. "That is magnificent. I hear growls sometimes, but I have never heard specific words before. And I have never seen a dragon spirit."

She looked upon Ash with wonder.

"I am crying because I am a prisoner here," the woman said, placing her hand on her belly. "I cannot escape from the man who is destroying this world. I'm afraid of what kind of person he'll raise my baby to be."

Ash's heart ached. She thought about transporting the woman to freedom through her blue flames, but she had only transported animals. She didn't know what would happen to humans, and she didn't want to try it on the sweet pregnant lady.

"Can you help me? Can you help us?" the woman pleaded.

I can't. Then Ash flew away, leaving the woman at the window. But Ash didn't venture far. She kept hearing the woman's words and seeing her eyes, pleading for help.

The mother and unborn baby reminded her of the mother dragon searching for her baby above the grassland. Ash had done nothing.

Maybe she could do something different this time.

She floated unseen amongst the dictator's soldiers, haunting the compound that secured the mansion.

One evening, she noticed a man peering up at the pregnant woman's window as he walked by on his rounds. Then again, the next night, and the next.

Ash followed him more closely and saw that he gathered supplies and transferred them across the compound. He went into the mansion, and she followed him, watched him go to a door and use a key to unlock the door to the woman's room.

"Clegg, thank you," Ash heard her say.

"Shhh, my lady," the man responded. And then he left as silently as he'd come.

Ash started to form a plan in her mind.

She watched the man, Clegg, and waited for the next time he stopped and looked up at the woman's window. Ash blended into the mansion walls, unseen.

Clegg, she said, pushing the word telepathically into his head.

"Huntra?" he asked, peering up toward her window.

Clegg. Help me escape.

"I can't do that, Huntra. They will kill me." Clegg shook his head.

You must take that chance. Get me out of here. We can fly off in one of those spaceships. Take me to the sister world.

"To Naldash?" He looked toward the field where a few newly built ships were waiting in the darkness. He looked up toward the skies. After a long silence, he finally spoke again.

"Alright," he said. "Be ready tonight."

And then, he headed off with protective determination in his step.

Ash realized she would have to prepare the woman that Clegg had called Huntra.

She drifted up toward the window and peered through the thin glass pane.

Huntra came to the window immediately, as if sensing her presence. She didn't open it this time.

"You came back," the woman said.

You must be ready to escape tonight. Clegg will free you. He will take you far away to safety.

"Thank you, but I have forgotten your name."

Ash thought for a moment. The young woman was beautiful, her features fierce but delicate, and she reminded her of her own mother, trying to protect her baby.

You may call me Ash, as my mother did, she said.

"Thank you, Ash."

Ash bowed her head slightly, and then drifted away, faded, and transformed into smoke.

That night, she watched Clegg enter the mansion. He

unlocked her door and she stepped softly in bare feet behind him, cloaked in a black robe. Once outside, you could barely see her move through the darkness beside him.

Clegg helped her into a spaceship, and they lifted off. Soldiers turned at the noise, but Ash tried to help hide the ship by appearing to be an enormous plume of smoke traveling with it into the sky.

She followed it into the blackness of space and toward the sister world. She watched as it landed much too hard in the middle of a forest and worried, watching nearby, and anxiously waited for them to emerge safely from the strange machine.

Clegg came out first, looked around, and then went back to carefully escort her down the ramp. They walked to the edge of the forest and Clegg immediately began to setup camp.

In the days that followed, he created tools and cut down trees, beginning the process of building a home.

Ash felt proud of her work. She'd helped rescue a woman and her unborn child. She had never felt so happy.

And then the screaming began.

Huntra was giving birth.

She had seen thousands of women give birth, but she knew that it was much safer on Denlerack. They had medicines and technology that didn't exist on Naldash.

There was a village, but it was far from where Clegg had built their house. He knew of the village but would not leave her side to try and find a midwife.

Ash had no magic that could help Huntra in this situation. She cringed every time Huntra's voice cried out in agony. The dragon floated back and forth in front of their home, waiting, and hoping.

The sun rose and Denlerack appeared in the sky, menacing and taunting. The screams continued until after the sun set and then finally, she heard a baby cry.

It was over.

But something was wrong.

Clegg stormed out of the small hut while the baby cried from inside. He had blood up to his biceps, and splatters all over his face, neck, and covering his shirt.

He ran his bloody fingers through his dark hair and then let out a deep, guttural yell to the sky. Then the man dropped to his knees and Ash knew.

Huntra was dead.

Dying during childbirth was common on Naldash. It even sometimes happened on Denlerack where they had better medical care.

But Clegg hadn't known what he was getting into.

Ash shrunk herself down to a furry rodent and crept into the house through the open door. Huntra was lying on a rug on the floor, her head on a pillow. The baby cried beside her, lightly swaddled but still covered in mucus and blood.

This is my fault. I'm so sorry.

She left the house and flew off toward the cliffside caves, where she stayed for years wallowing in her guilt and miserable loneliness.

When she finally descended, she went back to see the young baby, half expecting it to be dead. But there she was in all her fierce glory, looking exactly like her mother, and sword fighting with sticks with Clegg in front of the house he had built years before.

"KaLeah, step in and block like this," Clegg told the young girl.

She tossed her long brown hair back from her face and did as he said, successfully blocking his jab.

"Great. Again."

She realized that the young girl was being raised by a soldier, not a father. She had no mother and never spent time with children her age. She wondered about her ability to help this young KaLeah have a better life as she drifted between the sister worlds.

Visiting Denlerack, it seemed to have gotten much, much worse so very quickly. The air was thick with smoke, the lands had all but completely dried out, and the people fought each other for their survival.

She watched a young girl, about the same age as KaLeah but with dark brown skin and a head full of curls, try to fight off a group of boys determined to steal her boots. The girl drew a gun and stood firm, ready to fire.

A child should not have to live this way, she thought to herself.

She followed the girl back to her home, a warehouse garage at the edge of a dirty village and watched her give her mother scraps of metal she had collected.

"What are we supposed to do with this, Elektra?" the mother asked her child.

"There are so many possibilities, mother," she responded, smiling.

The dragon drifted again, thinking as she floated in space.

What if it isn't too late to help these people? she wondered. *What if I have a purpose here to help them do something great? What if they can make these sister worlds better?*

Ash was back on Naldash, standing on the lawns near the Belarone castle. She watched the blonde princess riding her draggot, looking careless and happy.

Three bandits jumped out from the trees, catching her and her draggot off-guard. They snatched the young girl and pulled her into the forest with them.

Ash felt helpless. She thought about transporting the kidnappers with her flames, but she was afraid she might hit the girl on accident.

Can I do this, mother? Is there some way I can help the princess?

Guttural growls, the voices of her mother and other dragon spirits long gone, filled her mind.

Suddenly, everything made sense and she knew what to do.

She would try to help them save their sister worlds.

She couldn't save the princess. But she knew someone who could.

1 QUEEN AMIRRA

Queen Amirra sat on her throne in a black dress with a silver crown on her head. She was in mourning after the loss of her father and both brothers.

Many of her soldiers had died during the siege of Extelli as well, and were constantly being picked off by Lisodanyan troops, who kept testing the Belarone borders.

Then there was Favor KaLeah, her best friend, who was like a sister to her. She had watched KaLeah be transported to the sister world, Denlerack, in order to help protect Naldash.

Months had passed since KaLeah had left and she hadn't seen the phantom dragon since. She worried that the dragon had burned and killed her friend, just as she had burned her brother, Prince Nikolat.

She didn't know how to do this alone and was afraid that KaLeah would never return home.

The doors to the throne room swung open, and a young man made an announcement.

"General Daven for her majesty, Queen Amirra Belarone," he called out.

She sat up straighter on her father's wooden throne, stretching out her white fingers to grasp the dragon faces carved into the armrests.

The general stalked forward, followed by a handful of soldiers all dressed in crisp white uniforms with the silver dragons encircling red balls of fire on their chests.

It had been a while since she had seen him. He had been in the countryside leading the troops and watching the situation in Extelli.

The sight of him reminded her painfully of KaLeah and the last time they had all stood together. That was the day the dragon had sent KaLeah through the blue flames.

General Daven bowed to the queen, his blond hair falling slightly on his brow. He casually tossed his head back as he rose.

"Your Highness," he started. "You seem to have aged since I saw you last."

"Death does that to a person, I suppose," she stated without emotion.

"Indeed."

"What is it?" she asked. She knew her father had always had a much more proper greeting, but she didn't have the energy to care about decorum.

"Lisodanya has taken Extelli, and troops are on their way to request your surrender," he said, straight to the point.

She rolled her eyes, sighed heavily, and slumped down into her throne.

"Haven't we already done this?" she asked no one in particular. "We are only a few kingdoms. Can't we just be happy with what we have? Why does everyone have to keep trying to conquer everyone else?"

There was silence in the throne room and then the general cleared his throat.

"I suppose it is because they see weakness and feel that they need to show strength or be conquered themselves."

Queen Amirra sat back up fast.

"What weakness?" she asked, narrowing her eyes at him.

Hilip responded quickly, as if he'd already thought at great length about the matter.

"Your father was a fiercely strategic leader, my queen, and your brothers were both groomed to be leaders in his likeness. There are not many kings or generals who wouldn't take the opportunity to conquer a land as rich as ours when there appears to be only a young girl standing in their way."

"But I am a young girl with an entire army," she said, raising her voice in both volume and pitch.

"Of course," Hilip said. "But there is a bit of wisdom that comes from an older king who has seen battles over the years."

"It does not take wisdom to see that men are greedy and just want to take things that do not belong to them. Why can't they just leave us alone?" Amirra felt exhausted by the months of death and doubt.

"Although I agree, we cannot waste time debating the idiocy of men," the general said. "The Lisodanyan army will come, and you will need to guide your own army."

"I don't even know what I'm supposed to do, though. How do I guide them?" Amirra threw up her arms, already feeling defeated.

General Daven stepped closer to her and lowered his voice so nobody behind them in the room could hear. "You first decide if we surrender the kingdom or fight for it," he instructed.

Amirra looked up into his blue eyes. He was a handsome man, and he had shown her a great amount of kindness since her father had been killed. However, she only trusted him because KaLeah trusted him.

The day they had watched the phantom dragon transport KaLeah to Denlerack, she noticed a change in General Hilip Daven. It was as if his heart had broken a little, and the only comfort he found was in making sure Amirra and her kingdom were safe.

Even if he was only loyal to her because of his love for

KaLeah, she didn't care because she loved the woman too. She leaned toward him.

"I will never surrender," Queen Amirra said.

"Good.   One decision down."   Hilip nodded approvingly. "But now, you need to make more."

Queen Amirra flopped back into her throne. The wood was covered in black and brown skins from wuvats the Belarone ranchers bred and raised for food, milk, and pelts. It helped make the wooden chair more comfortable, now that she had to sit upon it so regularly.

She didn't want to be sitting there. She wanted her father here, alive, and making all of the hard decisions for her. She wanted to be out riding draggots across the lawns or trying on new dresses in her expansive dressing room. She wanted to paint pictures, read books, and attend parties.

She wanted to continue being a princess, not a queen.

In the back of her mind, she wondered about what her life would be like if she did surrender to Lisodanya. Would the king take her as his daughter and let her live a comfortable life? He already had daughters and no sons, which was probably why he wanted to pull all three kingdoms under his reign while he was alive.

His actions didn't surprise her. She had met him as a young girl, and he'd seemed like just another friendly old man to her. She imagined him putting one of his daughter's husbands in charge of running Belarone Kingdom. Maybe she could marry a man in the village and live out a normal life as her own father had planned.

This is all KaLeah's fault, she told herself, thinking of her friend. *KaLeah was the one who had encouraged me to stand up and fight for the throne. If she had just kept quiet, I could have given it to Nikolat and gone on to live a much less stressful life as a wife and mother.*

Shivers floated up her spine. She knew even though KaLeah had supported her, Amirra was the one who had decided to take the throne.

Taking over the responsibilities of her kingdom was

frightening. The idea of hearing troops storming the castle made her heart race. But she felt a deep sense of responsibility to protect her home.

She had never liked her father's plan of being married off to a favor and existing only to produce more children to be bred back into the royal family someday. It made her feel like nothing more than a fat wuvat from the fields.

"I am not a wuvat," she said out loud to herself.

"I am sorry, Your Highness?" Captain Daven asked.

"When will their army be here?" she asked him instead of repeating her outburst.

"Our scouts say within a week or two," Hilip answered.

"Are our men ready?"

"Yes, they are coming in from the outlying villages, and we have been gathering supplies. More of the villagers are coming in also, concerned about their homes being burned by the troops moving this way."

"Are there any villages burning?" Amirra asked, feeling protective of the people there.

"No, not yet. It's just something that the Extellans did regularly, so there is the expectation that the Lisodanyan might as well."

"If they want to rule the kingdom, why would they hurt its people?" She couldn't wrap her mind around hurting people in order to control them later.

"To scare you into surrendering, Queen Amirra," he explained.

She took a deep breath. "I am not ready for this," she admitted.

"Please, you mustn't speak like that where others can hear you," Hilip whispered, sounding more like a caring brother than a general. "You cannot let your men hear you sound so unsure."

She leaned in even closer toward him, her hazel green eyes wide and her long silvery-blonde hair cascading over her shoulders.

"Fine, but by the spirits, what am I supposed to do if

they defeat us? What am I supposed to do if they march in here and remove me from my throne and from my home? Will the new king send me off to be some rancher's wife, or will he have me killed and buried beside my father and brother?"

Hilip's face was stern. "I do not know," he said.

She sat back so fast that her crown jostled to the side of her head. Amirra had to catch it and put it back in its place.

"But I assure you, if his men make it inside this castle, it'll only be because they have killed me and my soldiers first."

Queen Amirra blinked her long eyelashes a few times. "That does not actually make me feel any better, general," she said. She looked away from him, trying not to picture blood-drenched white uniforms lying outside the castle doors.

"I know you are not quite ready for war, but war is coming. I will work with General Array, who is on his way back here from Extelli, on a few different strategies. Your father was always heavily involved in the strategic planning of our defenses, but I know that won't come as naturally to you."

"Because I'm a girl?" she asked, jerking her eyes back to his.

"Because you have never been a soldier. You have never had to fight."

"I fought for my life when I was pulled off my draggot and carried through the woods. I fought off an Extellan soldier on the steps of this castle. I can stand on my own."

To emphasize her point, she clambered down from the throne and stood in front of it, her black skirts falling down like a waterfall from the fur-cushioned chair.

Hilip raised his hands slightly, as if she might jump toward him with fingernails extended.

Amirra opened her eyes wider at his protective stance.

"Please, calm down, Your Majesty," he said. "I did not mean that you are not strong and capable."

"Calm down?" She took one large step toward him. "My kingdom is on the verge of being invaded. My father and brothers are dead. One of them would have killed me for the throne. I am only ten-years-old, and you want me to *calm down?*"

"You mustn't let the others hear you speak like this," Hilip warned. There were soldiers standing in and outside of the throne room.

"These are my men," she said. "Why can't I speak as freely around them as I can around you, as I did around my father and brothers? They are men who are loyal to this crown, not to me, anyway."

She pulled the crown from her head and looked at its diamond jewels. One red ruby twinkled from the center, representing the blood and fire of the dragon.

It had been made especially for her, because her mother's crown was still a little too large. She knew that eventually she would grow out of this one and begin to wear her mother's, but she couldn't imagine that future.

She couldn't imagine herself at her mother's age and was afraid of what that might mean. She didn't see herself marrying a man and letting him become king. She didn't see herself leading an army and saving her kingdom.

Of course, she had heard murmurs among nurses and dress maids about the queen being married to 'save their kingdom'. Nobody thought she could manage all of this on her own.

If only KaLeah were here, she thought. Or the dragon.

"Where in dragon's blood is Klackire?"

"That's not her real name," General Daven corrected.

"Right," she said. "Anissa La…"

"Alani," he finished when she faltered.

Queen Amirra stood still for a moment, remembering the sight of the massive beast with green scales and translucent wings.

"Anissa La Alani," she repeated. "We have a great, mythical creature among us, and we still have to worry about invasions? She mustn't be that great if she can't protect us."

"Maybe she doesn't know which of us to protect when we are all her children," he said.

General Daven stood there all handsome and confident, and she knew he had protected her diligently. He was an intelligent man and although her frustrations were running high, she knew she needed to listen to him.

"What do you mean?" she asked with a sigh.

"Well, it is like when two fighters go up against each other in battle," he explained. "If they both ask the same dragon spirit to protect them, then who wins? How could she possibly choose one victor over another?"

Queen Amirra stood there in her crown and dark gown, looking so small in her enormous throne room, with soldiers she had seen but not come to know standing around the edges of the room. They were all there to look out for her, but she didn't trust any of them.

She only trusted General Daven because she had an instinctive hunch that he was in love with KaLeah.

"The dragon saved me instead of my brother, so obviously, the good one should win. The dragon should be here to help me win, but we haven't seen her or KaLeah in months."

Amirra's anger began growing with her frustration and fear. She was angry with Anissa La Alani.

"The dragon killed my brother and stood beside me, saving KaLeah in the process. I am supposed to be here, on this throne, in this castle, ruling this kingdom."

She wanted to believe the dragon spirits were on her side. She needed to believe that it was her destiny to save her kingdom, her planet, and herself.

But fear and anxiety called her hopes to the battlefield of her heart.

A fire in her cheeks burned down to her neck and her chest grew so hot she wanted to rip off the sleeves to cool off. She could see the soldiers in the back of the room whispering, looking at each other as if she had completely lost all sense and self-control.

But she hadn't. She knew who she was and what was happening.

Her parents and brothers were dead. Her best and only friend was gone. She was completely alone and expected to know exactly how to respond when told that her kingdom was about to be destroyed and then taken from her.

One kingdom taking over another seemed so petty and small compared to the threat she knew lingered above them in the skies.

Babies would die. Mothers and daughters would be brutalized. Trees and homes would burn. And then the planet would be invaded by Denlerack, and the winners of this trifle war would be enslaved anyway.

Her people would all cry out to her, wondering why she wasn't able to save them. She would fail before she even had a chance to try.

"I don't know how to try," she said to Hilip, standing there with a shocked and confused look on his face. "I don't know what to do next, what to say, who to command. I can't deal with this when I know what's really coming for us."

She was speaking to herself now more than to him.

"Why is it so hot in here?" Queen Amirra started pulling at the collar of her dress, thinking seriously about ripping tiny cuts in the fabric to let her skin access more air.

Her palms were sweaty, and drips of sweat trickled down her spine. Her underarms burned painfully, as if sweat was stabbing at her pores in an attempt to escape her skin.

She realized that she needed to leave the room before she said something she would truly regret.

Without a word, she pushed past General Daven, marched by the soldiers who stood there gawking at her, and the guards pulled open the heavy double doors just in time for her to slip through.

She heard Hilip stomping after her.

Maybe it was her comfort with him that made her care

less. He had been there since the beginning. He had seen the dragon. He had known KaLeah.

Amirra's door guards saw her coming and opened the doors to her room. She stormed in, immediately calling to her nurse maids.

"Dohori, Felair, where are you?" she yelled out to the empty suite.

The ladies were not meant to be there, expecting her to be in the throne room for much longer, but she hadn't thought to send a request out for them.

"Guards, send for my nurses," she beckoned.

"Yes, Your Highness," one responded.

"Queen Amirra, I implore you to please take a deep breath," General Daven said, as he cautiously entered her room with his hands extended.

"Do you even realize what is happening?" she asked, spinning around to face him.

She clawed at the fabric that extended down to her wrists, eager to be free from the restrictive lace. Hilip raised his hands higher and backed up, averting his eyes.

"I see that you are upset."

"The people of this kingdom, the Lisodanyan king, none of them have any idea what danger, what threats, lurk beyond our skies," she said, stepping closer to him while clawing at her lace sleeves.

"If KaLeah fails, then we will see ships on the horizon with weapons we have never dreamed of, twice the size of what killed my brother, Bylex, so easily. Lisodanya is nothing. Let them come. Let them see the ships descending. We will all be enslaved, so what is the use of trying to fight against the inevitable now?"

She turned and marched off toward her closet.

"We won't have any chance at surviving Denlerack if Lisodanya decimates our troops first," Hilip said, cautiously following her.

A plump nurse in a grey dress rushed past him and chased the queen into a doorway leading to a closet at the end of the room.

"None of us are going to survive this!" she yelled.

Dohori came into the closet and immediately began freeing the queen from the contraption. She had already torn some of the lace with her nails.

"Are you alright, dear?" the nurse asked.

"I am just so tired, and this dress is burning my skin. I need something light, something free."

"I understand, miss. I'll get you something better."

For a moment, she felt remorseful for giving Hilip such a hard time. He was clearly trying to help her, to help guide her, to encourage her to be stronger and make the best decisions. But he wasn't KaLeah, and he wasn't her father.

The nurse peeled the black dress from her thin body, and she almost started crying from the relief. She had grown up wearing gowns, of course, but she was feeling more and more uncomfortable in them lately. It was as if she had grown but the dresses had not.

She started breathing heavily, trying not to cry.

"Slower," said Dohori. "Breathe slower, child."

Dohori grabbed her shoulders and looked her in the eyes. The older woman drew in a deep breath through pursed lips, exaggerating the motion, letting it out, loud and heavy.

Amirra tried to mimic her on the next inhale, forcing herself to release it just as slowly as Dohori.

She failed, and it almost brought her to tears again, but Dohori stayed strong and focused, her hands gripping her shoulders solidly.

Dohori finally released her shoulders and slipped a loose-fitting, violet gown over her head. It was more of a spring dress, not meant to be worn during the colder season they were currently in, but she welcomed the cool silk against her skin.

She took another deep breath, in and out, and then stepped back into her bedroom suite. General Daven was standing by the closed double doors, eyes on the fireplace, patiently waiting.

"So, what are we supposed to do?" she asked, trying to maintain composure.

She wanted to be like her father. The memory of his smile behind his beard came back to her, almost overwhelming her. Blood rushed from her face and lips, her eyes blurred, and she quickly dropped into a chair.

"I know this is not easy for you," Hilip said, coming over. "You have lost everyone, but I swear to you that I will do everything I can to help protect you and your kingdom."

"My kingdom."

"Yes, it is your kingdom—or queendom, if you'd rather.

Queen Amirra let out a loud burst of laughter, surprising herself.

"This place, this planet, these men will never accept me as their queen. They want me to marry someone, literally anyone, just to feel better about the state of things. Can you imagine if I were to call this a *queendom*? That is the thing of childhood fairytales. That isn't my world or my reality."

"But it is," Hilip said. "You are technically ruling a queendom now."

"My father and brothers would be so angry to hear you say that," Amirra said, sitting in a chair and looking toward the fireplace.

"But they are not here," Hilip reminded her. "You are strong enough to make decisions for this land. We must discuss the coming Lisodanyan invasion, Your Highness."

The queen let out a very unladylike yell and stood up, storming over to the window.

"They will come and kill us all, is that what you want to discuss? I don't know how to make war-time decisions. I don't know how to fight. That's your job, not mine."

She closed her eyes and tapped her fingers to her forehead, over and over.

"What did we do before?" she asked. "We were attacked and KaLeah ran out into the castle yard to protect us. We didn't know we were going to be attacked. The soldiers just had to wake up and fight."

Hilip furrowed his brow and began pacing again. He stopped and looked up at her, standing by the window.

"We know they are coming, so we can prepare like we were not able to prepare before," he said. "All I need is for you to support us preparing to go to war."

"No," she said, spinning around quickly. "You can't go!"

Hilip furrowed his brow, confused. She stood there wringing her hands together nervously. Fearfully.

"Queen Amirra, we are not leaving you," he said, stepping closer. "We are simply gathering troops and weapons, with your authorization, in order to set up defenses around the castle. We will stand on the outskirts of the kingdom and fight off the invading army. We will not go far."

"You can't even leave the castle grounds," she said. "What if they get past you, what if they sneak in like that assassin and make it all the way to my doors again?"

Tears started to roll down her cheeks and she looked at her doors, remembering that frightening night.

"KaLeah should be here to protect me. She was the only one who protected me, and she's gone. Why isn't she back yet? She is the only one who can protect me, the only one who can keep me safe when Lisodanya attacks and when the sister world attacks. I can't do this without her. I can't survive here. Where is she?"

Amirra's heart thundered rapidly in her chest, and she looked toward the closet, as if nurse Dohori could breathing-exercise her back to calm, but the nurse was gone.

Her skin was itching and burning again, and she felt her pits and brow pinch with sweat threatening to escape from pores.

The lavender gown was too much, too restricting, too much like a prison and she started to claw at it, as if climbing out would save her from the panic filling up her entire body.

"No, Amirra, it's all going to be alright," General Daven

said, extending out his hands as if to protect her from herself.

"I need KaLeah," the queen screamed. "She's the only one who can save me from this. She knows what to do. She understands me. She can protect us. Where is KaLeah?"

The queen began clawing at her skin, and Hilip grabbed her arms.

"I miss her too," he said, trying to capture her eyes with his. "I lost her that day too. I want her back with us more than anything. More than… more than I can explain. I understand. I need her too."

"You do?" His words made her feel momentarily sorry for someone else besides herself.

"Yes. But she isn't here. I am here and your army is here. We can put a plan together. General Array is on his way back and we will make sure you and your kingdom are protected from any and all threats."

Amirra tried to calm herself, but sweat was rolling down her back. She wanted to believe this man, but he wasn't KaLeah. He wasn't a friend.

"I need air," she said.

She pulled herself from his grip and spun back to the window, marching over. He moved quickly to beat her to it and help get it open for her.

He pushed the glass panes outward, and she stuck her head through, closing her eyes and breathing in the cool air deeply. She felt him there, ready to catch her if she tipped out too far.

She was grateful for his presence. Loneliness had covered her like a dark cloud over the past few months, but now he was there, watching over her and ready to protect her from herself and others. He acted more like a big brother than her actual big brothers ever had.

She knew she was being odd and irrational. She had never felt so out of sorts before, but they kept telling her she was in mourning. She had lost everyone and had this new, heavy burden, upon her fragile, young, beautiful shoulders.

"I don't want to fight," she whispered. "To defeat the dictator from the sister world, we need Extelli and Lisodanya to join us. We need all the help we can get, general."

"I know, my queen, and I agree. I just don't know how we convince the war-hungry men to join your cause. They didn't see the phantom dragon."

"Spaceship," Amirra blurted out in shock.

"Yes, if they could only see the dragon or a Denlerackian flying ship, then maybe they would join with us."

"Spaceship!" Queen Amirra yelled, hardly believing what she was seeing.

A black, circular object was descending into the dark courtyard. She only barely saw it because of a reflection from castle lanterns.

General Daven leaned out of the window. "I don't see anything. Are you sure?"

"I saw it! KaLeah is home!"

She turned and ran for the doors. Hilip put his hand on his sword instinctively, and then ran to follow the young queen.

"Wait, you do not know if that is KaLeah."

"I know it is her. She has come back to us." The queen ran down the halls as fast as she could in her house slippers. She held her dress up as she ran, trying not to trip.

Love and joy filled her as she imagined giving her sister a hug.

Hilip caught up and got in front of her, trying to slow her down.

"We need to make sure that it is her," he said, raising his voice to sound authoritative.

"But it is her!" Queen Amirra knew in her heart her sister had returned.

"Please stay behind me," he pleaded. And then to the other guards, "Come with us to the yard, we have a visiting ship. Be prepared for anything."

They burst out of the doors and onto the courtyard. The black ovular object had smashed onto the lawn. Lights glittered about its edges.

Amirra was in awe of the strange craft but allowed Hilip to stand in front of her with his sword extended. He tried to hold her at bay with one hand.

"My queen, stay behind me."

"But it's KaLeah!"

"I hope so too. I really do," he said, his voice seeming to crack just a little. "But we need to be sure."

Amirra was sure and her heart was about to burst.

The craft's door opened, and a ramp extended out toward the ground.

A silhouetted figure stepped out.

2 FAVOR KALEAH

"Ladies and gentlemen, we are floating in space," Prince Nikolat said, gazing out of the craft's windows. A black expanse spread out ahead of them. Naldash and its moon were dots in the distance.

"When that little girl told me I was no longer on Naldash, I thought she was crazy and stupid," Nikolat said. "But it was my concept of the world—my understanding of the two planets—that was severely skewed all along."

He laughed, seemingly surprised at his own realization, and standing too close to KaLeah for her comfort. She slowly edged away from him while he spoke.

"To think that Denlerack wasn't a dead planet at all. There is an entire civilization and a leader with an army," he said with admiration.

"He is a leader who wants to invade our home world, Nik," KaLeah said. "And what little girl are you talking about?" she asked.

"Some slave girl helped me cross the mud lands to get me to this ship," he said, waving his hand dismissively as he inspected cabinet contents. "Is there nothing to eat or drink on his thing? How long do you think the flight will take?"

"Where is this girl now?" KaLeah asked, ignoring his

questions.

"Back in the compound," he said, not even making eye-contact.

"You left a child behind—a little girl who helped save your life—to continue being a slave for the dictator of a dying planet?"

"So what? Oh yeah, I forget you have a soft heart underneath that well-formed, abrasive exterior," Nikolat said, looking her body up and down for good measure.

KaLeah glared at him and crossed her arms, turning back toward the controls. She was still wearing the black, mechanical wings she had gotten while on Denlerack because she was afraid Nikolat would tamper with them if she set them down.

There was nothing for her to do on the ship. The top portion consisted of a rounded control room with a view of the universe nearly all the way around.

There were storage cabinets running along the edge, sitting beneath stations with various blinking lights, buttons, and knobs, although she had not ventured beyond using just voice controls.

Since Denlerack did not have ample resources, she was concerned the ships may not have been kept stocked with food or water. She left Nik on the top level and ventured below deck down a single, narrow set of stairs to look for supplies.

Lights flickered on as she entered the lower space. KaLeah saw a few rows of single beds with no linens or pillows, and one toilet beside a cabinet. Clearly, they had not gone to great lengths for comfort.

The wings had become extremely uncomfortable, and served no purpose on the ship, so she shrugged them off and laid them on one of the bare beds. She felt more comfortable with Nik upstairs.

Beside the cabinet was a metal door. She opened it into an area that was buzzing with noise.

"This must be where fuel and everything needed to

power this craft is kept," she whispered to herself.

"Most likely."

KaLeah jumped straight up at the voice, instinctively reaching for the sword strapped to her side. As she was spinning toward the threat, she knew that it was just Nikolat.

She forcefully shoved him back from her with one hand.

He doubled over laughing.

"That was not funny," KaLeah shouted.

"It was to me."

She noticed he wasn't holding Elektra's gun and wondered if it was in his pocket.

"This place is not big enough for the both of us," KaLeah said, shoving past him but trying to inconspicuously feel at his pockets.

Spirits, it isn't on his right side, which is where he'd most likely put it. Maybe he stashed it upstairs. I'll have to check the cabinets when he isn't looking.

She knew the damage that those things could do, and she also understood the power they held. With one gun, Prince Nikolat could take back his kingdom from the queen.

KaLeah couldn't let that happen. She had to find the gun and take control of it before they landed on Naldash.

"Don't be so cranky all the time, KaLeah," he said, following her back up the stairs and into the upper level of the ship. "You should really smile more. If you keep glaring like that, you'll get wrinkles."

He laughed at his own joke, and she rolled her eyes, trying to look annoyed while she focused on going through the cabinets.

"There's no food or water," he said. "I already checked all those."

"Well, I want to check for myself," she said.

Nikolat followed her step-for-step.

"There isn't anything useful in this place, KaLeah."

"Can you just give me some space, for dragon's sake?" she stood up from looking into a cabinet and gave him another firm shove.

The action caught him off-guard this time and he lost his balance. It gave her just enough time to dive back into the cabinet and pull out the gun she had seen stashed there.

He rammed his head straight into her side, knocking her down to the floor, grabbing at her arm and hand for the black metal object.

She wasn't as comfortable with hand-to-hand fighting, like she was with the sword. Nik was stronger and bigger than her, but he'd become emaciated while they had been apart. She assumed it was due to the lack of available food while he traversed Denlerack with the child he'd mentioned.

She was used to being light and limber, so she used that to her advantage. She was able to twist her body out from under him quickly, pinning his legs with hers and catapulting herself over and on top of him, mounting his torso. She clasped her thighs tightly, holding his arms to his side with her legs.

"Stop or I will put a bullet in your throat," she said, holding the gun to his neck with both hands.

"Go ahead," he said. The look in his sharp, blue eyes was playful, and his black hair didn't look half as disheveled as it should have after their tussle. His skin was just as smooth and olive toned as she remembered it, hers looking pale in comparison.

A memory of his lips on hers sent a shiver down her spine, and the smirk on his mouth grew wider.

"You won't kill me. You and I are meant to be together, Favor KaLeah," he said, his voice deep and smooth. "You can try to resist it, but there is a reason that the spirits keep bringing us together like this. Our destiny is to rule the sister worlds as king and queen. You know you still have feelings for me."

"Shut up," she said. "Don't tell me how I feel."

He jerked his head up, trying to smash her face, but she pulled back to avoid the blow. She lost her balance and her hand clenched, accidentally clicking the gun's trigger, firing off a bullet.

It grazed his neck, and he spun his entire body out from underneath her, then turned to grab at the gun while she was getting back to her feet.

They wrestled for it, and her finger squeezed the trigger again, sending another bullet off into the ship.

She heard a clank and a pop, and she could see smoke from the corner of her eye, but she didn't want to give the gun up to investigate.

Part of her wanted a bullet to accidentally kill him. She knew that she wasn't truly able to kill him on purpose, no matter how much she hated him.

The truth was, she did feel a strange pull toward him, as if they were supposed to be together. She couldn't help but feel attracted to him every time he caught her eye.

The hatred burned as ferociously as the attraction in her blood, and it angered her even more.

They kept fighting over the gun and it went off one more time. This time, the craft shifted and tilted to one side.

She started to slide, and in attempting to keep her footing, she lost her hold of the gun.

"Got it!" Nikolat exclaimed, trying to turn it on her.

Smoke caught her eye, and she took a quick account of the damage that had been done. Grey smoke billowed out of two separate control boxes.

"Ship, what is the damage?" she asked.

"Dama… land… ridge… larp…" crackled the robotic voice.

"Spirits, that's not good." KaLeah scrambled over to the main control box, as the ship continued to tilt to one side. "Manual controls. There must be manual controls here."

"What's happening?" Nik asked from the other side of the ship.

"The bullets damaged the voice commands. We have to land this thing manually. Ship, level-out, level-out," KaLeah tried yelling, hoping there was enough of it working to hear the command.

The craft stopped tilting but didn't level back out.

"This will have to do," she said, looking over the blinking lights and buttons.

KaLeah could see the planet Naldash through the front windows, but she didn't know how far off-course they were. They could end up on the opposite side of the planet or miss it completely and be stuck drifting through space for eternity.

She realized that she had to get it back level and on-course. She put her hands on the controls and closed her eyes, taking a deep breath.

"Spirits, please guide me," she said.

"You're going to need more than their help," Nik said from right beside her.

"Dragon's blood, Nik!" she said, jolting from the shock of hearing him suddenly so close.

"Are we going to crash?" he asked.

"Not if you leave me alone so I can figure this out," she grumbled through gritted teeth.

"What makes you think you can control this thing?"

She ignored him and looked at the levers. There was one that appeared to go up and down, so she grabbed that one first, slowly raising it toward her.

The craft lifted ever so slightly.

There were buttons to the left and right of the lever. She pressed the one to the left and the craft started to level out, its right side raising back up slightly.

"I knew you could figure this out, dragon-lady," Nik said, slapping her on the back.

"Shut up. I still have to get us safely to the ground. I don't see how to slow this thing down to secure a safe landing."

"Well, while you work on that, I'm going to get some water from that sink down below and take a little nap. Your little love tussle wore me out." He puckered his lips at her, feigning a kiss, and then walked away, taking the gun with him. She was so frustrated that she wanted to smash the controls with her fists.

"Maybe I should drive this thing straight into the ocean and save both planets from that useless waste of a prince. Why couldn't I just shoot him?"

"Shoo…ting."

The robotic voice crackled again, and she heard rapid fire. Two rows of lights shot out from beneath the window.

"Whoa, this thing has guns too."

She looked behind her but didn't see Nikolat anywhere in sight.

Good, she thought. She didn't want him to know about this. He didn't need any more weapons in his hands.

She stood and watched Naldash getting closer and closer in the window. The progress was so slow, she could only tell they were moving by making small marks on the window of where the planet was.

They were definitely getting closer. Even though it felt like they were crawling, she knew that at some point, they would be barreling down on the castle, and she didn't know how to slow the machine down.

And Nik had the gun.

She couldn't let them land if he still had the gun. He could easily walk out of the ship and shoot his sister down before anyone saw it coming.

She kicked herself again for not being able to shoot the man. She had only ever killed in self-defense, and those were men she hadn't known.

Even though she was angry at Nikolat for fighting her on the castle balcony when Amirra took the throne, she couldn't shake the memory of him holding her in the ballroom. She couldn't break free from the pain of him walking out of the library after she had begged him to stay.

She closed her eyes tight, trying to bury the memories of her early infatuation. She thought that she could get over him with time and with plenty of space but being cooped up together on the ship was the opposite of what she needed.

KaLeah was starting to feel sleepy after the long day and the earlier tussle. She hadn't had any food or water, either.

But she was too worried about the slightest miscalculation sending them off course from landing safely in Belarone. She didn't want to risk stepping away to get water or rest, even for a few moments.

She looked the control board over again.

"Ship, can you hear me?"

Static buzzed for a moment and stopped.

"Useless," she murmured.

KaLeah had figured out up, down, left, and right.

"Surely, I can find the slow down and landing gears."

KaLeah ran her fingers over all of the buttons, gently, hoping that her intuition or spirit would guide her as it did the first day she had ridden a draggot. She had instinctively known how to steer the dragon-like animal, pulling it to a stop and prodding it gently into a gallop.

"Where are you now, Anissa La Alani?" she asked, looking out into the stars.

The dragon spirit seemed to only show up sporadically, and never when KaLeah actually needed her help. She assumed a dragon wouldn't know how to land the craft anyway.

"This is all on me," she said. "I have to figure out how to land this thing. You look curious."

There was a blue knob the size of her palm, and when she placed her hand on it, a slight vibration buzzed through her skin.

She cautiously rolled her palm on it, trying to feel how the movement impacted the ship.

Please be the speed controls, please be the speed controls.

The button vibrated each time she moved her palm, but she couldn't tell if the ship was speeding up or slowing down.

"Useless," she said again, removing her hand.

She sat down in one of the captain's chairs and leaned her head back to rest.

"Wake up."

KaLeah jolted up in the chair at Nikolat's voice.

"How long was I out?" she asked, suddenly on high alert.

"How should I know?" he said, standing at the window.

KaLeah could see that the planet was much closer now, filling almost the entire window. "Spirits, Naldash is so close now."

"Did you figure out how to slow this thing down and land it?" Nikolat asked.

"While I was sleeping?" she clarified incredulously. No. Of course not."

"Well, that's no good," he said, looking the controls over. "I guess they don't believe in labels in Denlerack."

He started hitting at buttons and levers.

"What are you doing?" KaLeah jumped up and knocked him back from the control board. "You are going to get us killed," she said.

"We are going to die anyway if we can't land this thing," he said, accurately describing their predicament.

A crackling sound came over the ship's system.

"What's that?" Nik asked.

"The ship is probably warning us that we are coming in for a landing," KaLeah said.

"How do you know we are still pointed toward the Belarone castle's courtyard?" He looked intently out the front windows of the ship down at the planet that was growing larger by the moment.

"I don't," KaLeah said. "But I know how to steer the ship better now. I can make sure we are pointed in the right direction; I'm just not sure if I can slow us down or land us gently."

"You're the one with the wings," Nik said. "So, I hope that you can figure this flying thing out for us."

KaLeah's cheeks grew hot, and she was digging her nails into her palms. She turned sharply and headed downstairs to get some space to think.

She went to the sink and used her hands to drink and

then splash the water on her face and neck. She didn't come all this way to crash land on Naldash. She knew she was going to get back to Belarone Kingdom and the queen.

But how?

She looked at the black wings on the bed. There was a gear she'd used to increase and decrease the fan speed, and she had also spread the wings out further to slow down before she landed.

The spaceship didn't have wings, but maybe once they approached, she could find a way to decrease the speed. She just had to listen to the engines while she tried the different gears.

A sound like an inferno started to build and the ship began shaking. It was the same thing that had happened when they'd left Denlerack. They were now in Naldashian skies.

"I can do this," she told herself, and then she ran back upstairs.

Sure enough, the stars were gone and only blue and green came through the window.

Nikolat was still standing at the controls but doing nothing. She noticed a bulge where he had stored the gun in his side waste band as she shoved him out of the way and took the helm.

She placed her right palm on a gear that looked like a ball, and her left hand on the lever. While she lifted up the left, she rolled slightly back on the right.

Miraculously, the craft seemed to lift slightly and slow down.

"Did you feel that?" she asked.

"I think so," Nik said. "Feels like we slowed down slightly."

She rolled her hand back even more and there was a noticeable shift as her body tried to keep propelling forward but the craft had slowed.

"KaLeah…"

"I know."

The ground was coming closer at an alarming rate of speed. She could see trees clearly now, rivers, and the castle getting bigger.

She braced herself and rolled her palm back more and more, slowly, listening to the engines revving up as if the fans were reversing direction.

The castle lawns looked a lot smaller than she'd remembered. She kept hitting the buttons to the left and right, moving the lever up and down, trying to line up the craft to the tiny spot where she needed to land it.

They flew over the top of the forest, over the farmlands, and finally, panicking, she rolled the ball as far back as it would go, but the craft didn't feel as if it was stopping.

Dragon spirits were starting to growl inside her mind, warning her of danger.

"STOP!" she yelled, frustrated, lifting the nose of the craft up but feeling it sinking fast.

The ship smashed into the castle lawn, knocking KaLeah and Nikolat to the floor. She scrambled to pull herself back up and looked out of the window.

"We did it! We're home!" Nikolat said, coming up behind her and wrapping her up into a tight hug.

"I did it," she said, glaring at him as she shoved him back. "Why don't you go figure out how to open the hatch so we can get off this thing."

He pulled back and ran his hands through his black hair.

"I'm sure I can figure that out," he said with a smirk.

KaLeah dropped down to the lower floor to grab her wings. She smiled, pulling out the gun that she had just snatched away from Nik without him noticing.

She didn't have a holster, so she tucked it into her pants, under the longer side of her tunic. She slid the wings back on and secured her sword in the scabbard.

"Home," she said with a sigh, then headed back up to where Nik had opened the ramp.

He smiled at her as he waited for it to fully lower. She didn't smile back and kept her distance in case he realized that she'd taken the gun.

"It looks like the guards have their bows aimed at us, so you should go first," Nik said with a smirk.

KaLeah narrowed her eyes but maneuvered around him quickly to head down the ramp. She raised her hands up and eyed the crowd while walking down the ramp.

There were a dozen guards standing with arrows pointed directly at them, men with swords drawn behind them, and other soldiers running toward them from the castle.

"KaLeah, KaLeah."

She heard the young queen calling her name and quickly jumped from the ramp to look for her among the sea of men in the dim, moon-lit, and torch-lit evening.

Soldiers took a step back in shock at seeing her more closely and kept their arrows locked on her. She realized that she must look like some dragon-human beast with the black wings on.

"KaLeah, is that you?" Amirra asked from behind guards.

"Queen Amirra, stay back."

"Shut-up, she is Favor KaLeah," the young girl said.

Queen Amirra ran up to her in a violet gown, her long, shiny blonde hair flowing behind her. The tiny girl wrapped her arms around her waist tightly.

KaLeah was so relieved to see her young friend still alive, knowing how dangerous it was to be a queen. She enclosed the young girl in a hug and felt a sense of calm joy flow throughout her body.

"It is you. You're back. Are you alright? What happened out there? How did you get this ship?"

"Your Highness, Favor KaLeah."

KaLeah looked up and saw that Hilip was standing there. Her voice caught in her throat as she met his eyes, and she found herself smiling.

He smiled back at her.

"Are you injured at all?" he asked her softly.

She shook her head, still unable to speak. She felt

Amirra pull back from her.

"I am so glad that you have returned, KaLeah," she said. "There are so many things we need to discuss. There is so much work to be done. And we—"

She stopped speaking suddenly and KaLeah looked down into her blue eyes, which had locked onto something behind her.

"Hello, sister."

Queen Amirra released KaLeah and took two big steps back. Hilip drew his sword and stepped protectively in front of the queen.

The queen's shock turned to fury, and she whipped her head back toward KaLeah.

"How could you bring him back here?" she asked.

"I had no choice," KaLeah said quickly. She started to feel panicked, having not realized the emotional impact seeing Nikolat would have on Amirra.

"Guards, arrest the prince and take him to the dungeon," Hilip commanded.

"Arrest him? He needs to be shot. Now, general," Amirra commanded Hilip.

"Your Majesty, we cannot kill a member of the royal family. We shall take him under our control. Fear not."

KaLeah could tell that Hilip, now a general, was trying to be comforting, but there was a level of caution and concern in his tone that she knew meant trouble.

"You cannot arrest the prince for simply coming home," Nikolat said, reaching for his waist band.

Soldiers began to walk toward him with swords extended.

The confident smirk slowly faded from his face as Nik realized the gun was no longer on him. He looked up and met KaLeah's eyes. She smiled.

"You," was all he said before the soldiers grabbed and tied his hands behind his back.

She felt no remorse for him as they drug him toward the castle. She turned back toward Queen Amirra, who was glaring at her with her thin arms crossed.

"I truly had no choice," KaLeah said.

"You could have killed him." Hate and fear emanated from the young princess, who looked much older and angrier than KaLeah remembered.

The young queen shifted weight and looked at KaLeah with judgement on her face. "Lisodanya is on its way to attack us while we are weak. Were you able to stop the dictator on Denlerack from planning his invasion?"

KaLeah was embarrassed, remorseful, and angry with herself. "No," she admitted.

"No," Amirra repeated. "So, a kingdom is going to be invading Belarone. A planet is going to be invading Belarone. And now, my brother, who wants to kill me and take Belarone for himself, is back. Here. Alive. Were you able to accomplish anything useful while you were away, Favor KaLeah? Or did you just go on a trip to turn yourself into a dragon?"

Amirra motioned flippantly to the black wings that KaLeah was wearing.

KaLeah's embarrassment rose, and her cheeks began to burn. The child was right. She hadn't done anything useful to help protect Naldash or Belarone Kingdom.

"He is going to try to take the throne from me, and these people are going to want to give it to him because you have brought me nothing. Maybe you should not have come back at all." The queen turned around and stormed back off toward the castle. Hilip signaled for men to follow her. He then stepped up closer to KaLeah.

She felt even more embarrassed with him there.

"I failed," KaLeah whispered.

"You made it back alive, though," he said. "She's glad you are back; she just has a lot to deal with right now."

"And she's just a child, I know," KaLeah said, trying to put herself into Amirra's current situation.

"It is a tricky combination being a leader and a child," Hilip said.

"I failed her, I hurt her, and now there's a rift that I have to mend."

"You will mend it," he said. "Are you alright?"

Warmth spread throughout her body, and she nodded.

"Were you able to learn anything that we can use?" he asked.

"I learned a lot, yes. And I was able to bring this back with me." She pulled the black gun out from where she'd tucked it away.

"That's what killed Prince Bylex," he said, shocked, and taking a step back from her.

"Yes, but I know how to use it now," KaLeah said.

3 REBEL ELEKTRA

Elektra held Colt's hand tightly as the sounds of pain, the smell of blood, grew more intense with each step they took back toward their camp.

"They are all going to hate me for this," Elektra said.

"For what? For risking your life to try and save our world?"

"I failed and Felisha is dead," she said, squeezing his hand tighter.

Holding his hand was the only thing keeping her moving forward. She wanted to curl up into a ball on the ground. She wanted to use her golden wings to fly off into the sky. Anxiety filled her body like a stiffness with every step.

She did not want to face the rebels.

She did not want to find out who still lived and who had died during the attack of Lord Keldon's compound.

Elektra had one job—to assassinate the dictator, and she had failed.

The dictator still lived, and he had killed one of their own.

"How am I going to tell them about Felisha?"

"I will tell them everything," Colt said, protectively. "I

will give an update regarding the failed assassination attempt. They will all be disappointed. They may be angry. Some of them may leave but for veterans, for those who have fought for years, they know the cost of war and the cost of change. You don't always win. We may not win this war at all."

Elektra stopped on the dirt path, shocked. She was still wearing her wings, but Colt had taken his patchwork wings off and had the slung over one shoulder.

"Don't say that," she said. "Otherwise, what are we doing this for?"

She felt tears begin to sting her eyes. The responsibility of saving her entire world felt like a heavy burden on her, but it was one she still felt hope and commitment toward. If he didn't think they had a chance, it would eat away at her own confidence.

She saw herself back in the garage where she grew up, tinkering with scraps to sell for food. She saw the eyes of the slaves back at the compound. She saw the people living underground foraging for water.

Elektra shook her head to stop the images from overwhelming her.

Colt let go of her hand to stand in front of her, cupped her cheeks in his hands, and looked intensely into her eyes.

Elektra's heart fluttered for a moment, although she found his new affectionate attention slightly uncomfortable. She and her mother had never been affectionate, and she had never kissed a boy before. She had finally kissed him after a rush of hope and adrenaline at seeing a young girl morph into the mythical dragon, but it was all still very new to her.

It felt strange to have feelings for someone while the world seemed to be collapsing around her. Guilt mixed in with excitement and fear, and it left her feeling flustered.

"No matter what happens, I am ready to fight beside you until we die," Colt said. His golden-brown skin was so soft in the smoky air, and his hands were so reassuring, holding her in place.

"I don't want us to die, Colt," Elektra said, pulling back from him and trying to reclaim control of her emotions. "This isn't some romantic adventure. We are now leaders of this thing, and it lives and dies with us. We either march back into that camp and convince everyone to try again, or we go back to the way things have always been. And I would rather die."

Elektra took a moment to step away and collect her thoughts. It did not matter that she had newly formed feelings for Colt. She would not let those feelings distract her from her lifelong goal of improving Denlerack and the lives of thousands of people.

The people deserved clean water and fresh air. They deserved to see the sunshine on their skin. She lifted her own brown hand up in front of her face. Her skin had never seen sunshine. She envied KaLeah the world she had gotten to grow up on, a world untouched by mechanical and industrial pollution.

"I am going to save this place, Colt. I am going to let those people know that our friends did not die for nothing. We will keep fighting. We have to keep fighting."

She turned to look at Colt, who stood there somber, but smiling.

"You will get no argument from me, Elektra," he said. "I am in this with you all the way. My parents died fighting for this cause, and for a long time, I wanted nothing more than to disappear into an underground village somewhere and just forget them. But they are all around me. They are in this smoky air that itches my throat on really bad days. They are in the fiery sun that's blocked behind the haze. They are inside of me when I feel hunger and burning thirst. Either I will die, and my family is lost forever, or I will help other families bring children into a better world. Either way, I have to do something."

Elektra knew that it was easy to say. But now they had to walk into a camp full of people who had just lost a battle.

He held his hand out to her again and she took it, ready to face whatever may come.

They walked together back toward the camp where everyone had gathered after the battle. Various sizes and types of fabrics were strewn about on thin poles and hanging between crumbling buildings. Most people just camped out in the open, on the ground, sitting on the hard dirt. There were a few small fires burning with brush only as needed to cook or boil water, since tinder was so scarce.

The air was warm and still, and every person she passed was covered in a thin layer of dust, kicked up from walking. She was also fairly coated in dirt.

Some people were sitting quietly, cleaning weapons with far-off looks in their eyes. Other people frantically tended to the wounds of their friends or worked together to carry the body of someone too injured to walk, or worse.

She could feel eyes boring into her, but she kept her own eyes straight ahead, looking for their small band of rebels.

"Colt! Elektra!" The young man's voice filled her with relief and her heart pounded harder in her chest. She saw Rustin running through the crowd to them. He bent down and gave her a hug, reaching around and underneath the brown wings she wore. She stood on her toes to squeeze him tightly around his neck.

Although he was much taller, she thought of him like a little brother. He seemed too young and innocent to be orphaned and fighting battles.

"Spirits am I glad to see you two," Rustin said.

Elektra had tears in her eyes and a lump in her throat, but she swallowed it back down and asked, "Are you hurt at all?"

"Me? No, I'm good," he said, with a smirk. "But we've been worried about you. Where's Felisha?"

Colt dropped his strong, firm hand up onto Rustin's shoulder. "She didn't make it," Colt said.

Rustin's brown eyes darted between the two of them,

and then out behind them as if confirming that Felisha wasn't just slowly trailing behind them. Rustin looked down at his hands and nodded slowly. "I see," he said.

"Let's go talk to the others," Colt said, leaving his hand in place as Rustin turned back toward the center of camp.

The three of them walked slow and somber toward their tents, and Elektra felt a nervous tension in her body as she got closer to her compatriots.

Spotting Elektra and Colt, the group stopped what they were doing and came to meet them. They were not smiling or as happy to see them as Rustin had been.

Alister came up first with an air of calm authority, seemingly always ready to step in and lead if ever needed. His black hair was disheveled over his olive complexion, but his face had been wiped clean. She noticed a bloody bandage around his wrist and forearm.

Von came up next with his shaggy dark hair covering his shoulders and stubble across his chin. Then gentle Zuri, stepping quietly and knowingly, but limping slightly.

"Where are Lina and Lainie," Elektra asked, looking around for their wild blonde locks.

"They are trying to help heal some of the wounded," Alister said. And then getting down to business, "What happened at the compound?"

"Team," Colt said, taking control of the next part of the conversation. "Felisha went into the dictator's room ahead of us and he shot her before we could get to her. We lost her. We were imprisoned and couldn't get back to her."

There was silence as the news sunk in that one of their own had been killed. It wasn't that they had expected to get out of battle unscathed, and they were probably more surprised to see that Colt and Elektra both survived, but it was still upsetting.

"How did you two manage to escape?" Alister asked, showing no emotional response to the news.

"KaLeah broke us out," Elektra said.

"KaLeah?" Von interrupted. "But I thought she had

vanished."

"I thought she was working for the dictator?" Zuri asked.

Elektra sighed. "It's complicated."

"Help us understand, Elektra," Alister said. "When you left us, she was our enemy."

Elektra wrung her hands together, looking over the small group of men who had become friends. They had all thought that KaLeah had betrayed them, and it was Elektra who had driven that idea more than anyone.

She was used to only relying on herself, only trusting herself, and having no friends. Friends stabbed you in the back. Friends took things from you. Friends abandoned you.

It had been easy to jump to that story in her mind when she'd woken up to find KaLeah gone from the hideout. But she'd been wrong.

She now trusted KaLeah as much as she trusted the people who had gone to battle with her and as much as she trusted Colt standing beside her.

"KaLeah hadn't told us her whole story and even though I am still angry at her, I understand why she didn't," Elektra started to explain.

KaLeah leaving them all in the middle of the night, vanishing with no explanation, had made Elektra feel abandoned. She had been hurt and frustrated. The entire group had to leave the safety of the hideout for fear that KaLeah would send the dictator's men to capture or kill them all.

"She didn't leave us to betray us," Elektra said. "She came here to try to save her world, Naldash, yes, but the dragon spirits sent her because she is the dictator's lost daughter."

They gasped in shock and murmured their disbelief.

"No."

"What?"

"How can that be?"

"It's true," she continued. "KaLeah is the dictator's daughter and she thought that she could get through to him. She hoped that she could find a good part of his soul and guide him toward saving the planet. But after he killed Felisha, she realized there was nothing she could do, and she decided to risk her life to rescue us. KaLeah flew off in a spaceship back to Naldash, and here we are."

There was stunned silence among her friends while the camp went on noisily around them.

"I did not expect that," said Alister.

"I'm glad that she isn't our enemy," added Rustin with his big smile. "She was nice."

Elektra had missed that smile and positive attitude. She was so glad he had survived the battle. The kid was a bright light for her on this dark, dingy planet, and his optimism reminded her about the future she was fighting for.

"We must regroup," Alister said, looking to Colt. "What are our orders?"

Colt looked around at the people in the camp. Elektra followed his gaze.

All the tribes who had come to fight were now in disarray, tending to their dead and injured. The tribes that had led the fray had come back dragging more of their friends.

"We need to see how many of those people are still willing to fight," Colt said, nodding out at the camp folk. "We need to see how much artillery we have left, how many bullets. And then we'll need to come up with an offensive plan. The dictator may send some of his men out after us and so we should plan to take more defensive measures."

Elektra scrunched up her face. She had feelings for Colt, but she wasn't ready for him to make all of the decisions all the time.

"I'm not sure he'd waste the resources to come after us," Elektra countered. "From what I saw, we are just minor annoyances to him. He isn't going to waste his resources on us. We flew into his compound, but we won't be able to do that again. I'm sure they will be watching out for us now that they know some of us have wings. He will expect us to come at him through the air again. I say we make a plan to attack on foot next time."

"We need to talk to the tribe leaders before we make any decisions," Colt said. "They need to be involved so we can get their buy-in for any plan we come up with."

"You won't need to wait long for that," Rustin said, nodding his head.

Colt and Elektra turned and saw the massive leader of the Mud Shadows people walking their way. He was bare-chested with a blood-soaked bandage wrapped around his mid-section.

The red-haired woman walked behind him, along with a few other tribe leaders. She did not see the third Mud Shadows leader and wondered if he had been killed.

"Colt and Elektra," the man said, his voice reverberating throughout the camp. Many others working around them stopped and turned to watch his approach.

"Ludwig," Elektra said. "I am so glad that you survived."

"Did you assassinate the dictator?" he asked.

"We did not," Elektra answered, trying not to sound scared or ashamed. "He was alerted to our presence too early, and we were captured."

"Then how are you here now?" Deep lines of doubt creased the man's brow.

Elektra's palms were sweaty, and she hesitated. This man didn't know KaLeah. He wouldn't understand the entire story. She wondered if it would make her seem weaker than she already felt.

"The dictator's daughter actually set us free," she said, finally.

Ludwig blinked, confused. He brought his hand up to run it through his black, bushy beard.

"The dictator does not have a daughter," he said, very slowly, as if he didn't believe that catching a girl in a lie could be so easy.

Elektra took a deep breath. It was an unbelievable story, but she didn't have a choice now.

"About sixteen or seventeen years ago, the dictator captured a woman named Huntra. She was a rebel, like us."

Ludwig nodded. "I have heard this name."

"Huntra was able to escape from the dictator while she was pregnant. She had a daughter but died after childbirth," Elektra recounted the story. "This daughter recently returned to get to know him, but she realized that he is an evil man."

"Gone for so long, though? Where was she? Where had she been hiding?"

Elektra hesitated again. This was the most unbelievable part. "She had been living on Naldash, the sister planet."

He looked up to the hazy sky and nodded at the orb none of them could see. "I remember seeing Naldash in my youth," he said, nodding. "But how could this child set you free and you escape past the hordes of soldiers who did so much damage to my people?"

"We stole a ship."

"Excellent. Where is this ship?" he swiveled his head, looking for it.

Her heart sank deeper into her stomach and sweat trickled down her back. She kicked herself for not realizing how beneficial a stolen ship could have been to their cause.

"KaLeah, the dictator's daughter, flew it back to Naldash."

Ludwig's expression stayed the same, but he looked directly into her eyes and held there for an uncomfortable amount of time. She felt more and more stupid for the mistake the longer he stared at her.

"Battles are not always won," he finally said. "This war has been going on for longer than you have been alive. I did not expect you to succeed but I also did not expect you to come back alive. You may have failed at your mission, but you surprise me by still being here. Maybe there is more to you and your small band of rebels than I expected."

Relief started to slowly refill her body, and her shoulders relaxed just a tiny bit. The man wasn't angry, at least.

"I wish you luck," he said. "We are heading back to our underground community. We must ensure that those who survived this battle can still survive the harsh Denlerack life."

"You're leaving?" she asked, surprised.

"Yes, we are."

"No, you can't leave! We have so much work to do. We have to regroup and attack again, Ludwig. You have more fighters than any of the other tribes. We need your people."

Ludwig took a step toward her and appeared twice as tall, all of a sudden. Or maybe she just felt a lot smaller.

"You need to realize we can't stand up against a wall of armed soldiers without proper weapons, resources, or information. I won't lose any more of my people."

She was intimidated by his ferocity and stature. She knew that he was only trying to keep his people safe, and her heart ached thinking about how many he may have lost, while she still stood there unharmed.

But she wasn't ready to give up. "We can take the time to make more weapons, make bullets, and come up with more resources," Elektra said, trying to keep her fear in check. She didn't want to sound desperate, but she also knew that if the Mud Shadows people left, other tribes might follow, and they would be right back where they started.

"We'll have another chance at taking the dictator out, Ludwig," she said, trying to believe the words herself.

"When, young Elektra?" Ludwig pressed. "He has more men, more ammunition, and a fortress secured by high walls and gates. When and how are we supposed to have any chance against all of that?"

"When they invade Naldash," Colt said.

Elektra and Ludwig both turned to look at him.

"That's what they are preparing for," Colt continued. "That's what KaLeah was hoping to prevent, right? The dictator has been building ships in order to send his army to take over Naldash. When that happens, the compound will be exposed. There may be guards left, but not as many. We just need to attack after the majority of the army has left Denlerack. We can burn his mansion and his factories to the ground. We can free all the slaves. That's our next opportunity. We simply need to be ready for it."

Of course, Elektra thought, nodding with pride at Colt.

They didn't know when it would happen, but maybe they could find out or at least be ready for when they saw the ships all leave the atmosphere.

She turned to look at Ludwig, who was stroking his black beard again. "The ships will return, once they have taken over Naldash," he said.

"Only to pick up anyone wealthy enough to afford a ride back to Naldash," Elektra said, feeling optimistic about changing Ludwig's mind. "The dictator will want to rule his new planet and forget about this one. He may expect that the soldiers he leaves behind will run this world, or he may abandon it completely. He wants his new, cleaner, better world. Regardless, we will make sure he has nothing left here to return to."

Ludwig nodded slowly and Elektra was starting to feel hopeful again. She didn't know what the dictator had been waiting for, since his father had created the ships so long ago. Maybe he'd been nervous about leaving this planet, not knowing how to conquer Naldash. Or maybe he had just been laying the plans all this time.

But whatever his hesitation, if the dictator finally left Denlerack behind, that would be the perfect time for the rebels to take over and shift the power back to the people.

Elektra noticed that the camp had quieted around them. There were still a few painful cries and even screams as people were getting bullets removed or limbs amputated, but anyone who was close enough to hear their conversation had stopped to listen.

"We don't know how many ships will return once they have conquered Naldash," Ludwig said.

Elektra nodded but his hesitation didn't concern her.

"We will know how many ships leave, and how many are left behind, if any," she said. "And if they all leave, then we have another opportunity to strike."

"You are asking me to put more lives at risk." His tone was softening, and Elektra stepped closer to the big man.

She spoke loudly, so that everyone around them could hear her. "I am asking for everyone to keep fighting until we take this world back. I know that things didn't go the way we had planned, but I still have hope that we can win this. We have to all stick together. We need each and every one of your people, each and every person in this camp, and if we work together and prep for the day when the ships head to Naldash, then we have a chance."

Elektra noticed that even more people had stopped what they were doing and had come closer to listen.

"You are a good speaker, and a good leader, and I understand what you are asking all of us to do." Ludwig made a grand sweeping gesture over the onlooking crowd that had grown around them. "But I need to give my people time to recover and recoup before I sign up for your new plan."

Blood rushed up to Elektra's cheeks in anger and frustration. She scrambled to try to find the next right words to say to convince him and all of the tribespeople standing around them that this would be their only chance to save future generations.

She opened her mouth to speak but as she did, horns began to ring out in alarm. They all turned toward the sound of gunfire, and something else…

Black spaceships were coming toward them out of the thick haze.

"We are under attack," Ludwig yelled. "Get the guns,

return fire!"

"Find cover," Elektra called out, realizing that everyone was out in the open and would be fired upon from above.

She turned to her friends, who had already begun drawing weapons.

"We need our wings. We have to attack the ships from the sky. It's our only chance."

Colt, Rustin, and the others nodded in agreement. They dove into their campsite to grab wings and more guns.

Elektra didn't wait for them. She was still wearing her golden and synthetic animal hide wings, so she flipped on the engines and lifted into the sky. She drew out only one gun, since the young man, Nikolat, had taken and kept her other one.

There seemed to only be two ships attacking their camp. She felt slightly insulted that Keldon thought so low of them that he assumed he could destroy their entire camp with only two ships.

So far, his pilots were already doing a good job of razing the people who had no cover. Elektra knew that she had no time to waste in shutting the flying machines down.

She flew straight to the closest one. The pilot didn't see her, but she could see him at the control board firing away at the people as they ran away below.

The man barely had to lift a finger. He just hit buttons and the ship did the work for him, killing in swaths.

"You cowards," she growled, then propelled herself straight at the glass window.

The soldiers were shocked to see her, and their shots died down for a moment while they tried to figure out what was happening and if they were in any immediate danger from the winged woman.

Elektra aimed her gun and fired at the glass.

But the rounds only bounced, ricocheting off of the edges.

"The glass isn't breaking," she said as Colt and her friends joined her, flying near her in their own sets of wings.

They all tried aiming at different areas of the ship, firing shots into what she hoped were chinks in the metal armor of the machine.

"We need something stronger than bullets to break through the glass or metal," Rustin said.

"Maybe if we all cover the glass, they won't be able to see where they are shooting," Alister added.

Rustin dropped out of sight to find something stronger and bigger than bullets while the others flew off to find materials to use that would cover the glass and block their view.

The pilots were getting more aggressive in their maneuvers. The men spun the ship around, trying to aim at her, but she maneuvered fast, dodging their guns.

Elektra flew up over the top of the craft, catching a view of the carnage around her.

The second black spaceship floated near the entrance to the camp, firing indiscriminately into the crowd as the people tried to hide or fire back as best as they could. The bullets bounced off the black orb without even denting it.

Her heart sank every time she saw another person fall to the ground. "This can't happen. We can't lose all these people with just two ships."

A sharp pain sliced through her cheek. Elektra spun away quickly, reaching up to touch her face. Her fingers came back covered with blood. She'd been hit by a bullet, and for a moment she wondered if it was all over. She waited for a deeper pain to set in. She expected to feel faint.

"Spirits. Keep your wits," she said to herself. "It's only a scratch and I have to figure this out. I have to save these people."

She saw Rustin fly up toward the rear of a spacecraft holding a long, sharp metal pole in his hands. He flew straight toward a thin line of the hatch, barely visible on the opposite side from where the windows were.

Maybe he thinks that the glass is too strong and he's trying to break in another way, Elektra thought.

The pole hit the craft but bounced right back, and Rustin went flying onto the back of the craft, hitting it hard.

"Rustin!" she screamed, feeling helpless and panicked.

The young boy was now falling to the ground, and she was too far away to catch him. Von was closer, and she watched him whisk down fast, catching the boy right before he hit the ground.

She was awash with relief but even more fearful, turning back toward the ship, looking it over with more determination.

"How do we break into this thing?" she asked out loud.

Her friends were getting injured. She had been shot in the face. And the people who she was trying to save were dying below her, calling out for help.

And then it hit her. "It's voice activated." Elektra flew around to the back of the ship.

"Elektra!" she heard Colt call out to her, but she was too excited to see if she was right.

"Spaceship, open the hatch!" she yelled.

Like magic, the door clicked loudly and began to slowly open to reveal a ramp. There was so much commotion with Alister and Zuri trying to cover the windows with tarps while the pilots swerved the ship back and forth to shake them off, that they didn't notice the door opening wide right behind them.

Colt flew up beside her and they both dove through as soon as the space was wide enough. They landed with their guns pointed at the two men inside.

Elektra pictured Rustin falling and people dying, and she had to stop herself from shooting the two men. She turned her gun and shot at the control boards first, and when the pilots turned around, she noticed they were not armed. In their hubris, they had come to battle thinking the spaceships were all they needed.

"I should kill you both now, you cowards," she said, redirecting her gun back on them. Their eyes were wide with fear.

"You are lazily killing people down there who just want to make this world a better place," Elektra accused. "You want to work blindly for someone, taking orders without any care for how they impact the rest of the people on this world, and would kill us all without a thought. Well, maybe it's time I let you have a taste of what that feels like, you mindless beasts."

Anger boiled up inside of her and she felt her cheeks flush with heat.

"Elektra, I can tie them up," Colt offered. "We have them."

"Do we?" she asked. "We are in a war, Colt. These wretched men are just casualties of this war."

"I've got this, Elektra," he said, and then he stepped toward them as if protecting them.

She knew he was technically the leader of the rebel pack, but she had never answered to any leader.

"Spaceship, turn the windows toward the sky," she commanded.

The spaceship began to turn skyward. Elektra let her engines lift her, and gently floated with her wings spread out. Colt lost his footing as the ship angled, and he also began to float upright.

The soldiers were slow to catch on as the machine lifted its nose. The men scrambled to keep their footing, and then struggled to hold on to the backs of their chairs before being dumped out onto the floor.

They screamed as they slid across the floor beneath her, tumbled out the back hatch, and fell toward the ground.

"Spaceship, level out and turn toward the other spaceship." Elektra sunk to the floor, holstered her gun and ran to the controls. She nodded at Alister and Zuri through the window, motioning for them to get out of the way.

They looked shocked and confused at seeing Elektra at the controls.

"You didn't have to do that," Colt said, coming up beside her.

"They would have killed us and our friends, so yes, I did," she shot back. "The other pilots don't realize that their comrades have been tossed out. We need to shoot them down as soon as we can."

"But we could use that ship if we were to get control of it undamaged," Colt said, trying to reason with her.

Elektra paused, watching as one machine lined up with the other. She wanted to blow it away, using immediate force to neutralize the threat.

But she knew he was right. Two ships would be better than one. They didn't have the luxury to waste the opportunity to have more artillery.

"Alright," she agreed. "I can draw their fire and confuse them, if you want to take the others to sneak in and take that ship."

He nodded curtly and then flew out of the back of the craft.

She sensed he could be upset with her over letting the soldiers fall to their potential deaths or for giving him an order to go take the other ship, but she shrugged off the feeling. Even though she liked him, she didn't have time to be soft and gentle with his feelings.

Colt gathered their friends from the air, and they drifted stealthily around to the rear of the craft. As soon as they were out of sight, she commanded the ship to fire across at the other.

Dictator Keldon's pilots stopped firing at the ground and began to return fire at the ship she had taken control of. It was only a matter of moments later when the firing stopped completely, and she saw Colt waving at her from the windows.

They captured the pilots instead of dumping them out onto the ground and then commanded both ships to land.

She walked down the ramp to cheers and many patted her on the shoulder, head, and wings as she passed.

The four soldiers were already tied up, and she saw Rustin sitting with Von, both of them looking shaken but alive.

Her small band of rebels reunited in the middle of the two black ships. Blonde-haired twins, Lina and Lainie, appeared out of nowhere, both throwing their thin arms around her and then the others.

She was so thankful all of her friends were alive, and then she remembered Felisha and guilt washed over her again.

She didn't have a moment to mourn, however, because Ludwig was stomping toward them. He seemed to be covered in more blood than before the ships had arrived.

Ludwig stopped and looked her and her friends over, towering menacingly over them all. Then he looked at each of the black spaceships sitting behind them and the pilots tied up at their feet.

"Maybe I have underestimated you and your friends, Elektra," he finally said.

She took a deep breath and held it, waiting for him to say more.

"You just took two ships and four men with wings and engines that you built yourselves. I am impressed and I have rarely been impressed in my life. We will keep our people in this fight, but we can't stay out in the open like this. We will go back underground, but leave scouts here, waiting for Keldon to take his army to Naldash, as you say he will. Then we will return here and use these ships to lay his compound and his factories to waste. We will save and rebuild this world together."

"Yes," Elektra said, feeling a mix of fear, relief, and anxiety. Her hands were shaking but her voice was smooth. "We will."

4 TOGETHER AGAIN

Queen Amirra stomped across the lawns and back to the castle with the guards right behind her. As soon as she passed the gate and onto the stone courtyard, she lifted the skirt of her black gown and started to run.

The clanking of the armored guard behind her grew louder as the men tried to keep up. But she was small and fast, flying into the castle, racing through the hallways, and dodging servants as she turned up the staircase.

Hot tears threatened to fall down her cheeks, but she knew what those tears meant.

Those tears told everyone around her that she was still a little girl; that she was weak and emotional. The tears told others how angry and fearful she was, and they made her feel ashamed.

Her soldiers didn't cry.

Her generals didn't cry.

KaLeah didn't cry.

Queen Amirra rounded the top of the staircase and headed down the hallway that led to her suite. The two guards opened the large, wooden doors for her as soon as they saw her coming, and she ran into her room, immediately collapsing onto her bed.

She didn't know what she felt.

She breathed in short, fast bursts, lying face down on the soft bedding, sinking into the bed.

Amirra had waited so long to see her friend, KaLeah, hoping she would bring back reassurances that Denlerack was no longer a threat to their planet.

She had mourned the loss of her father and her oldest brother. She had tried to forgive and mourn her brother Nikolat for trying to kill her and take the kingdom.

KaLeah had been the one who had convinced her to fight for her kingdom. She'd been the one to defend the princess' right to be queen.

"But she brought him back here to Naldash," she said, screaming her frustrations into a pillow.

"Are you alright, Your Majesty?" asked one of the guards from the other side of the closed doors.

"Leave me alone!" she yelled back at him. And then to the room she yelled out, "Why did she have to bring him back? He was supposed to be dead. He was supposed to leave me alone."

She was torn.

10-year-old Amirra wanted nothing more than to wrap her delicate frame around her friend and feel that everything would be alright. KaLeah was like a sister, and she had been gone for so long.

But Queen Amirra was writhing in anger, clawing at the dress that had become itchy and constricting after her run back to her room. "How could she do this to me?"

There was a loud bang on the door.

"Your Majesty, Favor KaLeah is requesting to speak with you."

"Tell her to go away. I don't want to see her."

Her heart ached within her chest. She had wanted nothing but to see her friend for months, but now she was so angry.

"Amirra, let me in," KaLeah begged from the hallway. "Let's talk about this."

"What is there to talk about? You brought my brother back here, and you know I am going to suffer because of that decision. I am not safe while he is alive."

"Let me in."

"No."

"Amirra."

The queen rolled around on her bed, bringing herself to a seated position, and dug her nails into her palms.

"Fine. She can come in." *But I won't look at her*, Amirra decided. She stood up and marched to the window, staring out across the darkened lawns to the forest.

She heard a door open and KaLeah's footsteps on the stone entrance, going silent once she stepped onto the rugs.

"I am so glad to see you and really happy you are well, Your Majesty," KaLeah said, speaking gently. "I want to explain to you why your brother was on that ship. Prince Nikolat climbed aboard the spaceship, and I could not make him leave because he had a gun."

The queen spun around fast with her brow furrowed. "A gun? Is that the thing that killed Bylex in the throne room?"

"Yes, the same device," KaLeah said, nodding. "The ammunition is different. It doesn't kill as quickly and can be removed. But nonetheless, I did not want to get shot. I had to wait for the right time to take it from him."

"So, you did get it? Do you have it now?" Queen Amirra looked her friend up and down for a moment, as if the gun might be concealed on her.

"Yes, it is safe, and I know how to use it properly now."

"Then why didn't you kill him, if you were able to get the gun from him?" The queen crossed her arms and narrowed her eyes.

KaLeah's cheeks flushed with shame. "I fought with him, but I could not bring myself to shoot him. I assumed that once we arrived, your soldiers would secure him, and he wouldn't be a threat any longer."

"But he is a threat! I will never be safe as long as my

brother lives."

"My queen, he is locked up," KaLeah tried to reason, but Amirra wasn't having any of it.

"And prisoners never escape?" The queen took two steps closer to KaLeah, arms crossed, eyebrows raised. "Can you promise me that he won't get out and come after me?"

"I am here now, and I promise to always protect you," KaLeah said, looking earnest.

Amirra didn't feel convinced. She knew KaLeah was her friend, but she was disappointed the woman had been unable to prevent her brother from coming back to Naldash. The queen lowered her voice to a whisper. "Where is the dragon spirit? Can *she* kill the prince for us?"

"I don't think she has the ability to kill," KaLeah said. "I think she can only transport."

"Then have him transported back to Denlerack," Amirra yelled, flailing her arms in exasperation. "Let the people on the dead planet have him."

"He would only find a way back on another one of their ships," KaLeah said. "We are going to have to deal with him here."

"Well, I don't want to deal with him at all, KaLeah." The queen huffed loudly and marched back to her bed. She threw her little body onto it while KaLeah stood in the middle of her room. They were both silent for a few uncomfortable moments.

Amirra didn't know what else to say. KaLeah was back but hadn't actually solved any problems. It was as if she'd caused her all of this pain for nothing.

Her eyes started welling up with tears again. "Everything is worse now than before you left."

"Please don't say that, Amirra." KaLeah moved to sit at the foot of the queen's large bed.

"I know things did not turn out the way we had hoped, but I learned so much on Denlerack. We are still in a better place knowing more than if I hadn't gone there at all."

"What did you learn? What did you do there?" Amirra sat up and wiped away tears. "What is Denlerack like?" she asked, her tone softening slightly.

"The world is so much different from ours," KaLeah started. "Where we have villages and castles made of stone, they build huge towers they call buildings within walls that keep entire villages separated from the outside. Their air is thick and smoky, polluted and hard to breath. You can't see Naldash from there. You can't even see the sun." KaLeah sat down onto the edge of her bed before continuing.

"But I met a few of the most wonderful people there who were all trying to help make their world better. A young woman named Elektra saved my life on the very first day. She had made wings that allowed her to fly, and her friend gave me a pair of wings too."

"That's what I saw you wearing at the ship. The black ones. You can actually fly in those?" Amirra asked.

"Yes, I can."

"Can I try them?" Amirra felt a flutter of fear and excitement, remembering how impressive KaLeah had looked in the black dragon wings.

"Of course," KaLeah answered, smiling. "I left them next door in my room, but we can definitely try them out soon. I'll teach you how to fly."

"I guess that would be fun." Amirra started fiddling with the bedding, trying to hang onto why she had been so angry with KaLeah.

Having her there made Amirra yearn for the mother that she never had. She wanted to lay her head in KaLeah's lap and snuggle up to her, hoping to hear that everything would be alright. She wanted to feel safe and protected.

But the young woman had brought back a man intent on harming her and taking everything away from her. She wondered if there was more behind KaLeah being unable to kill him on the ship.

"Do you want Nikolat to be king?" Amirra asked, giving KaLeah a side-eyed glance.

"No. Why would you think that?" KaLeah shrunk away as if struck.

"Because you loved him once. There was a time when you wanted to go with him to rule the Extelli Kingdom on the cliffs."

KaLeah stood up and stepped toward the window. Her long brown hair draped down over her brown tunic and her skin was paler than Amirra had remembered. *Maybe it was the lack of sun on Denlerack*, she assumed.

"I thought that I had feelings for him at first," KaLeah said, her back to Amirra. "But I was just confused. I had never liked a boy before. Boys in my village paid me no attention. Nikolat was the first boy to show me any sort of attention and I was confused about what that meant. I thought it was something special, but it wasn't. He thought I was attractive, and I realize now being attractive isn't a very important characteristic in a person." KaLeah turned back to face Queen Amirra.

"We women are a lot more than our ability to procreate. We are more than our soft lips and skin. When your brother showed me affection, I thought he was appreciating something that no other man could. But I was wrong. He was just appreciating something about me that I hadn't learned to appreciate yet about myself."

Queen Amirra was quiet, considering KaLeah's words. The young woman claimed she no longer had feelings for Nikolat and hadn't brought him back on purpose to take the kingdom from her.

Amirra started to feel the stress lift from her shoulders. "So, you are still my friend, and you will help me keep the kingdom?"

"Yes, of course," KaLeah said.

"Good, because we need your help." Amirra spun around on the bed and sat on the edge, her feet barely touching the floor.

"Why? What's happening?" KaLeah asked, stepping toward her.

"The Lisodanyan King wanted to marry his daughters to my brothers, but that isn't an option now. He still wants Belarone Kingdom, but since there isn't a king for one of his girls to marry, his only other option is to invade and take the throne from me himself."

"Do you know what his plan is? Has General Daven said when the Lisodanyan army might attack us?" KaLeah sounded concerned.

"They are nearing the border now and it could be very soon. I'm scared," Amirra admitted. "My father led all of the battles before. The generals, they all listened to him and now he's gone. They shouldn't listen to me anyway because I didn't study things like warfare. I don't even like playing the strategy games in the library or reading about war history. This isn't me. I can't lead these men into battle. What do I do?"

KaLeah walked toward the bed and placed her hand on the young queen's shoulder. "You give a command to simply protect the kingdom, and the generals will come up with when, where, and how. It may have been part of your father's role, and you can learn it over time. But right now, you can lean on them to make wartime decisions. Follow your instincts. That is where you will be the strongest. That is what you can do as a leader, as the protector of Belarone, that your soldiers and generals cannot do as well."

"My instincts?" Amirra asked.

"Yes. Follow what your heart tells you. Follow your first reaction. You can answer all of your own questions just by paying attention to how you feel."

"If I pay attention to how I feel, I will just curl up into my bed and cry. I feel lost. I feel afraid. I feel angry about my brother being back in Belarone."

KaLeah nodded. "I understand and can see the confusion between the two. Let me think."

KaLeah took a step back and paced for a few moments. Then she drew her sword and spun back toward the queen, arching the sharp object up and then down at Amirra.

The queen screamed and ducked quickly out of the way. KaLeah stopped the swing in mid-air.

"Why did you do that?" Amirra squealed.

"To show you the difference between instinctive reaction and feelings. You acted instinctively, without thinking, to avoid the sword."

"And now I'm angry at you for pretending to kill me!" Amirra yelled.

"Exactly. Those are your feelings about the situation. You must make sure you separate the two. Trust your first response to duck instead of questioning whether or not I intended to hurt you."

"What does that have to do with protecting my kingdom?"

"Your instinct is first to protect yourself," KaLeah explained. "You don't think about it. You just react. Your feelings of being betrayed that I raised my sword against you, or afraid of me actually hurting you, come next, after the reaction. It is that reaction, that lack of hesitancy, that ingrained instinct to save your life, which will help you to save your kingdom and the lives of those who live within it."

"I think I understand, KaLeah. I need to think more about it, though."

"That's good, my queen. Is it alright if I return to my room? I'm exhausted from not being able to rest on the spaceship."

"Yes, but the door between our rooms was boarded up for security. We will need to have the guards remove the boards."

KaLeah smiled warmly. "I'll take the long way around. It is good to be back. And it is really good to see you, Amirra. We will make sure we keep you and this kingdom safe. I promise."

Amirra's heart ached, feeling grateful to have her friend back and on her side. She stood up and wrapped her arms around KaLeah's waist. "It is good to see you too, my friend. I am glad you are back safe."

❦KaLeah❧

KaLeah left the queen's room. The guards closed the door behind her, and she headed toward her own room with her head hung slightly.

She hadn't expected Amirra to be so upset with her. It wasn't that she didn't understand the girl's fear about her brother being back, but there seemed to be lost trust between them and it made her feel sad but determined to win that trust back.

KaLeah looked up and saw General Hilip Daven standing outside of her door in his full white uniform. She slowed her steps, took a deep breath, and tried to calm her racing heart. He stood up a little straighter, squaring his broad shoulders, and then bowed.

"Good evening, Favor KaLeah," he said, shifting his kind, hazel eyes downward and then back into hers when he rose up from his bow.

She just stood there and watched him move his blond hair off his forehead, before remembering she was supposed to curtsy.

"Oh," she said, quickly moving into the motion, finding it awkward in pants. "Hello, General Daven."

"You can just call me Hilip."

"Then you may call me KaLeah."

She laughed suddenly, surprising herself. "Why are we being so formal and awkward, anyway?"

"I'm not sure," he said, smiling back. "Maybe because we haven't seen one another for a while."

"That must be it. Did you need something?"

He shifted his weight from one leg to another and pulled his hands in front of his body before answering. "I wanted to check in with you after the queen's concerns earlier."

"You mean after her emotional outburst?" KaLeah

asked, raising an eyebrow sharply.

"I'm trying to be diplomatic, KaLeah," he said.

"I know." She thought for a moment about Hilip, while she looked him over. When she first met him, he was a captain, and now, he had risen up quickly to general, probably due to his heroics and support of the queen after the king was murdered.

He had always been kind to her and the queen, and she felt protected in his presence. He was a man she could easily talk to and he'd given her no reason not to trust him. KaLeah sighed.

"She is upset with me for bringing her brother back alive, but I really had no choice. I even fought him on the ship and took—" She paused, not knowing if she should tell anyone else that she was now in possession of a dangerous weapon.

"I took control of the ship," she finished. "But I couldn't bring myself to kill him."

Hilip nodded and stepped up to stand right in front of her. He put his hand on her shoulder. "I understand."

A charge of energy flowed through her, surprising her again. She looked at his hand and he quickly removed it. He was a handsome man, and she had thought of him often on Denlerack, but standing in front of him again, she realized she didn't know him at all.

He had been kind to her and seemed to look out for her from the very first moment they met. Hilip had taught her the secret passageways and given her the dagger she kept on her at all times. She knew he was a good man, but she wasn't sure if she should allow herself to consider him as anything more than a general doing his job.

She cleared her throat and her thoughts, trying to refocus. "Amirra and I talked, and she doesn't seem as angry with me anymore. I am hoping this will all blow over and the prince will simply rot away down there alone in the dungeon."

"I will put my best men outside of her room, just in

case," Hilip declared.

"In case of what?" KaLeah asked, tilting her head and suddenly on high alert.

Hilip looked up and down the hallway and then took a step closer to her, lowering his voice. Chills ran across her skin, but she didn't know if it was anticipation of what he was about to tell her or his sudden proximity.

"There may still be soldiers, and even generals, who would welcome Prince Nikolat as our next king. I don't need to tell you how uncommon it is for a queen to rule alone. And she is a very young one, at that."

KaLeah was instantly on the defensive, protective of the queen and of women in general. "I don't understand what the issue is. Why can't these men accept that there is now a woman in charge?" She whispered a little louder than she had intended.

"Why can't they accept it?" Hilip asked, standing up straighter. "KaLeah, she isn't even a woman yet. She is a child; a little girl who just lost her entire family. She is still attending her lessons on math and history, has just learned to write, and we expect her to make decisions for an entire kingdom? The people and the soldiers in this kingdom have never seen a little girl on the throne. They have struggled. They have fought wars. They have farmed land and starved. So, when they look to a leader, they expect to see someone who has overcome the same hardships they have endured, at the very least."

"But what hardship did the king, or his sons ever have to endure, really?" KaLeah asked.

"They fought in battles."

"So did I," KaLeah said, remembering the night she'd caught Lamone sneaking an assassin into the castle, the night she'd been stabbed, the night Amirra had almost died.

"But the queen did not fight any battles, KaLeah. And you are not the one on the throne; she is."

"On Naldash, the royalty is as sacred as the dragon ancestors, the spirits that supposedly guide us and watch after us," KaLeah said, raising her hands in frustration. "She should be revered for being the king's daughter."

"She is and there is no debate about that," Hilip agreed. "The debate is whether or not her brother should sit on the throne as king now that he has returned."

"I should have killed him," KaLeah said, knowing the truth of it.

"Don't say things like that, KaLeah. It's dangerous." Hilip's voice was low and cautious, trying to protect her.

She nodded, understanding, but she was angry and frustrated about the entire thing. She knew it wasn't Hilip's fault, but why should Amirra fear her brother's return?

Anissa La Alani, the dragon spirit, had floated above them on the balcony on the day Amirra became the Belarone queen. She hoped the dragon spirit would show herself again if they needed help. She was starting to feel like it was her, Hilip, and the queen against the entire world; against two entire worlds.

And she didn't feel ready.

She put her hands up in front of her and looked them over. They were bruised from her squabble with the prince, and they weren't ready to truly battle.

"It's been too long since I've had a good sword fight," KaLeah said. "I would love to practice with you. When do you do drills?"

"First light, out by the stables," Hilip answered.

"I'll be there tomorrow morning. Just go easy on me. I haven't been keeping up with my swordplay."

"It'll be my pleasure to be gentle, Favor KaLeah."

He bowed, but his cheeks reddened before he turned away to walk back down the hallway. She felt a mix of relief and sudden loneliness at seeing him leave.

KaLeah went into her room and locked the door behind her, surprised by how good it felt to be back in her room after traveling to Denlerack and back.

There was a fireplace, a large bed stacked with fur blankets, an armoire she knew led to secret passageways, and a small basin with water. It was familiar and comfortable. Stable.

She kicked off her black boots and sat on the small sofa, stretching her legs out. The room was cold, and she looked at the pile of wood beside the fireplace, wondering if she had the energy to light a fire.

Even the bed seemed too far away as she leaned back and rested her head onto the back of the sofa instead of walking across her room.

The dark colors and dim light from a few burning candles began to lull her to sleep.

She saw Hilip when she closed her eyes. His smile wide across his lovely, clean-shaven face. His eyes, light blue with dark blue speckles, glittering at her as if he had been waiting for her to return.

No," she told herself.

She sat up, jerking her body into a rigid stance, and shook thoughts of Hilip from her head. KaLeah walked to the window, looked across the lawn, and then up into the dark sky.

He is just like the others, she told herself. *He is just another man who doesn't think Amirra and I can stand on our own and save the world.*

He might think I'm attractive and strong, and maybe even smart, but there is no way that he could have real feelings for me.

He is a general and he has a job to do. I can't be distracted by him, and I can't let him distract me like Nik did not so long ago.

I won't let that happen to me again.

❧Hilip❧

Hilip noticed his palms were sweaty.

He had been in the king's army since he was eight, starting off as an errand runner in order to help make money for his family. He had grown up sword fighting, earned the trust of many of the men, became the youngest captain and now he was the youngest general in Belarone history. He had been in more battles than men twice his age.

And he had never been nervous. He wasn't the type to show emotions, whether positive or negative.

He just did whatever needed to be done and whatever was best for the kingdom and for his family.

So, he was surprised to find himself feeling a mix of feelings whenever he was around KaLeah.

He had been excited to see her step out of the ship, and then angry at seeing that the prince had been in there with her.

Jealousy crept into his chest, and that feeling drove him to follow her to the queen's room, where he waited anxiously for her.

He had felt nervous standing in front of her, watching her face and her stormy blue eyes for any clue, any hint, that she might have feelings for him.

He couldn't believe the array of emotions he was experiencing. It was embarrassing to be so vulnerable, hoping she had missed him like he had missed her.

But things were delicate. He was a general now, and in addition to protecting the young queen, multiple invasions were threatening their borders and skies.

He knew that's where his mind should be focused. And yet, his heart was beating faster in anticipation of practicing with KaLeah the following morning.

Any normal man would be anxious about the impending battles, but Hilip had never feared a fight. He had never truly feared anything, until he had watched KaLeah vanish into blue flames. He had been afraid he'd never see her again. He had been afraid she'd be in danger, and he wouldn't be there to save her.

And now, he was afraid that KaLeah would only ever see him as a general performing his duties.

He wiped his palms on his pant legs, nodding at the guards that he had placed in front of Queen Amirra's doors as he walked by.

He truly was concerned about the young girl's safety,

even more so now that her brother had returned.

Hilip put men on her he knew he could trust. They were men who were protective of their own mothers and sisters, and other females, out of a respectful ownership of that responsibility.

They were the type of men who never gawked or made sexual innuendos when younger ladies were nearby. They didn't sleep with the servants or nurses. They were loyal to their duty, but their hearts were also in their job.

He knew they would protect the queen against any threat, not because she was the queen, but because she was a helpless young girl.

Unfortunately, those men were hard to find.

There was a masculine part to being a soldier, and some men liked to compete for who could be not just the strongest, toughest fighter, but the best with the ladies.

He had never participated in that type of thinking, and so his path to go up the hierarchy within the king's army was a lot easier. He only focused on achieving his goals and didn't let the men's games distract him.

Most of the men he fought beside had different lives and concerns than he did, though. It wasn't until a father died and a young man had to step up, that he'd recognize a change in maturity.

Sometimes, there was anger and resentment that the man now had to take care of a family, even though it was his own, before he was ready. But Hilip had already experienced those reactions at a young age, and had been forced to grow up so quickly, he hardly remembered those emotions.

There were traditions and expectations that ran deep throughout history. Husbands and fathers were expected to take care of everything. Kings, leaders, the heads of favor families, store owners, soldiers, generals—all men.

So, when his own father suddenly passed away, Hilip stepped up as the head of the family to ensure his mother and sisters were taken care of.

He was too young then to think about being with a woman or creating a new family of his own.

Other men who grew up with that expectation, who were suddenly burdened with a very different life, either reacted by taking ownership of that responsibility, or they became angry and resentful.

And Hilip could spot the difference. He had never been a talker, choosing to spend all his free time becoming an expert swordsman and learning about battle strategies instead.

The unexpected benefit of being quiet was that he heard and saw everything.

He had known for years he could not trust Prince Nikolat or his friend, Favor Lamone, but he didn't know why until the night KaLeah had found Lamone to be a traitor to the kingdom.

Hilip had his suspicions about the prince then, but he could never obtain any proof. Even with proof, once the king and the elder Prince Bylex were killed, Hilip had no authority or recourse to call out Prince Nikolat for his treason.

Belarone Kingdom had always been ruled by kings. Even if kings died, the queens had remarried from the Favor families, and only a man who the generals had approved of.

But now, Hilip was a general.

He knew that General Zoseff Array was the only wild card. As well as he knew most of the men in the legion, General Array was sometimes a mystery to him.

The large, dark-skinned, bald-headed man was domineering and exuded leadership. He commanded every room he walked into, but it wasn't just his stature. He had a great, wide smile and a personality that everyone loved and trusted.

His laugh could be heard throughout the castle, as could his jokes.

But General Array had been loyal to the king and princes. He seemed to have a good heart and cared for the princess, for her safety, but Hilip did not know if General Array would embrace the tradition of Belarone desiring a king in place of a queen.

Now that Prince Nikolat was back, he would need to act quickly to find out where General Array stood.

He heard boots running toward him and he instinctively placed his hand on his sword.

A young soldier with pale skin and red hair approached, bowing slightly.

"General Daven," he said, breathing heavily. "I've been looking for you."

"What have you heard?"

They both looked up and down the hallways to make sure they were alone.

"There is talk that the men want Prince Nikolat released from the dungeon. They want him restored to the throne. They don't think it is right for a young girl to be queen. They say she is too emotional—that she isn't ready and can't make decisions."

"Which men?" Hilip asked.

"Soldiers."

"General Array?" Hilip pressed. If General Array supported Nikolat on the throne, Hilip was afraid there would be nothing to prevent it.

"I am not certain, sir. And there is more. Lisodanyan troops were falling back when they heard Prince Nikolat had returned with a flying weapon. But now, word has reached them that he is in the dungeon, so they are beginning to creep back toward our borders. The soldiers believe if we put the prince on the throne, Lisodanya will cease to be a threat. And if we don't, and the army does come, they don't think the queen will be able to protect us."

"Thank you for your report," Hilip said. "Stay vigilant and keep me posted if you hear anything more."

"Yes, general."

The boy bowed and ran off, leaving General Daven even more concerned than before.

He knew the time was coming when he would have to make some very difficult decisions.

5 EXPECTATIONS

Nikolat Belarone cracked his knuckles and smiled knowingly. He could see the soldiers whispering among themselves in the hallway that led to the stairs up and out of the dungeon.

"When I am king, I will remember the men who brought me steak and drinks down here," he said, his voice carrying across the cavernous space.

It was inconvenient and uncomfortable to be sitting on the stone ground, to be sure. The air was stuffy, and he would give his right arm for a warm bath.

No, he said to himself, *my left arm. I'll need to kill my sister and KaLeah with my right one.*

KaLeah… his mind drifted back to wrestling with her on the ship. He was angry that she'd gotten the better of him by taking the gun.

Of course, it didn't matter. He wouldn't need the gun once he was back in charge of commanding his father's army.

It was embarrassing and demeaning to be stuck in the dungeon, covered with layers of dirt and dust from the dark planet, Denlerack, starving and thirsty, while his sister played with her dolls in the throne room. He assumed she still needed people to help her cut her meat, and nurse maids to dress her. She was a child, a princess, and not a leader.

He was meant to be a king.

He'd barely survived on Denlerack and now he was so close to the kitchens that he could smell cooked foods wafting down the stairwell. He was so painfully close to everything he wanted.

One thing for certain, he was going to get out of there. He was going to be clean again, eat until he felt full, and sit on his father's throne.

Nikolat needed a plan, but his mind was so clouded with the lack of nutrition. All he could think about was food, juices, meats, fruits, water…

He leaned against the bars of the cell; his legs stretched out in front of him. The soldiers were still there watching him, but maybe not truly guarding him, he hoped.

"It is almost time, men," he said loudly enough for them to hear from across the room. "We will rise again as men of Belarone. We are my father's men. Remember my father, the king? Spirits rest his soul. I fought beside him when we were invaded. I fought beside him when we took Extelli. Doesn't that mean anything to you wretched soldiers?" Nik tsked and shook his head, conveying his disappointment in these men who had served the king now reduced to milkmaids.

"What would my father think about this kingdom now that it has fallen to my baby sister? How do you feel about being ruled by a little girl? I am already a king. I have traveled to Denlerack and back. I have seen true desolation and destruction and survived. I know how to fly a metal sky craft through the stars. What other king in history can say these things? What kind of kingdom would this be if we allowed ourselves to be ruled by women? You think Lisodanya will stand for that? Do you think the people of Extelli or Lisodanya would allow themselves to be ruled by a little girl? Absolutely not! They would join together in the streets, march to their castles, and take their kingdoms back, bestowing a rightful man to their thrones."

He knew the soldiers, the guards, were listening to him intently, so he spoke to them directly from his dungeon cell. "But what will you men do? You men of Belarone, if you can call yourselves that. Lisodanyan troops are on their way here to invade us right now and who will lead you all into battle? A child?"

Nikolat rambled on for some time. He stopped caring about whether or not anyone was listening. Talking kept his mind alive while his body starved.

"Your Majesty," said a man's voice, finally.

Nikolat looked up toward the sound and saw a soldier standing with the gate open. The man handed Nik a steak and a potato on a plate. Another man came in and set down a pitcher of clear liquid.

"Ah, may the dragon spirits bless you," Nikolat said.

And then he ate.

❧KaLeah☙

KaLeah woke up still fully dressed in her pants and tunic, but she had managed to leave the chair and get into the bed sometime during the night.

While her brain was foggy from sleep, she thought she was still on Denlerack, sleeping in her biological father's mansion. She opened her eyes to see the bedposts and curtains bathed in light from the open window and smiled wide.

Sunshine meant she was back home; safe on Naldash.

Sunshine meant it was time to meet General Daven on the lawn for swordplay.

Hilip…

She jumped up, used the chamber pot, and splashed cold water on her face. For a moment, she wondered if she smelled.

That's a weird thought. Why does that matter?

She resisted the urge to see if there were fresh clothes

in the armoire. Seeing that piece of furniture reminded her of the dresses Amirra had forced her to wear and how strange it had been putting a dress on for the first time.

Clean clothes, dresses. Why am I thinking about these things? It's just Hilip, she told herself.

KaLeah left her room, looking at the guards briefly as she passed Queen Amirra's room.

She was proud of the young girl for continuing to own her position but scared for her too. Amirra was only ten, tiny and tenacious, full of attitude and now coping with loss.

KaLeah didn't remember her own mother enough to mourn her. She'd barely thought of the father who raised her, or the father who didn't, since meeting him.

Even though she once mourned the loss of Prince Nikolat, thinking that he had died, she no longer cared about him.

She couldn't empathize with Amirra's loss, so she didn't know how to comfort the girl. All she knew was that she needed to keep encouraging her to be strong. Wisdom would come. The queen had plenty of people around her now who were willing to help her be successful.

KaLeah walked down a servant's staircase, slipping into the kitchens, and grabbed half a loaf of bread. She munched on it all the way through the main corridors, the entry doors, and out onto the stone courtyard.

A few men were tending to draggots, marching, and drilling. But it was mostly quiet in the early morning. She took a deep breath, smelling the sweet dewy grass.

It was crazy how much she used to take the fresh air for granted. After living on the polluted, smelly planet of Denlerack, where everything tasted like sulfur, she was so grateful to be breathing clean air and eating freshly baked bread.

She had honestly never been happier. There was a skip in her step as she looked for Hilip.

Handsome Hilip. Kind Hilip.

Spirits, no. Stop that, she told herself, wiping the smile from her own face.

She stretched her fingers, opening and closing her palm, and started doing lunges across the yard, heading toward the area where the soldiers were exercising and sparring.

KaLeah was acutely aware of how odd she looked, lunging painfully slow toward the practice field. She took a break, stood up, leaned to one side, stretched her right arm high above her head, her scabbard dipping low on the left, and then stretched the other side.

A few soldiers looked at her, some laughed, and she thought she saw one roll his eyes.

Never mind them, she told herself. *I am a fighter, even if I am a woman. I killed an assassin right in front of the queen's room. These men just don't understand what I can do because they haven't seen it.*

But they will today.

General Daven spotted her and came jogging up to her in plain clothing.

"Good morning, Favor KaLeah," he said.

He was already glistening with sweat, and his blond hair was slicked back by the moisture. His cheeks were slightly pink, and his light blue eyes were wide and bright.

"Good morning, general," she said.

"Are you ready to spar? Do you need to warm up?"

"I stretched on the way over. I'm ready," she said, drawing out her sword.

"On your guard, then."

He raised his sword up and stepped back on one foot. She mirrored his stance and made the first move, lunging forward.

Hilip easily deflected.

They exchanged hits and blocks, moving around the yard, and KaLeah noticed some men around them had stopped practicing.

"They are watching us," she said.

"They have never seen a woman sword fight."

"Some of them have seen me fight." She thrusted

forward and he pivoted to avoid the blow.

"Not in the daylight," he said, winking.

"Did you see me that night—the night the castle was attacked?" KaLeah asked.

"I saw you," he said. But then his expression changed. His brow furrowed and his smile vanished. His movements seemed to become more aggressive as he attacked.

"I saw you surrounded, and I couldn't get to you," he said, stepping toward her with his eyes on her sword.

Was he sad? Disappointed? Guilty? She couldn't tell from his expression and tone. She had a strange swirling in her stomach, and wished she knew what he was remembering.

"Why did you want to get to me? You hardly knew me."

The general's cheeks flushed again, and a grin came to the corners of her lips at seeing him so exposed.

"I didn't want you to get hurt, KaLeah. You'd been through a lot, and I knew how much you meant to the princess."

"I see," KaLeah said, disappointed. She narrowed her focus and leapt toward him, striking at him. He swatted her sword away.

Of course, he only cared about my safety because he was concerned about the princess. This has nothing to do with me, she told herself.

"It seems that you've been taking good care of her; keeping her safe." Her tone was almost accusatory, and she hated her inability to hide the jealousy. Her reaction surprised her.

"I have been practicing with her in the armory," Hilip said. "She has become quite good with the sword and can hit a target consistently with both arrows and daggers. She has been practicing dutifully and with a passionate focus. She seems determined to be as good a warrior as you are."

"Well, being a young woman in her position, she needs to be prepared for anything. I'm grateful you've been teaching her in my absence. My father's teachings saved me many times. This world isn't safe for women who go against tradition."

She took a step back to regroup and saw Denlerack, the dark sister planet, hanging in the sky beyond Hilip's back. The sight of it and remembering the threat still lingering there sent shivers up her spine. "We aren't safe on either world, really."

Movement behind Hilip caught her eye, and she pulled her sword back, standing at attention.

"What is it?" Hilip turned to see what she was looking at.

Clegg Trapper, the man who had raised her, had emerged from the road, and was walking toward them across the castle lawns.

The last time she had seen him, she had set him free from the dungeon during the night. His presence was confusing. She assumed he was no longer a wanted man, since the guards had let him come this far.

His face was stoic behind his dark beard. He nodded to Hilip and then looked her in the eyes.

"KaLeah, it is good to see you," Clegg said.

KaLeah shifted uncomfortably from foot to foot, feeling awkward in the man's presence after meeting her real father.

Hilip seemed to pick up on her energy, looking between the two. "Excuse me, sir, may I ask why you have returned to the castle?"

Although Hilip had sheathed his sword, he still stood protectively on the lawn with one hand on the hilt.

"I was hoping to have words with my daughter," Clegg said, looking past the general toward her.

She had no issue with talking to the man, she just felt disappointed to have to leave Hilip—her practice with Hilip, so soon.

The handsome general turned back to look into her eyes. He closed the distance between them so officially, leaning down toward her face to whisper.

Her heart fluttered and then pounded at his closeness.

"Are you alright?" he asked.

"Yes, I'll speak with him," she said, barely able to hear her own words amongst the sound of her heart pounding in her head.

"I enjoyed this and hope we can do it again soon." His eyes pierced hers and he smiled ever so slightly. She couldn't move. She couldn't even bring herself to nod.

Hilip bowed slightly to them both and turned, heading toward a group of soldiers sparring on the lawn.

She immediately wished he hadn't left and resisted the urge to call him back.

"Father," she said, and then corrected herself. "Clegg, what are you doing back here?"

"I saw the Denlerack ship break through the atmosphere and knew you had returned. I was hoping for news from the other world and to see that you were unharmed during your travels."

"I am fine," she said.

She noticed many of the soldiers were still watching them.

"Can we go somewhere more private? I am feeling a bit exposed out here," she said.

"Of course, after you." Clegg made a sweeping gesture with his arm for her to lead the way.

KaLeah led him through the yard and toward a garden on the other side of the castle. She knew there were benches throughout the garden they could sit on and not be disturbed or overheard.

He followed silently, but he had always been a quiet man. He was a stealth-like hunter and had been a soldier on Denlerack. It was strange to think about how she'd been raised by a man she now felt she hardly knew at all.

Bushes lined the parameter of the garden. They walked through an archway of vines, and a sweet smell flooded her senses.

Beyond the archway, there was a stone walkway leading to a small fountain. She headed for one of the wooden benches across from it and took a seat.

Clegg Trapper sat down across from her, on the stone wall edge of the fountain.

"How was Denlerack? What happened?" he asked.

She found she couldn't keep eye-contact for long. It felt strange knowing a man who was not her biological father had raised her without her knowledge.

Do I feel resentment? she wondered, looking at the flowers growing around her.

"I met my father," she told him.

"I see," he said with no emotion. "I am surprised he let you go."

"I escaped. My friends tried to assassinate him and failed. I rescued them and we stole the ship so I could return."

"Keldon still lives then. This doesn't bode well for the people of Naldash." His words felt laced with judgement, and she felt like a failure.

Disappointing the man felt different now that she knew he wasn't her real father. It felt less defeating and painful than when she had made mistakes as a child, but there was still an uncomfortable feeling gripping her chest.

"Don't you think I know that?" She stood up and took a few hard steps away from him, crossing her arms as if to protect herself. She felt as if she were being chastised again for not bringing home any game after a long day of hunting.

"I am not sure what I was supposed to do on Denlerack, but I am well aware that I failed, regardless. The dictator is still alive and he's going to bring his ships here."

KaLeah looked up into the sky at the dark orb floating just a bit lower than the sun. She looked until her eyes started to burn, then gazed back at the ground, blinking.

"I couldn't kill him, father... I mean, Clegg."

"You don't need to do that, KaLeah. I raised you as my own daughter. You may call me father. Keldon may be your real father, but I am the man who taught you how to be the woman you are today."

KaLeah shook her head violently at his words, then turned to him. "You taught me how to be a man, not a woman. And now I am someone in between. I'm in between two worlds. In between two fathers. In between a man and a woman. I don't know who I am or who I am supposed to be, Clegg."

He shrugged off her outburst. "None of us do. Do you think I knew how to be a father? All I ever knew was war, hunger, fighting, and struggling to survive. I had no idea that one day I would be asked to protect and raise a child alone. Mothers are supposed to raise children."

"My mother…" KaLeah uncrossed her arms and went back to the bench, slumping down into it. "I saw a picture of her. I slept in her bed. I looked out of the same window she had once. I think that I even wore her clothes."

She lifted her eyes to Clegg's. "How could she be with *him*?"

Clegg held her gaze for a moment, and then looked away, off into the gardens. "Sometimes, when a person only knows a life of terror where one is surrounded by terrible things, then a level of comfort begins to develop in order to protect the heart and mind. When pain is the only thing you have known, but you crave love so desperately, you find ways to turn that pain into love."

Clegg motioned to her. "Take that bench you are sitting on, for example. If that were the only bed you had ever known, then you would eventually learn to sleep on it. You would be tired and desire that bench so you could rest. It would not matter if the bench caused you pain. The bench was there for you to rest, and it was better than no bench at all."

His words made her heart ache for her mother. The woman must have endured so much emotional pain that Keldon's abuse had seemed normal.

"So, what you are saying is my mother had a painful childhood and fell in love with my father because he was a slight improvement?"

"I did not know your mother well," Clegg admitted. "I helped her escape the dictator and the planet, but we had a very short time together before you were born. I wish I had asked her more about herself and her life. Had I known I was going to end up raising her daughter, I would have tried to learn more about her, for you."

He shook his head back and forth and looked to be sincerely regretful before continuing. "I have seen her kind before. I have seen children raised in abusive homes grow up to confuse fear with love. They accept the bench because they think that is the best they can get, and it is the best they deserve. Or they choose to avoid it altogether, sleeping on the ground. Some are so low they don't even think they deserve the bench."

Things started clicking together in her mind as she listened to the man who had raised her. He could have just left her on the doorstep of one of the villagers. He could have taken the ship and gone back to Denlerack. But he made the choice to raise her.

He had been abused. Her mother had been abused. And he didn't want KaLeah to repeat the same pattern.

"You," KaLeah said, understanding. "You came from an abusive home."

Clegg nodded slowly and she thought she saw his eyes become glassy. "Even though I didn't raise you with the kind of love that you deserved, I was never abusive toward you. I knew I could help you channel your frustration and loss into hunting and fighting and provide you with lessons when I lacked the ability to provide you with familial love. I know I wasn't a good father to you, KaLeah, but I'm not a monster. I have seen how people who grow up without love can end up loving any monstrous thing that gives them attention. I swore long ago I would not become like the man who raised me. We make the best choices we can in this life. Your mother left the dictator because she did not want you to be raised by a monster. She was afraid of what you might become. She knew you were special. "Maybe it is because the spirits spoke to her. Maybe she knew they would one day call to you." Clegg shrugged and shifted his weight on the garden wall where he sat.

"You may never think of me as your father, and that is alright, as long as you know I tried my best to raise a daughter Huntra would be proud of. I raised a young woman *I* am proud of. And although there is no easy solution to protect this planet from the Denlerack invasion, I believe you will try your best to keep this planet safe. You can do hard things. You are a survivor."

KaLeah stood up and placed her hand on her sword. "I am what you made me. I am a fighter. And I am grateful for that, father."

The man stood up and stepped toward her. She tilted her head up to look at him. "When the Denlerack army does come, I would like to fight beside you, if you'll have me," he said.

There was a pang in her chest and a burning sensation at the corners of her eyes.

"I would be honored," she said in a whisper.

They nodded their heads in slight shows of respect to each other, and KaLeah cleared the lump growing in her throat.

"General Daven can provide you with your quarters and prepare you for battle," she said.

"I will go check in with him and leave you to the garden," Clegg said. He nodded again and left her alone with her thoughts.

She fell back onto the bench, feeling exhausted from trying to hold in her emotions.

She was still angry and resentful, but it was harder for her to understand why. More than anything, she felt a deep longing for loving, attentive parents. She closed her eyes and saw her mother and Clegg, smiling together, landing the ship in the woods, and building their hut.

She saw her true father Keldon back on Denlerack pulling her chair out for her in the mansion, walking her back to her room after dinner, and kissing her sweetly on the cheek.

Two visions. Two different men. And a mother she never knew. She longed for a normal, comfortable family.

And then another vision came to her mind.

It was the day Queen Amirra and General Daven had walked her to the lawn. The dragon spirit Anissa La Alani was standing there, large and regal, green scales, and translucent wings.

She had been sad leaving them behind and felt a great relief at seeing them again on the same lawn when she returned from Denlerack.

KaLeah slowly opened her eyes, looking at the fountain. In the center was a large, stone dragon, wings spread out wide. A stream of water came up and out of the dragon's mouth, shooting into the air and then coming down in two different streams.

The streams fell onto the heads of two smaller dragons—her children.

"I have family here," KaLeah said out loud. Then she stood up and took a few steps toward the fountain. "And I have to save my family. I have to figure out how to save them."

She turned and marched back into the castle, heading toward one of the tapestries in the main corridor.

It was the one she had walked by numerous times, initially thinking there was a man with long hair riding on a dragon's back, flying into a battle.

But now she knew it was actually a woman warrior, which went against everything the Naldashian people believed.

Women did not rule kingdoms alone and women were not warriors. Amirra and KaLeah were not what the men expected but looking at the tapestry made her wonder if it was only that the stories had been changed over time.

Was this a depiction of history, or just someone's dream turned to art? she wondered.

She stood in front of the woven image. The sky was a dark blue, nearly black, with grey clouds threatening the edges of the image. A woman rode a black dragon down from the cliffs, sword drawn and extended, as they headed into a battle.

But where? What battle and for what purpose?

Is this the past or the future?

She ran her fingers over the image.

"Anissa La Alani, where are you? Is this our future? Am I to ride you into battle against the Denlerack spaceships when they come? Can you tell me how to save the sister worlds?"

If I knew, I would have saved everyone by now.

The words drifted into KaLeah's mind, and she knew them to be from the phantom dragon. She looked around the corridor but saw nothing and no one.

"Can't you kill Keldon and stop this invasion?"

Killing is not a magic that I possess. There is nothing I can do.

Hope spilled out as KaLeah exhaled a breath she had been holding inside her tight chest. She pulled her hands to her head and rubbed at her temples, trying to temper a slow pain building there.

It was just stress, at least, and not the spirits warning of danger. It had been a while since the angry voices had penetrated her mind.

"Why are you the only one I can talk to, when I hear all of the guttural growls and whispers of other spirits in my head?"

I hear them too. Some are the spirits of the Dynack dragons. Some are the spirits of the Nala dragons. The Nalas want to warn you of danger so you will protect their world. The Dyancks want their dictator, your father, to take Naldash. They want to finish a war they started while they were still living—a war I ended by splitting the planets apart.

"But why me? Why aren't they speaking to kings, queens, or generals? Why am I hearing them if I have no idea how I could save either world?"

That might be my fault.

What do you mean?

I spoke to your mother.

KaLeah stopped pacing and turned back toward the tapestry, as if the dragon was speaking to her from it.

"My mother?"

Yes, I was the one who encouraged her to come here. I was concerned for her. I wanted to help her.

"You knew my mother and you encouraged her to come here? I can't... I don't..."

KaLeah put her hands to her temples again, rubbing back the throbbing pain that had suddenly come upon her.

"But I thought that dragons had always spoken to her? Couldn't she hear them the same way I can?"

She heard me when I chose to speak to her, and to Clegg. I was trying to help her. She and others like you hear the growls from time to time, especially if the spirits think the human has a particular advantage they could use. But she did not hear words until I spoke to her directly.

"But why her? Why did you interfere in her life? Why did you interfere in mine if we aren't supposed to somehow save this world? Can't you just tell me what I need to do?"

I do not know how to repair the damage I have done. I do not know why you can hear all of us. All I know is the dragons want to finish their war, both sides want to win, and if you can hear them, then they believe you can help them win.

Maybe you hear them because you are like me; you are of both worlds. Conceived in one, born in the other.

The pain suddenly vanished from KaLeah's mind, as if a clarity had been revealed.

KaLeah wasn't magical. She had so special abilities. There was no prophecy about her. She just belonged in both and yet in neither world—just like Anissa La Alani.

"What side are you on?"

I want peace, but I am cursed to neither live nor die. Until the war is won, I will not have peace.

"Anissa,"

You may call me Ash, as my mother and your mother did.

"Alright, Ash," KaLeah said, starting to pace the floor in front of the tapestry again. She tried to make sense of all of the details.

"I have no power to stop the war. I am just a young woman. You cannot rest without peace. Elektra is back on Denlerack trying to protect her friends. What can I do? You transported me across space. Do you have some powers we can use to stop my father, Keldon, from enslaving the people on this planet?"

My magic is elemental. I can manipulate water, earth, air, and fire, Ash answered.

KaLeah tried to think of ways those powers could be useful. She realized by talking to Ash, the dragon was not a warrior. She had never fought or killed. This was not a monster in any sense.

It would be up to KaLeah to come up with a strategy. She would need to coach Ash on what to do when ships broke through their atmosphere.

"Elemental. We may need to practice and see what you can do."

"Favor KaLeah, is everything alright?"

She jumped and spun around, face-to-face with the general.

"Hilip, you startled me," she said, removing her hand from her scabbard and placing it on her heart.

He cocked a slight grin.

"I didn't think anybody could sneak up on you."

She smiled and laughed slightly.

"Don't tell anyone that it can be done," she said.

"I promise. But seriously, are you alright after speaking to your father earlier?"

"Clegg, the man who raised me, who isn't my real father, yes. I am fine. He is a good man, and my real father is a monster. Clegg wants to fight with us."

"Yes, he told me as much on the lawns and I set him to sparring with my men." Hilip eyed the tapestry and then looked back to her. "What are you doing here? I heard you talking."

"I was just seeking counsel." KaLeah shrugged as if pacing in front of a tapestry and talking to herself was totally normal.

Hilip furrowed his brow and looked at the wall.

"From a tapestry?"

"No, silly." She reached out and lightly shoved him. He didn't move, but his smile grew wider across his face. "I was talking to Anissa La Alani, the dragon spirit."

"Oh, I see. And is she going to help us defeat Lisodanya and your real father's invading army?"

KaLeah took in a deep breath and let it out slowly, looking back over the tapestry.

"I don't think she can," KaLeah admitted, feeling defeated.

General Daven placed his hand on her shoulder, and a jolt of energy unexpectedly surged through her entire body. The feeling surprised and delighted her. It was getting harder for her to deny there was something between them.

"We will figure this out together, KaLeah," he said.

His voice was calm and confident, and she wanted to believe him. She looked up into his eyes and felt lost there for a moment. KaLeah felt a pull toward him, as if she needed to place her head against his chest. She wanted to wrap herself up into his arms.

What is this urge? she wondered. She shook her head to expunge the desire building within her. "I hope you are right. If you'll excuse me, I need to clean up before breakfast with the queen."

"Do you think she is still angry about you bringing Nikolat back?"

"Maybe a little, although I managed to get her to calm down yesterday. I have never seen her like this. It is like I came back to a completely different queen than the one I left behind."

"Things have been difficult since you left. There is a lot

of pressure resting on her small shoulders."

"She can feel all of those emotions," KaLeah said, "but at the end of the day, she has to be strong enough to rule this kingdom. We have to all figure this out together."

"Together?" Hilip's eyebrows raised.

"Yes. You, Amirra, and I have to figure out how to use the dragon's magic. We are here for a reason. Ash spoke to me and made herself visible to the kingdom the day she sent the prince away.

"Who is Ash?"

"That's what Anissa has asked that we call her. She can manipulate elements, like sending people through the blue flames."

Hilip nodded since he had seen both Nik and KaLeah disappear into the flames.

"I know the looming invasions may seem like too large of a burden for the queen alone, but I am here now. I can support and encourage her."

"I have been here too, you know," Hilip said. "I've never stopped supporting you both."

KaLeah smiled up at him and placed her hand gently on his forearm. He looked at her hand as if he wanted to grab it with his own.

"And I am so grateful to you for that. You have watched over her. It doesn't matter that she is a young girl ruling a kingdom. You have chosen to protect her and her rightful place. You are an honorable man. Her father would be grateful to you for protecting her."

Hilip looked away from her hand on his arm and into her eyes, a sadness crossing over his features.

"Her father would want me to place her brother on the throne," he admitted.

KaLeah pulled her hand back and took a step away from Hilip, the smile vanishing from her face.

He reacted quickly, stepping toward her to close the gap, and grabbed both of her hands in his. He looked into her eyes.

"But I am not going to do that, KaLeah," he said, speaking slowly. "She is the queen, and I will stand by her, no matter what. I will stand by you, too. Always."

KaLeah squinted her eyes and cocked her head to one side. "Me?"

Hilip's cheeks flushed. He turned to look up and down the corridor, making sure they were alone.

"I have missed you, KaLeah," he admitted in a low tone.

A heavy silence filled the air around them. She felt both flustered and fearful. She wanted to run to him and from him at the same time.

"I was hoping you missed me too," he continued. "I was hoping you might want to spend more time together."

Panic rippled through her body. KaLeah took in a deep breath and yanked her hands free from his.

"I have to go," she said.

And then she turned and ran off down the hallway toward her room.

6 THE RIGHTFUL HEIR

Queen Amirra sat in a heavy violet dress at the head of an extremely long, wooden dining table. Every single chair was empty except for hers, exemplifying exactly how alone she felt most of the time.

Her chair was really more of a throne and had been specially made for her so she could sit higher at the table.

She still hadn't gotten used to sitting in her father's place. She expected him to come bounding into the room at any moment, playfully telling her she is too tiny for his chair, and then lifting her up to carry her back to her place at the table.

She smiled thinking about him.

The servants came in with silver trays loaded with breakfast foods and juices. She watched the girls, who were not much older than her, place dishes before her.

"This is too much," she said, anger bubbling up in her tone. "I have told you before this is way too much food for me. Why do you all keep bringing me so much when you know I can't eat all this? It is wasteful."

True to form, the servants said nothing, avoided eye-contact, and kept placing food from their trays onto the table.

Amirra reached out and grabbed one of their thin, white wrists. The girl she grabbed squealed slightly but the queen got her to look her in the eye, finally.

The girl had red hair pulled back into a braid, bright blue eyes, and freckles all along her cheeks. Her eyes were wide, and she stood frozen in place.

Amirra started to laugh.

She couldn't help it. It was the squeal and the look of fear in the girl's eyes. It was as if Amirra had taken the place of her own brothers.

The queen's laugh echoed throughout the space and the young servant girl finally smiled back at her in return.

"You squealed like a juliebee with its tail caught in a trap."

The servant girl laughed cautiously after seeing the look on Amirra's face. She let go of the servant's wrists and noticed all the other servants had fled the room.

"I didn't mean to scare you," said the queen. "I just feel like no one around here listens to me. Everyone wants to keep acting like I am my father, but I am not my father. And I am not my brothers. I am just a girl who has no idea what she is doing most of the time and I don't like wasting food when there are starving people working to make this food in the villages and farms."

She leaned forward and put her face into her hands, feeling her eyes fill with tears. She felt a warm hand on her back, moving in a circular motion.

Amirra took a deep breath to calm herself and then wiped her tears, sitting back up straight. The servant removed her hand quickly.

"My apologies, Your Highness. I know I am not to touch royalty, but you appeared in need of a friend." The servant clasped her hands together in front of her grey dress and bowed her head as she slowly backed away.

"Thank you," Amirra said. "What is your name?"

"I am Tasis, Your Highness. Daughter of Aris Ardatu."

"Tasis," Queen Amirra repeated, smiling at the young

servant. Amirra found the servant girl to be very lovely and demure.

Amirra suddenly wanted to be normal. She wanted to be able to sit and braid this girl's hair while they giggled about nothing important.

The pain of having no friends her own age and of being a ruler so young pressed down on her like a great weight.

"Will you tell the kitchen to only bring me a single portion and they can choose the meal for me? I don't care what it is, I just care that it isn't wasted. My father and brothers had the appetites of dragons, but I do not."

"I understand, Your Highness."

The girl curtsied and left the room, leaving Amirra alone in a stillness she had become accustomed to since KaLeah had left for Denlerack.

Her fork made loud clanking sounds as she began to eat the eggs.

A door opened and the sound startled her. She turned and saw KaLeah sauntering into the room with a big smile on her face.

Amirra was instantly annoyed but wasn't sure why. She knew she should feel happy KaLeah was back and happy to finally have company at mealtimes again.

"Good morning, my queen," she said, bowing.

Amirra rolled her eyes. "You are supposed to curtsy, not bow."

"Oh right, sorry. I just keep seeing so many men around here bowing that I forget."

"You forget that you aren't a man?" Amirra asked, not caring that it sounded rude.

"That's not what I mean, Amirra. You grew up around all of this, so it comes more naturally to you."

"When will you learn the correct way to live in a castle, KaLeah?"

KaLeah froze for a moment, standing beside the table, but Amirra looked down to select another bite of eggs. KaLeah grabbed a heavy wooden chair and slowly dragged it across the stone floor to sit closer to her. The favor sat heavily and loudly, then pulled a plate closer to her, piling on it from other plates.

"Maybe if you practiced your swordplay, you'd be hungry enough to eat all this," KaLeah jabbed back.

"I do practice," the queen exclaimed. "Even though I don't need to practice when I have these guards and soldiers all over the castle, following me from room to room all the time."

"It doesn't hurt to be skilled at protecting yourself. Hilip says you have been doing your archery." KaLeah's tone softened.

"I practice swordplay, archery, and even knife throwing, yes, but not enough to eat all of this. This much food is…obscene."

"It is delicious, at least," KaLeah said, scooping some into her mouth. "It is so quiet in here. Where is everybody?"

"I am the only one who eats in here. I don't know if you have noticed but all of my family is dead, except for the one who *wants* me dead, who is currently in the dungeon."

"This is true." KaLeah set her fork down and leaned back in her chair. Amirra tried not to make eye-contact. "I am sorry about all that you are going through right now," KaLeah said. "I feel that even though we talked last night, you are still angry with me. What do we need to do to just get past it?"

"Get past it? I can't just get past it. You brought him back and he wants my throne!"

"I was trying to get back here, and he was on the ship. I fought him but it was no good. I'm sorry I brought him back. I'm sorry I couldn't kill him."

"If you truly loved me, you would kill him to protect me."

"That isn't fair. I cared about him once too and if he is only being himself, and not actively trying to hurt us, I can't *just* murder him. It isn't right, Amirra."

"Was it right when he tried to kill me on the balcony?"

"You were trying to claim the throne he thought belonged to him, but no, of course it wasn't right. But that's what men do. They fight for what they want."

"And we don't?" Amirra couldn't help but look at KaLeah, her cheeks flushing with anger.

"We do, absolutely. I fought him that day. I fought to protect you because I believe you belong on the throne. But I didn't know how to kill him then, I didn't know how to kill him in the spaceship, and I don't know how to kill him now."

"I will," Amirra stated plainly, looking back at her plate. Amirra felt KaLeah watching her as she lifted another bite to her lips, chewed her food, then swallowed it.

She had once idolized her older brother. He was handsome and smart, always wielding his charm to get his way. It was impressive and she had wanted to be just like him.

"What do you mean?" KaLeah asked.

"I will have him tried for treason."

"With what proof?"

"He tried to take my throne and he will try again."

"But that isn't proof, Amirra. He is trying to claim a throne he believes belongs to him and some people in the kingdom may believe the same thing. We need to be careful."

"We?" Amirra nearly choked on her food. "You and I are not in this together. I am dealing with this alone. I have to go counsel the townsfolk alone. I have to command the army to prepare for war with Lisodanya alone. I have to save the world from a Denlerack invasion alone."

"Stop it. You are not alone in any of this. You are just angry with me."

"I am angry, and I am alone," Amirra yelled. "You left me for nothing. You didn't stop Denlerack, and you brought my brother back!"

Queen Amirra pushed herself away from the table, slid

out of the chair, and marched toward the doors that led to the throne room.

If KaLeah liked the massive amounts of food and the solitude, then she could have it. Amirra had more important things to do than eat and yell at the woman. She had to greet and counsel the people who came to see her every morning after breakfast.

She knew many of them were scared, but she didn't know how to promise them everything would be alright when she felt scared herself.

A guard standing silently beside the throne room doors opened one for her and announced her arrival to an empty room. She heard another guard then shout out toward the front of the throne room to the crowd of towns people waiting to speak to her beyond the doors.

She climbed up onto her father's throne and placed her hands on the dragon carved armrests. She took a deep breath and then nodded to the guard standing to her left.

He shouted out again for the guard at the doors to begin letting a few people inside at a time.

General Daven walked in with the first few, escorting them to their place many feet in front of the queen.

She felt safer with the general around. She knew he would always protect her. He had been a loyal and yet distant presence ever since KaLeah had left for Denlerack.

The first man stepped up with his hat in his hand. His skin was dark brown, and he had no hair. His hands were rough and worn.

He bowed to her before speaking. "Majesty, I come from the border. Lisodanyan troops are stealing my ranch animals. They are coming onto my lands at night. I don't know what to do."

Hilip stepped up onto the dais to speak quietly with her.

"Can we send men to help him protect his ranch at night?" she whispered.

"If we send him men, other border ranches will want men," General Daven instructed. "We must keep our troops close to protect the castle and the market center."

"Then he must leave his ranch?"

"At least until Lisodanya retreats." Hilip stood back up and returned to his post.

Queen Amirra sat up straight and gave the rancher the bad news.

Her day carried on like that for some time. KaLeah came in and stood toward the back, watching. Amirra assumed the young woman had nothing better to do.

She would have traded places with her if she could. She was bored listening to each story, all so similar, and depressed by having to disappoint person after person.

They wanted her to save them, but she didn't have magic powers. She couldn't thwart an army, make their crops grow, or solve their feuds with a wave of a hand.

The morning was dragging on and she was starting to feel tired. She wanted to let Hilip know she was done for the day and started to lean over toward him when there was a commotion at the door.

She saw some of her soldiers push through the crowd, knocking a few people down.

Her brother Nikolat walked proudly behind them, clean, shaven, dark brown locks brushed back, and wearing his best bright red royal regalia.

Amirra stood up and Hilip drew his sword, moving to stand in front of her.

"Little sister, no need to stand up for me," he said, fanning out his arms as he kept confidently walking forward into the throne room.

"Halt," Hilip said. Other soldiers came up quickly to stand beside him, protecting the queen. She saw Hilip look at each man carefully, as if making sure he knew which soldiers were standing with him.

Standing with her.

Face-to-face with her brother who had been freed by her own men, she suddenly realized how dire the situation was. Her heart was pounding, and she didn't know what to say.

This man wanted the throne.

Maybe I should just give it to him, she thought.

And then, KaLeah was beside her. She grabbed and gave the queen's hand a quick squeeze before drawing her sword.

"I am here to let you know that the throne is mine," Nikolat called out. "I can help all of these people, where you have been unsuccessful, baby sister. It isn't your fault. You have tried your absolute best, and I applaud your efforts. But we all know that Lisodanya will go away if you simply give me back my throne. There needs to be no discord between us. We can go back to having happy meals together in the dining hall. You can play with your dolls or ride your draggot in the garden while I tend to all this business."

Nikolat swept his arm, motioning to the townsfolk who were now being slowly escorted out of the throne room. "Tell me sister, isn't that what you truly want?"

There was silence in the room. No one would speak until she answered.

She hated that he was right. Living a child's carefree life was what she really wanted, she knew. She missed riding her draggot across the lawns. It was much too risky now. The soldiers hadn't let her leave the castle in so long that she couldn't remember what the markets looked like.

But she wasn't a child anymore. She had been stuffed into a bag and kidnapped because of her brother. She had been attacked by assassins and rescued by KaLeah because of her brother. A war was started because of him.

Nikolat was not a good brother. He was not a good man. He had toyed with KaLeah's emotions and tricked their father, the king.

Queen Amirra turned to look at KaLeah. Maybe she was being too hard on the woman for bringing her brother back. Maybe this was just something the two of them would have to end together.

She turned her eyes back to Nikolat. "I want my people to have the best ruler, and that is not you, brother," she said, loud and defiant.

"You wound me deeply, sister. I was always the better man of my father's sons. I fought better, rode better, and led better on the battlefield. I understand this planet and all of her kingdoms. I can get Lisodanya to back off by marrying one of Mikroth's daughters. You can't do that, sweet sister. It is obvious I am the best leader for Belarone. I have been preparing for this my entire life. You have been preparing to marry into a favor family."

Amirra's blood felt hot under her skin and sweat beaded on her forehead. "The best leader for Belarone is a woman. I am the queen, and you are to be taken back to the dungeon to face trial for treason."

"Tsk, tsk, tsk. You can't charge the rightful heir to the throne with treason. That would be like accusing a farmer of stealing the crops he grew. I am destined to rule Belarone. You may be a queen, but you are just a weak little girl. No queen has ever ruled without a man at her side."

"I do *not* need a man. I do *not* need a king. And you will never rule Belarone."

"Very big words from such a little girl. Alas, I have done my best to reason with you, but as you see, you are a typical girl. You cannot reason with the emotions of girls."

Amirra was fuming. Her fists were clenched, and she felt her nails digging into her own palms.

She wasn't used to fighting with words, and although she was angry, she was also afraid. She was worried her father's ghost would walk up behind her and tell her that she was an idiot for not letting her brother take over now.

"I, Nikolat Belarone, challenge you, Amirra Belarone, for rule of my kingdom. I challenge you to a duel."

Murmurs from remaining townsfolk and soldiers flowed through the room, washing over her. Her stomach sunk down lower in her gut, making her feel sick as acid rushed up her throat.

She stood perfectly still, trying not to make a move or alter her expression. She watched her brother take another step toward her throne.

"And this time, we will duel indoors, right here. There won't be a dragon ghost dropping out of the sky to create a distraction."

"I will fight in the queen's place," KaLeah said, stepping toward the edge of the dais. "As the current ruler, she is forbidden to participate in any activity which could do her harm."

"KaLeah, no," Hilip said, his eyes shooting over to her with a look of concern.

"Of course, KaLeah, the woodland warrior," Nikolat said, almost gleefully with a big grin on his face. "Although I think you are just making that rule up, I am more than happy to accommodate your request. Whether I kill her or you, I will still get my kingdom back. I will see you tomorrow, late morning, here. Until then, I will be sleeping in my own room with soldiers loyal to me standing guard. Until tomorrow, ladies." Nik bowed slightly and left the room, looking smug. He sauntered and exaggerated every step with his red and gold cloak swaying behind him.

"KaLeah, what have you done?" General Daven asked her, stepping close, grabbing her arm, and quickly turning her to face him. Amirra could sense the protective tone and worry in his words.

The other guards stepped away, and it was just the three of them left standing on the dais.

"I am protecting my queen," KaLeah said. "I haven't always done a good job at that, and I am the reason that Nik is here. I need to finish what I started."

"I will fight instead. I should be the one dueling for the queen, not you. It is not your place," Hilip said.

"Not my place? And what exactly is my place, general? I have rescued her, fought for her, wore very restricting dresses for her, and nearly lost her. This is my friend and my sister. How is it not my place now to fight for her?"

"Can you both stop talking about me like I am not standing right here?" the queen asked, rolling her eyes at them. "You two fight like an old married couple. General Daven, I know you are trying to be protective, but if KaLeah fails, then I will still need you to get me out of here. I don't trust my brother and now I can't trust his men."

"You don't think I can win?" KaLeah asked, putting her hands on her hips.

"I hope you do, but if I have learned anything in my short time as queen, it's that one needs a backup plan. Now, will you two please stop bickering and escort me back to my room? Find Dohori. I need to get out of this dress and rest in a nice hot bath. I cannot handle anything else going wrong today."

❧Hilip❧

Hilip and KaLeah walked the queen to her room. They stayed outside of her door after ensuring the secret passage doors were bolted shut, except for the one connecting hers and KaLeah's room. The boards had been removed that morning to ensure KaLeah could reach the queen quickly.

Hilip took a step toward KaLeah and lightly grabbed her hands. Her expression was part confusion and hesitation.

"I am going to stand guard here for a while and rotate with only the men I know I can trust throughout the day and tonight. I will go to Nikolat's room later and negotiate a trade. You do not need to fight him."

"What is your problem with me fighting him?" she asked, pulling her hands free from his. The loss of her touch was disconcerting.

Hilip shifted his weight from one foot to the other, looking down the dimly lit corridor.

He had feelings for KaLeah and wanted to keep her safe, but this wasn't the way he had envisioned telling her.

He wished he could go back to the sunny and beautiful

morning when they were sparring together in the dewy air. He should have told her then. When he tried to tell her after meeting with Clegg, standing in the hallway, she had simply fled from him. He had chosen the wrong moment and was afraid the moment was gone forever.

"Nikolat is a blood-thirsty monster," Hilip said, trying to reason with her. "I have never liked him, and I have never trusted him. I am afraid he will go to any length to win. He will cheat. He will fight dirty."

"You think I will lose because he's a dirty fighter?" KaLeah asked, crossing her arms.

Hilip wanted to grab her face in his hands. He wanted to pull her to him. He wanted to shake some sense into the stubborn young woman and demand she allow him to fight on her behalf.

He momentarily considered locking her up in her room, but he clenched his fists instead.

"You are *not* a warrior. You are *not* a soldier. You may be excellent with the sword, but Nikolat has been training to be a soldier his entire life. He has killed numerous men in battle. He is more experienced, and he is so much bigger than you are."

"Are you kidding me?" KaLeah scoffed. "That evil idiot can't see past his own ego. I can move around him and dodge him faster than you realize."

He hated seeing her upset. She backed away from him, which made him want to pull her in even more.

"Don't you have any faith in my ability?" she asked, her words sounding more sad than angry. Her face melted a bit and his heart started to ache. He wanted to yell at her and force her off this course of action. But he didn't want to hurt her.

"I *do* believe in you and in your ability," Hilip said, trying to be reassuring. "You are a wonderful fighter."

Looking into her stormy blue eyes, he finally lost control of his reservations. He closed the distance between them and softly placed a hand on her cheek.

"You are small and delicate, beautiful and precious, and I just can't bear to see you get hurt. If he gets in a single blow, I'm not going to be able to stop myself from rushing in to stop him. If he hurts you, I'll murder him."

KaLeah's eyes were brimming with tears, and she took in a quick, sharp breath.

"I don't think I can handle losing you again," Hilip declared.

"Again?"

"When you left for Denlerack, I didn't know if I would ever see you again. All I wanted was to have you back home safe. Please, KaLeah, let me fight this fight for you."

She started blinking back her tears, holding her head up and back, moving slightly away from him and the light grip he had on her cheek.

She shook her head back and forth, sniffing back a hint of emotion. "I cannot let a man fight this battle for me. Not against him." Her voice was a soft whisper but resolute.

He knew at that moment there was nothing he could do. He took a step back to resume his post in front of Amirra's door, knowing he would be keeping his eyes on KaLeah's door as well.

He turned his eyes away from her, focusing on the light flickering on the other side of the hall.

"You should go get some rest," he said, removing all emotion from his voice. "I am glad we practiced today. I hope that it helps you tomorrow."

He kept his voice flat and switched into soldier mode, trying to ignore the pain of rejection.

"Hilip..."

"Good day, Favor KaLeah."

He kept his eyes straight ahead, forcing himself not to watch her walk away.

7 TAKE OFF

Elektra Dean stood on the open field and looked from ship to ship. She had machines. She had men and women ready to fight for their planet.

But she had no idea what to do next.

She knew exactly what she could not do. She knew that by taking two ships to attack the compound, the dictator's army would get into their fleet and destroy her and her friends quickly and easily.

She saw Colt walking toward her and smiled. Seeing him always lifted her spirits, no matter how scared and unsure she felt.

"What are you thinking about?" he asked, kissing her on the cheek.

"Our next move," she answered.

Colt stood beside her, took her hand in his, and then looked out at the two black ships with her.

"We are all exposed out here," he said. "If Keldon sends more ships, we will have to go through all of that again."

Elektra looked around at the people cleaning up and wrapping wounds after the attack. She knew he was right. They were not safe just because they captured two ships.

The dictator had many more he could send at any time. They needed to protect their newly acquired treasures.

"We need to send everyone back home and hide the ships until the dictator heads off to Naldash," Colt advised.

Losing the people made her nervous, but they had no intelligence to suggest when the dictator would begin his invasion, leaving Denlerack behind.

It had already been years since the first ship had been built and she wasn't sure what the dictator's motivation was for waiting.

But she also didn't want to bury the ships underground or tuck them away somewhere. For the first time, they had their own army and ships. They had come too far to just slip back into the hideout.

"Maybe we don't have to hide the ships," Elektra said.

"What do you mean?"

"I agree that we are all too vulnerable if we stay here out in the open, but what if we use the ships instead of hiding them?" Elektra's mind was buzzing.

"Use them to do what?" Colt asked.

Ideas swirled in her head. She saw her mom's face first and then she saw her holding her new brother. An uncomfortable feeling swirled in her belly. "What if we go steal supplies from a diamond district?"

Colt let go of her hand to laugh and then turned to face her. But his smile faded when he saw the expression on her smooth, brown features. "You aren't kidding?"

"Think about it rationally," she said. "We are running out of resources. We need to feed these people. We need more water. We need more ammunition. We don't want to lose these hordes of warriors. What if they all leave but can't come back quickly enough? Or what if they go home and don't want to come back at all?

"We can do more today than we could yesterday. We have ships. We can go anywhere. I think we need to consider the possibilities."

Colt shifted on his feet and tucked his hands into his

pockets.

"I don't know, Elektra. There are soldiers guarding districts. There are families there. I'm not sure it would be worth the risk just to get food and ammunition."

"What if we can remove some of the risk?" she asked. "They grow food underground. What if we can get access to the farms without going through the entrance and higher district levels?"

"You mean, what if there are tunnels?" Colt clarified.

"Exactly, just like the tunnels around our building here." Elektra motioned to the land around them.

"But even if they actually exist, we don't know where those entrances are," Colt said, his voice laced with caution. "And do you know where the ammunition and artillery are stored?"

"No, but I know they don't use a lot of it, so their armory should be stocked." Elektra was excited considering the amount of supplies they could steal and how that could turn everything in their favor. "And even though I don't know for sure, I know someone who might. He's seen them being built and might have blueprints."

"Who?"

"Professor Wheelwright." Elektra was confident the professor would have blueprints of the districts and know how they could sneak into the tunnels for the lower levels.

Colt was quiet for a few moments, looking off into the distance, over the people moving around the camp.

"From what I have heard over the years, if anybody would know how to get into a diamond district, it would be him." Colt's brow was pulled down as if he was trying to think of an argument. And then he sighed. "When do you want to leave?"

"Now," Elektra said.

They walked back toward their part of the camp to gather supplies and let the others know about their plan.

"This time, I am coming with you," said Rustin.

"What do you mean, 'this time.' You came with us to

find the Mud Shadows people," Elektra said, feeling like an older sister.

"But you went to go kill the dictator without me," Rustin said.

"And it's a good thing since we almost got killed and Felisha…" Elektra couldn't finish. She swallowed down an uncomfortable lump in her throat and Rustin put a comforting hand on her shoulder.

"It wasn't your fault," he said.

He was such a sweet, young boy. She looked up into his brown eyes.

"It feels like it was," she said in a whisper.

Alister walked up then, intensely focused on the new situation at hand. "What is the plan? Are we all going with you to see the professor? Are we taking a ship?"

Elektra took a step back. The man would definitely be in charge if Colt wasn't. She felt relieved when Colt took a step forward, letting them all know what decisions she and Colt had made together.

"I think you should stay here and keep an eye on things," Colt stated firmly. "Try to find a place to hide the other ship."

Colt nodded at Rustin. "Rustin can come with us to talk to the professor. We are just talking, so there is no need for all of us to go. We can travel tonight and lay low. The ship will be the fastest way."

"Shouldn't we conserve it's fuel?" Alister asked.

"We are hoping that the professor can help us with that too," Elektra answered. "He built the engines for the wings, so maybe he'll know a fuel source for the ships. If not, then maybe there will be something at the district. We need his guidance, regardless, and we have time to get it, since we don't know Keldon's plans."

"You'll come back here after you learn more from the professor?" Alister asked, looking at Colt as if he was telling him and not asking at all.

"Of course," Colt said. "We will find out information

first before we decide to take any action. Elektra lived in a district and thinks we can get food and ammunition through underground tunnels. I don't want us to take any unnecessary risks, though."

The two men nodded at each other in understanding, but Elektra had her own ideas.

If they refused to support the mission for one reason or another, she knew she would take a ship and go get supplies on her own.

"I will take the leaders and some of their troops back to our building," Alister said, nodding at the small band of rebels who were packing up.

"That's good. We have enough room for them to go in and get some rest," Colt said. "Make sure to connect with the leaders and show them the way in."

"Von, Zuri and I will get the word out, and try to hide the remaining ship in the rubble," Alister said.

"Colt, we should get going," Elektra nudged.

Elektra started to walk across the camp toward the ships, with Colt and Rustin following close behind.

The Mud Shadows people were packing up their tents, and she could overhear Ludwig shouting out orders and identifying those who would stay behind as scouts.

Other tribe leaders were doing the same thing.

She was nervous about seeing them all getting ready to leave, but she understood that it wasn't safe for this many to be above ground in one location. Keldon could decide to send more ships to attack the again at any moment.

She was excited about visiting the professor and hoped he would have information she could use.

The trio climbed into one of the black ships and gave it verbal commands to close the hatch and start its engines. They took the helm, looking out over the active camp.

"Ship, take us up and slightly northeast," Elektra commanded.

"How will we find him?" Rustin asked.

"I can keep an eye out and guide the ship there," she

explained. "We are looking for two buildings that have collapsed into each other."

"Cool," Rustin said.

They lifted into the sky and began the flight. After a little while, Elektra told the ship to level out and head east. They watched for the crooked buildings through the haze as the sky began to darken.

"How much further?" Rustin asked.

"Any moment… there. There it is." Elektra pointed out the two buildings in the distance.

"Ship, slow down and prepare to land," Elektra said. "I wish I knew the coordinates or more specific information about how to command this thing."

"We are doing well, I think," Colt said, smiling.

"Ship, land in front of the two buildings straight ahead," Elektra told the ship.

"Preparing to land," said the ship's robotic voice.

The machine slowed and began to lower where Elektra had commanded. She was relieved.

They walked down the ramp and she looked over the familiar scene. There was a black iron gate around two condemned buildings, each about eight floors high, that had fallen into one another. It appeared as if the collapse had happened slowly over time due to poor foundations and perhaps weakening soil between them.

Aside from the gate, it was hard to see a way into the building. The lower floors were halfway underground, and every window had been boarded up, even the higher ones.

"Someone lives in there?" Rustin asked, surprised.

Elektra nodded and stepped closer to the gate. Although she expected the cameras bolted to the gate to whir to life, it still made her jump a little bit when they started to buzz and move toward her.

"Professor, it's Elektra and two of my friends here for advice," she said, looking into one of the cameras.

There was a loud clanking noise and the sound of locks, followed by tremors in the ground.

"What's happening?" Colt asked.

"The metal grate there is sliding open for us," Elektra explained, familiar with the place. "We climb down into the tunnel below. Let's go."

They walked through the tunnels to a staircase leading up to a wooden door. Elektra led them into a large room covered with mismatched rugs, hanging lights, and décor.

The space smelled like rotten wood and metal, but it was comfortable in its familiarity. She heard Rascal, the professor's metal doquer, tromping up before she saw it.

"What is that?" Rustin asked, stepping back in shock.

"A mechanical doquer," Colt responded, smiling wide. "I've never seen anything like it."

"Hi Rascal," Elektra said, crouching down to look the machine in its eyes, knowing that's where the camera was. Its snout was long, and it had sharp, metal teeth, and pointy ears she knew picked up sound.

"Follow me," said the robotic voice of the doquer, repeating a command Professor Wheelwright had given from somewhere deeper in the building.

They followed the doquer through the dilapidated building, feeling as if they were walking up a ramp due to the tilt of the floors.

The doquer led them to a sitting room that had an artificial fireplace blowing out heat that smelled like burnt dust. She saw the professor sitting on his favorite, tattered chair.

"Elektra, you have come back to see me so soon," he said, standing up slowly. "I hope everything is alright?"

"We attacked the compound, and we suffered some losses. Now we are regrouping and managed to get our hands on a couple of the dictator's ships," Elektra said.

"Hold on, now. This is a lot of information. I am going to need to sit back down. I assume these are friends of yours?"

The elderly, brown-skinned man sat back down in his chair, looking to make himself comfortable.

"Oh, yes," she motioned to the young men while she introduced them. They each took a seat in a scrappy chair, and she resumed her story.

"I found the band of rebels I was looking for and they made us feel right at home. We recruited tribes' people to join with us, we copied your wing design, and then we flew over the walls of the dictator's compound. We had planned on killing him but were unsuccessful."

"What about your friend, KaLeah?" the professor asked.

Elektra looked toward the ceiling for a brief moment, switching from excitement to hesitation.

"She's flown back to her home planet," Elektra said.

"Ah, so that was the secret she was hiding. Did she find what she was looking for here?" Professor Wheelwright had known that something was amiss with KaLeah from the beginning.

"Yes," Elektra answered. "She met her real father, who happens to be the dictator."

The professor shook his head and looked toward the fireplace, sadly. "And she saw for herself the monster he truly is, I assume," he said. "She returns to Naldash with a heavy heart. I had a feeling she was Huntra's lost daughter. She looks so much like her."

"You knew Huntra?" Colt asked.

"I did, young man," the professor said. "We were all rebels, back when I could still run and hold a gun. We almost took a couple diamond districts, and nearly took over the dictator's compound together. But that was many, many years ago, and nobody has seen Huntra since."

"Huntra was captured and held by Keldon, but she managed to escape to Naldash with an unborn KaLeah," Elektra explained. "She died during childbirth."

The professor looked Elektra over solemnly. "Seems to me you both experienced a challenging upbringing, missing out on a lot of good. The children of this world deserve better."

The room was quiet for a time, the only sound coming from the heater and blower inside the fireplace.

"We want to do something to make the world better, and we've got two of the dictator's ships now," Rustin said, almost gleefully. "You said you tried to take a diamond district once?"

"They are all identical, so if you know how to get into one, you'd know how to get into all of them, right?" Elektra asked. "Do you still know how to get into them?"

"Hmm…" was all the professor said before getting up and going over to a cabinet sitting beneath a large piecemeal map on the wall.

He began opening and closing drawers, pulling out pieces of paper, and flipping through old, yellowed documents.

Elektra stood up to get a better look.

"Here," he said, laying out a few papers. They were blueprints of a diamond district. Her jaw dropped. It was exactly as she had hoped.

The structure was made of nine tall buildings connected by wide bridges at every floor. From the sky, the buildings looked like a diamond. Windows around the edges helped it to reflect what minimal light came through the clouds. It must have once sparkled like a diamond, or at least, that was the intention of the original design.

The blueprints showed layer on layer, how the center markets were organized in the middle heart tower, where the stairs and elevators were, and toward the bottom page of the last document, there were the schematics for the tunnels.

"Do you know where they store the guns and ammunition?" Elektra asked.

"And the food and water," Colt added.

"Food and water come from underground, but once it is grown or collected, they move it up elevators through the center of the diamond district to disperse it through the upper-level markets—the heart of the district," said the professor, pointing out the locations on the maps. "There are tunnels underground that lead to reinforced grow rooms and recycling moisture rooms."

"Can we access those rooms without going through the front gates?" Elektra asked.

"There should be deep tunnel entrances, but they aren't explicitly marked on all of the blueprints. Maybe on another one…" he went back to the drawers.

"And what about where the weapons and fuel cells for the ships are stored?" Colt asked.

"The armory, yes," the professor said, nodding. "It should also be underground. If you can find an exterior entrance to the tunnels, you could travel through to the underground rooms without going through the main gates."

Elektra started to bite her nails while she waited, watching Professor Wheelwright scouring the old blueprints. Colt and Rustin were silent beside her, and she wondered what they thought about the professor and his odd house.

She wondered if he had guns and things to protect him from the gangs living in the slums, but assumed he was too far out to capture their interest.

"This could be a tunnel entrance, here," he said finally, tapping a spot on the blueprint.

Elektra slid in beside him and looked carefully. The drawing was crinkled and faded in a few places, but it looked to be on the east side of the entrance, far out from the walls but within the boundary of the metal fencing.

"I see it, thank you," she said.

"Here, take this with you." She reached for the blueprint in his hand, but he held firmly and looked her in the eye.

"Huntra and I never wanted this for the kids of this planet," he said, a serious tone in his voice. "We wanted Dayne Keldon's family to stop polluting, but we never wanted all this death. We were trying to prevent more death. You understand?"

Elektra nodded, but his speech wasn't over.

"You, all of you, all the youth of this planet are fading like the stars did from our skies. If you can help save more of the youth without getting anybody else killed, then that is the most important calling. That is your purpose."

"I understand," Elektra said, feeling guilty about how Felisha had died. "I don't want anyone else to die either."

"Good to remember that out there," the professor said, pointing toward the outside world. "Now, I have a few more things you are going to need."

They followed the old man around the buildings while he gathered and handed them inventions.

"These are not ordinary lanterns," he said, handing them each a metal contraption. "Once you light it, you can adjust these nobs to move the mirrors inside. That will direct the light to where you need it, instead of filling an entire space. This will help you see where you are going without being seen by the guards. And here, take this rope ladder."

Elektra handed her lantern to Rustin and then took an oval bundle of rope into her hands. It was heavy and bulky with two metal hooks attached to the ends.

"You lock those hooks onto your craft and then throw the ladder down into the entrance," he instructed. "It'll be a long way down, but the ladder is your best bet. If any metal ladder exists, it could be worn away by now."

Their arms were filling up fast, but Elektra could see the usefulness of it all. Each item brought the professor's history to life for her. He had been an adventurer and a rebel once. She felt even more grateful to know him and excited about making him proud.

"Let me get you something to eat and drink as well, before you head off on your mission."

"I don't think we have time, professor," Elektra said, which was true, although the thought of consuming his sulfur and dirt-flavored food and water turned her stomach.

They thanked him for his help and left the way they had

come, through the tunnel and out through the gate, carrying their helpful tools with them.

Elektra took the helm and gave the ship the command. "Ship, start engines, take off, and head toward the Morbel diamond district."

"What are you doing?" Colt asked. "We need to head back to get the others."

"There's no time," Elektra said. "They are busy moving the camp back into the hideout. We don't know how much fuel we have, and we are almost halfway there already."

"Halfway where?" Rustin asked, innocently looking out of the glass windows.

"Morbel, the diamond district closest to us."

"Elektra, isn't that where your mother lives?" Colt asked in an accusatory tone.

She looked at Colt for a quick moment and then back out through the windows.

"We will be going through the underground tunnels to steal supplies. We will move in and out quickly, without being seen by anybody, especially my mother, who lives on the upper floors."

"I have a bad feeling about this," Colt said. "Alister and the others are going to be upset."

"Not when we bring back supplies and save half the time. Besides, we are risking fewer lives this way," Elektra said, truly believing it. "Those tunnels may not be very big, and we have to move fast. The others would just hold us back."

Colt finally dropped it, but she could tell he was upset. She hoped he would shake it off and focus on the mission.

He was technically the leader of the rebel group, but she was abusing the fact that she didn't fully belong in any group, and she knew his feelings for her. That helped her get away with taking more control than he would have let anyone else take.

They flew through the darkness for a while until she could see the lights of the diamond district on the horizon.

"Ship, extinguish your external lights and dim the cabin lights," Elektra ordered.

"Lights off and dimmed," the ship repeated back.

She had seen the district lit up at night from the streets or from the rooftop of a nearby building but flying toward it was a different experience.

The district appeared to be impossibly massive, and the lights made it twinkle like a diamond in the night. It was both menacing and beautiful.

"How do you know where to go?" Colt asked.

Elektra looked at the blueprints laid out on the console.

"The entrance is there, straight ahead," she said, looking through the window. "According to this, if we go around to the right side and drop down here, inside the perimeter, we should be close to the tunnel entrance."

"I don't like this, Elektra," Colt says. "It feels like we are flying into the belly of a beast. Won't the guards hear the ship?"

"The district buildings create a lot of white noise," she said, remembering her time living in the slums and moving through the streets outside of the district. "The guards won't be able to distinguish these sounds from the fans, moisture generators, artificial light machines, air filters, and other sounds coming from the buildings."

She used the lights from the slums and from the district's buildings to guide her, and she commanded the ship to fly toward an area she knew would not be guarded. It also happened to be close to the tunnel entrance the professor had pointed to on the blueprint.

"Land gently, ship," she commanded, hoping it understood the word. When they landed, she told the ship to dim the interior lights even more and then open the ramp.

The ramp opened onto a pitch-black yard. Elektra followed the small glow from emergency lights to peer through the open door.

"How are we supposed to find the tunnel entrance with no light?" Colt asked, walking up behind her. He had his hands on his hips and she had the feeling he was either angry or frustrated with her. "We can't use a light without drawing attention."

"There are always two guards at the main entrance, which is far around the corner, and they never make rounds. Nobody ever climbs over these fences," she explained. The high fences were designed in a way where if anybody made it to the top, they'd be lacerated, but if they crawled over the razor sharp edges, the fence curved back around, so they'd be hanging upside down and fall to their deaths. "We are far enough around the buildings and back that a little light won't be noticed."

She lit one of the small lanterns from the professor and adjusted the knobs that moved the interior mirrors, directing the light where she wanted it to go.

The light pointed directly to the ground in front of her. She then began searching for a manhole cover based on her best estimate from the blueprint. Rustin grabbed a lantern and started looking too, but Colt stayed in the ship, squinting through the front windows above the control board.

Finding the tunnel entrance was not a fast process, but when she did, a flood of adrenalin filled her. She called to the young men, half expecting Colt to stay behind on the ship.

But both of them came and helped her lift the heavy manhole cover. They armed themselves with guns, lanterns, and carried big empty packs on their backs. Elektra secured the rope ladder and flung it down into the hole. She saw there was also a metal ladder built into the side of the hole, but she didn't trust it as much as the professor's rope.

The three of them began their descent, not knowing how deep the hole would go.

Elektra climbed down through cobwebs and ignored the creepy crawly things that flittered across her skin, hoping nothing climbed into her ears. She moved fast, leading the way, and only paused to look down every twenty steps or so.

Her foot hit the end of the ladder and she almost fell the rest of the way down. She was quick to recover and then called up to the men.

"There's no more ladder. I'm going to see how much distance is left."

Elektra shone the lantern down, gauging that the remaining distance was half her height. "Alright, we can drop from the last rung. It isn't far."

She secured her things and released her hold, dropping into the darkness. She let her knees buckle and extended her hands to catch herself on the ground.

She hoped the sound of her boots smacking onto the hard dirt wouldn't alert any guards to their presence. She heard the sound echoing down a tunnel she couldn't even see.

She lifted her lantern and looked all around, seeing only one tunnel in one direction—into the diamond district.

Rustin, and then Colt, dropped and joined her, and then they headed into the long tunnel together.

She expected another metal gate or an impenetrable door, but instead, she found rotten wood pieces loosely nailed together into a makeshift door, barely closing off the end of the tunnel.

"That doesn't seem very secure," Rustin said.

"To me it means this door and this tunnel are never used," Elektra said. "That's a good thing for us."

Elektra and Colt carefully maneuvered the door open, trying not to completely break it off of its rusty hinges. There was more darkness beyond the door, with a faint light shining at the end of the hall.

They nodded at each other and headed into the diamond district building. Elektra pulled the blueprints from her pocket and began surmising where the armory could be. She wanted to find the weapons first and take all they could carry back to the tunnel before searching for the food storage.

They walked as fast as they could without making noise, peeking into doors, and going up stairs as they came across them. Each floor was a perfect square with a hallway separating rooms, doors on each side. Each side of the square had one staircase.

It was simple to check the rooms on each floor, taking a right turn at the end of each hallway, circling back to a staircase that they'd take up to the next level. They only had to check a few levels before they found the armory.

Elektra was surprised the room wasn't guarded at first and then realized the guards must have become complacent within their peaceful paradise.

There were no rebels banging down their gates and no one on the inside was disgruntled enough with their lives to risk being thrown out. The guards had probably never even seen a real gun fight.

The trio filled their bags to the brim with guns and ammunition, then headed back down the stairs to the lowest level, through the tunnel, and deposited their loot in the darkness at the bottom of the rope ladder before heading back for more.

"I think I saw fuel cells for the ships," Colt said. "I'm not sure, but the boxes had an ovular design on them. I think we should see what is in those boxes and if they are the fuel cells, grab as many of those as we can, and any ammunition that looks like it may be for the ships."

"What does the ship ammunition look like?" Rustin asked.

"It should look like regular bullets, but maybe bigger," Elektra said.

They headed back through the tunnels, up the staircases, and into the armory again.

There were boxes stacked in one corner that had a picture of a spaceship on them.

Colt carefully pried off the top of the metal box and pulled out a long cylinder canister. "Yes, this looks like a fuel cell. We will have to figure out where to plug these into the ship."

"We have enough fuel for now to make it back to camp and then we can figure that out," Elektra said. "We should figure out where to load the bullets too."

"We should have a few books on these ships back at the hideout with instructions," Colt said.

They found a stack of boxes containing ammunition rounds for the ships and made multiple trips back to the rope ladder, stacking their items to carry up to the ship after they returned with the food.

"We should probably find the food now and then head back out. Maybe just make one trip," Colt said. "I think we have already been here too long."

"We can't get enough food for our people in just one trip," Elektra argued.

She looked at the blueprints again for where the food and recycled water was kept, but it was many floors higher than where they currently were. There was no way they could move as quickly and easily.

She put her hand on her holster but remembered what the professor had said. She didn't want to kill any of the guards, especially since a few had been kind to her when she lived there with her mother.

Elektra led Colt and Rustin through hallways and up more stairways, stopping to listen for sounds of movement or for voices.

She peered more carefully around corners as she ascended.

Finally, they reached the correct floor and she peered down the hallway. She knew the door was there, but from where they were, she couldn't tell if it was guarded.

"I need to check for a guard," Elektra whispered.

"I don't like this, Elektra," Colt said, reaching out and grabbing her wrist gently. "We are so far up into the buildings now. We should go back and find where the food is grown. Maybe we can get scraps or pretend to be harvesters working the crops."

"No, we are almost there," Elektra said. "I just need to head out a little bit and check to make sure the way is clear."

"It's too dangerous," Colt protested.

"I have lived through a lot of dangerous things, Colt." She yanked her wrist free and crept down the hallway, leaving Colt and Rustin cowering in the stairwell.

She was annoyed by how cautious Colt always seemed to be. For a leader, he didn't ever appear to take risks. Elektra had grown up stealing food, hiding, and running for her life. This was just another challenge to overcome.

The hallway was the same as the others, with doors on either side of her and a turn up ahead that would take her around the square floor. She crept quietly, listening intently around her, while she tried the knob on the first door. It was locked, so she moved further down the hall to the next one, which clicked open when she turned the knob.

Elektra was awash with relief. She could feel cold air coming through the cracks as she slowly pushed the door open, so she knew the room probably held perishable items.

The door hit something on the other side, and she froze.

"Hey," came a man's voice.

She spun around but a hand clasped down hard onto her shoulder, stopping her. The hand turned her back around and she was staring at man in a crisp, clean, blue guard's uniform.

"How did slum trash get all the way in here?" he asked.

"I'm not slum trash; I live here," she said.

"Prove it."

Elektra started to reach for her pockets, wondering if she had her forged identification card still stashed away.

"Hands back up where I can see them. Are you armed?" The guard grabbed her arm and shoved her against the nearest wall, pulling and bending her other arm back to cuff her hands together.

Colt and Rustin jumped out from the stairway and ran at them. The guard pushed her face flat against the wall while he tried to pin her with one arm and drew out his gun with the other.

Elektra had experienced no fear or stress until that moment. The man began to pull his gun from his holster, and she immediately feared the excruciating loss of both Colt and Rustin. She saw their faces, beautiful and brown, lying on the floor before her, their eyes wide open, blood spilling from their chests.

"Stop, we surrender!" she yelled. "We surrender. Don't shoot them!"

Colt furrowed his brow and looked at her, gun in his hand. "What?"

"Colt, put the gun down," she begged. "It isn't worth it. I don't want anyone to get hurt."

The guard was pointing his gun at the men but didn't shoot it.

"Please, we are just starving. We meant no harm." She put her hands up high, and Colt and Rustin set their guns down before raising their hands. She heard the boots of more guards running up behind them and saw two guards coming from the stairwell.

"Let's go, slum trash." The guard holding Elektra finished cuffing her hands together with cold metal locks. She watched two guards snatch up Colt and Rustin and do the same to them.

She winced as Rustin's face contorted with the force and pain of being placed in cuffs. Colt looked angrier than she had ever seen him. His eyes were narrowed, brow furrowed, and nostrils flared.

They are going to hate me now, she thought to herself. *How will I get us out of this?*

The guards marched them up multiple stairwells and then through a metal door that led them across the open courtyard.

The artificial lights were coming on, simulating dawn. Citizens were already out, doing morning chores and opening stores. Their hand woven, colorful clothing contrasted greatly to the dirty brown outfits that Elektra and her friends were wearing. She noticed how Rustin seemed intrigued by the onlookers. Most of the people looked shocked to see slum trash within their walls.

Elektra tried not to look at the people, trying to avoid detection. If anyone connected her to her mother and stepfather, they could get into trouble. She kept her eyes on the polished marble floors as they walked through a courtyard.

They were drug through another metal door and to a wide elevator that Elektra had never seen before.

The three of them were shoved into the elevator and pushed to the back wall, and then the guards joined them.

Nobody spoke on the long journey high up within the district tower.

Pulled and pushed through multiple doorways, they finally reached a large metal door with at least five deadbolt locks on it.

"We rarely get to use this space," one of the guards said. He pulled open the heavy door, removed their cuffs and shoved them inside one at a time.

It was a small square room with one window on one side, a toilet, and a chair. The floor was stone, and nothing had been cleaned in a very long time. There were no linens.

"You'll stay here tonight," said another guard. "The elders are sleeping, but they'll decide what to do with you all later this morning."

Elektra's heart sank as she listened to the guard's boots stomping away down the hall.

"What happened back there?" Colt asked, his voice loud and angry.

Elektra walked to the window, feeling defeated. The others were going to be so worried and upset when they didn't return. And she didn't know what to tell Colt.

She knew the only way they could have escaped back there was to pull her gun, but she couldn't fight that young guard. She couldn't risk hurting the man or risk her friends getting hurt. The guards were just victims of this world trying to make their way in it. Everyone was just trying to survive the best way they knew how.

"We got caught, that's what happened," she said finally, turning to face Colt. "You were right. I shouldn't have gone out of the stairwell that high up into the levels. There were too many people. We should have backtracked to the grow rooms or just left with the artillery. This is my fault."

"This is your fault," Colt confirmed. "I just can't believe that after all we have been through, after all of this, you could get us into this situation. What will the others think when we can't get back to them? Did you think about that? They are going to think that we are dead, Elektra. They are going to try to take on the dictator's army without us. They are going to put themselves in more danger just because you couldn't listen to me for one dragon's blood moment. You rush from one dangerous decision to another. You don't think. You don't consider anyone else's opinions. I am supposed to be the leader of this band and all you have done is ignore my leadership."

"That is not true, and you know it," Elektra finally yelled back. "I have listened to you when you had good ideas."

"Then why are we here?" Colt asked, accusatory. "Why did you get us into this mess—into this prison? I could handle it before when you put me in jeopardy, but now you have Rustin imprisoned with us. You should have listened to me this time."

Elektra bit her lip and dug her nails into her palm. Her own mother had been meek, so she wasn't used to taking anyone's direction or consulting with others. She wasn't used to considering how others would approach a situation. Growing up, making the important decisions, and acting fast to stay out of trouble, was all she knew.

She knew she was stubborn, but she wasn't so stuck in her own mind that she couldn't admit when she was wrong. And she had done that, but Colt was still fuming mad.

It wouldn't do any good to dwell on what happened or let guilt destroy her emotions. She had to keep a clear head.

She tried to turn the tension around.

"Rustin, are you alright?" she asked, lowering her voice to be softer and gentler.

"What are they going to do with us?" Rustin asked, worry in his voice.

"Ideally, they will just throw us out into the slums," she said. "We may have to perform some slave labor for them first in some way or another."

"What kind of labor?" he asked.

"Cleaning common bathrooms, polishing floors, and maybe helping pick up trash in the markets. Nothing too taxing."

"Nothing too taxing?" Colt asked, repeating her. "We are stuck in a prison tower with no food or water, our friends are going to think that we are dead, which we may be eventually if they don't let us out of here, and we are incapable of achieving all of our goals now. Is that not taxing?" Colt crouched down in a corner and put his hands to his head.

Rustin looked at her with wide, innocent, fearful brown eyes. She put her hand on his shoulder.

"It will be alright," she said. "We are not going to die. I lived here and they never killed people from the slums or people they imprisoned for stealing or small crimes. We will be alright."

Elektra turned back to look out of the window, trying not to look at Colt in his fury. She didn't want to add any fuel to his fire.

She was ashamed she hadn't listened to him. He was calm. He was smart. He was a good man, and she was dismissing him too easily.

"It's late. We should try to rest," she suggested.

Lights appeared on the horizon in the dimly lit part of the sky they could see through a small window.

"What is that?" she asked, gasping.

There were lights traveling upwards, far off in the distance. Orbs of lights, one after another, drifted up into the hazy clouds and disappeared.

"The dictator's ships?" Colt asked.

She was startled by his sudden presence behind her. "I think you're right. Keldon must have started the invasion. He's heading to Naldash."

Rustin came up beside them to look.

"May the dragon spirits watch over KaLeah," Rustin said.

Panic crept into Elektra's mind, making her palms sweat. "We better hope the dragon spirits watch over us too. We have to get out of here before we miss our chance."

8 DUEL

KaLeah stood on the dais of the empty throne room. It was where she had been standing the first time she saw Prince Nikolat.

She remembered the anxious fluttering in her stomach, the tightness of the red dress on her body, and the intensity of his gaze.

He hadn't *turned* into a monster, she told herself. He had always been one and it just took her too long to see him for who he truly was. And she knew in less than a few hours, she would kill him on that marble floor.

She drew her sword and took a deep breath, trying to relax into the inevitability of her situation.

"Dragon spirits, guide my sword." She flexed out her arm, extending to look down the edge of her blade.

"Even though I wish Ash could just light him up in flames and send him back to Denlerack. That would be a lot easier, don't you think?" She didn't know if Ash was there, but she addressed the dragon spirit as if she was, and then the spirit responded.

He will only keep coming back, as the dragon spirits did even after I sent them to different worlds.

KaLeah rolled her eyes. She wanted someone, anyone,

but especially a magical creature to make this easier for her. KaLeah didn't want to fight or kill the man she had experienced feelings for, even if she did hate him now.

The doors opened and Hilip walked through them. KaLeah felt an immediate shift in her own emotions and energy. There was an electric charge between them. Part of it was nervous attraction, some of it was frustration about him wanting to rescue her, and a little bit was her desire for him to take her away from all of this and indeed rescue her from what was coming.

"You are here early," Hilip said, walking into the room and closing the doors behind him.

He was dressed in the crisp white uniform of a Belarone general and KaLeah looked him up and down, shamelessly admiring how fit and amazing he looked.

"I want to make sure we keep the crowd to a minimum," he said, immediately getting down to business. She appreciated his battle-focused mind. "We cannot have his men outnumbering our own, and since we don't know who is and isn't loyal, we need to limit the audience size. I am also keeping townsfolk out of the castle gates." His voice filled the cavernous throne room as he walked toward her. "The word has spread fast, and we can't have disgruntled foes trying to force their way in if they don't like the outcome of this duel."

KaLeah nodded, agreeing with all the precautions he was taking. He was clearly thinking more about this than she was. She wasn't thinking further than her sword and the future pool of blood on the white marble tile.

She wanted to be more militant; more strategic. But she couldn't shake a small sliver of fear and doubt that had begun to creep in the moment she'd seen Hilip.

He wanted to take her spot in the duel. Did that mean she wasn't ready for this type of fight? She had grown up learning how to swordfight against the man who raised her. But what if Clegg had just been going easy on her the entire time? What if Hilip had been going easy on her during their practice sessions?

Am I really good enough to defeat the prince? she wondered.

"Are you alright?" Hilip asked.

She looked into his eyes and felt a small lump in her throat. For a moment, she wanted to confide in him. She wanted to tell him she was afraid.

But she knew his response would be to rush in and rescue her. She knew the overwhelming wave of relief from his offer would mean an immediate fear of losing him in return. There would be shame in not being the one to protect her friend, the queen, from the brother they had both once loved.

KaLeah calmed her heart and moved her eyes up to the cathedral ceilings.

"I am visualizing the fight with Nik," she said, truthfully. He seemed to believe her response and moved on quickly.

"Have you spoken with the queen today?"

"No," KaLeah answered, tucking her sword away and stepping down from the dais.

"She hasn't been very friendly with me since I returned and hasn't spoken to me since yesterday. I don't know what more I can do to earn her forgiveness."

"Sometimes, when people are grieving, or feel an incredible amount of pain, they take it out on those closest because they are the safest. She knows that you will still love her no matter what, even if she is angry at you for a little while."

"I'm trying to have empathy for her. I am," KaLeah said. "But I have lost a lot through all of this too. It's as if my struggles don't matter to her. I traveled all the way across space in order to try and find a way to save us, and all I experienced was more loss. I made and then lost new friends. I met and then lost my real father, who turned out to be nothing but a wealthy, selfish, abusive monster. By being in my mother's room, I felt like I lost the mother I never knew; it was like I lost her twice. I had to watch my real father kill a girl, and then I decided to abandon him and rescue my friends. We barely escaped with our lives. I was even shot down out of the sky and had to overcome a bullet wound."

Hilip moved quickly toward her then, looking her over as if the wound was fresh.

"You were shot? Where? Are you still hurting? Are you fully healed?"

"I'm healed. I'm fine," she said, brushing him off and stepping away.

She pulled her sword out again and pretended to be interested in swinging her sword in practice arches in another part of the throne room, leaving him standing in the middle of the floor alone.

"I just don't understand why Amirra is acting so selfish when I've been trying so hard to help save this kingdom. I have experienced pain for her. I have bled for her and for this kingdom." KaLeah took a deep breath and crossed her arms, starting to feel embarrassed for how much of her personal thoughts and emotions she was sharing with the general. He stood there listening to her vent, but she couldn't look at him.

Admittedly, it felt good to unload a little bit.

"I understand your frustration," Hilip said, taking a small step toward her. "We have to understand that no matter what we have gone through, Amirra is still a child who has lost her parents. She is the youngest one of us here. She is the first child ruler. The first female ruler. Her only living family member wants to dethrone her and marry her off to the richest favor family. You may be empathetic to her, but you aren't completely living in her situation. We have to be patient with her, which is easier said than done."

KaLeah bristled at his words, feeling slightly attacked. She wanted to argue with him and continue with her diatribe of the queen being spoiled and selfish and overly emotional.

This man was a fighter. He was tall, strong, and skilled. Although he was now a war general, he had patience and took great care in everything he did.

She knew he was protective of Amirra, and she was grateful for that, even if it didn't result in him taking KaLeah's side.

She knew Hilip was protective of her too. He would step in front of a sword blade or arrow for both of them. He was only in that room with her, talking with her, because he cared for her. He wanted to protect her from the upcoming duel with Nikolat. He would trade places with her to save her in a heartbeat.

She was a little stunned for a moment, realizing the kind of man who stood before her. He was sensible and stoic, but he was caring too. She knew he cared for both KaLeah and Amirra.

Hilip held her gaze as if he was unable to look away. Nervous energy flowed through her the longer they held eye contact.

He took a few more steps toward her and this time, she stayed put.

"Let me fight for you, please," he said.

He placed a hand on each of her shoulders, taking another step closer.

A wave of heat swept through her entire body, flushing her cheeks.

He lifted his hands and cupped her face. His fingers were slightly callused from sword fighting, and the touch sent a tickle through her body.

This was the room where Nikolat had first kissed her and here she was, about to kiss another man before dueling against Nikolat to save Amirra and her crown.

But all she could see was Hilip. All she could feel was his rough hands on her skin.

"Please?" he asked again, and then he leaned forward, gently placing his lips on hers.

She closed her eyes, kissing him back. She let go and gave into his lips. His grasp of her body seemed to reach all the way to her heart. Her legs softened as a weakness melted her body and soul.

It was a short, soft kiss, but the moment lingered. That word *please* echoed through her mind, and she hung on tightly to the waves of emotions flooding through her.

He pulled back and scanned her eyes for an answer or a reaction.

She opened her eyes slowly, smiled sweetly up at him, took a deep breath and said, "No. I am going to face this on my own. I have to be the one who defeats him. Can you accept that?"

He released her face from his fingers, and a cool rush of air filled the emptiness, but he didn't step away.

"I don't like it," he said. "I don't want to see you in danger, and it will take every bit of strength I possess to stop myself from running to your aid. But I will respect your wishes in this and in everything. Always."

She reached up, grabbed the fabric of his uniform, and pulled him back into her, kissing him deeply. She wanted to close every molecule of space between them, until one couldn't tell their lips apart. His arms wrapped around her, holding her in a way that pledged his desire to protect her.

She knew she was a strong fighter. She knew Ash was there, and maybe even the spirit of her mother, watching out for her. But there was no guarantee she would survive the day. KaLeah was going up against a ruthless man who was determined to take back the throne at any cost.

Where Nik would happily kill her, Hilip would die for her, and that was a man worth kissing in what could be her last hours on Naldash.

They gently separated and stood in quiet admiration of one another and what they had just shared. Her body hummed with new life and energy. Her mind was suddenly clear.

"We need to go get Queen Amirra," KaLeah said, breaking the spell.

"It would be my pleasure to escort you, Favor KaLeah."

Hilip held out his arm and she hooked hers in his,

smiling.

❧Amirra☙

"You are shaking," Dohori said, tightening the ribbons on the queen's dress.

"I am not," the queen argued.

"And you look pale. Did you eat anything this morning?" Dohori, the portly, gray-haired nurse said.

"I'm not hungry. And you can't make a queen eat if she doesn't want to."

Amirra could tell Dohori wanted to say more to her but was holding back. The nurse had taken care of her for ten years, ever since the day her mother hadn't survived her birth.

As much as she cared for the nurse, and knew that Dohori cared for her, she was not interested in her opinions. She was still a servant and Amirra was a queen.

"You have been more stubborn and distant lately," Dohori said, pushing the limits of her position. "I see that you are hurting and pushing everyone away. Even me."

"I don't want to talk about this anymore," Amirra said. Amirra was barely holding it together. If she kept emotion off her face and out of her mind, she was fine.

She didn't want anyone asking her how she was or showing her sympathy. She knew that if someone talked about the loss of her father, brother, or mother one more time, or if anyone mentioned KaLeah possibly being killed by Nikolat, she would lose herself. The best course of action was to be angry.

Queen Amirra bit the inside of her cheek in frustration. She let herself think about how angry she was with Nikolat, how much she hated him, and how angry she was that KaLeah had brought him back to Naldash.

They would both get what they deserved by trying to kill each other, she told herself.

"It is alright to be scared for KaLeah, you know,"

Dohori said.

Amirra walked away from the woman wearing the gray dress all servants wore and marched over to where she'd placed her calming tea on a table.

"I said that I don't want to discuss this and if you can't understand that, then you need to leave me, old woman. I don't have to eat, and I don't have to talk. Do you not understand me when I speak?"

"My apologies, Excellency. Here are your slippers when you are ready. Your escorts will knock once they have arrived."

Dohori curtsied as best she could in her stiff gray uniform and slowly left the room.

Amirra wasn't sure if being alone with her thoughts was any better than being poked to provide her thoughts.

She walked to the full-length mirror and looked upon her new black dress. She had only worn very dark colors for months, except for the short stint in lavender. Dark clothing was the only way she felt comfortable expressing her response to her losses.

Mourning.

So strange a concept when all she wanted to do was forget everything and just move on. She wanted the kingdom to accept her and move on. She wanted her father's room to be cleaned out and completely redecorated so she could move in and move on.

Amirra hadn't been in the king's chambers since he had passed, although it was expected of her to take that massive space over as queen. She was afraid of the memories of him it would bring.

It was hard enough sitting on the throne without him beside her and sitting at the head of the dining room table in a chair that had been made just for her where her father's chair used to be.

She had to look into the eyes of his men and somehow convince them they all belonged to her now, as if he had never existed; as if he hadn't been the great military mind and mentor to them, leading them through battles long before Amirra was even born.

"Why didn't you train me like you did them?" she asked him through her reflection. "Why didn't you make sure I could do this, that I could lead this kingdom, if anything were to happen to you and my brothers? Did you not think I could be strong, father? Did you think my brothers were stronger? I can fight very well. I hope you see me practicing with Hilip every day. I hope you realize the damage you did by not preparing me for this. And don't you dare think just because Nik is back that justifies you not preparing me. I am one hundred times the leader he could ever be. I have the heart and the brains and the strength."

She sighed deeply, wishing she could hear her father's response to her words. "The only thing I don't have is your people and that is your fault. You perpetuated this tradition of marrying off the women to the richest favor family. You were going to sell me off at the first chance. But you didn't get that chance and nobody, especially not my brother, will ever get that chance. I would rather die fighting for my kingdom than become a servant in an arranged marriage."

Queen Amirra shook her head back and forth, realizing the truth of her own words. There was a time when she thought she could accept the tradition of leaving the castle, moving in with a husband in the village, but now that she had sat on the throne, she knew she could never leave this place. The castle was her home.

"I will serve my people. I will change these archaic ideals and traditions."

A realization came to her, turning her anger into trepidation. "But KaLeah has to win. Spirits please, KaLeah has to win today."

There was a knock at her chamber door.

"Come in," she said.

The guards opened the door, and she saw KaLeah and Hilip standing in the hallway. Her heart was instantly warmed, as she tried to push down the aching fear in her gut.

"Yes?" she asked, holding onto her composure.

"Your Majesty, we are here to escort you to the throne room for the duel," General Daven said.

"Are you ready, Favor KaLeah?" Amirra asked the young woman, hoping to feel convinced and comforted by her response.

"Yes, I am. I can win this for you," KaLeah said.

"Good. Let's go." Amirra tried to focus on her breathing and steps, especially since her black skirt was so big and bulky. Two soldiers walked in front of them, two soldiers behind them, with KaLeah and Hilip slightly behind and to each side of her.

She didn't know what to say or how to keep her emotions pinned down, so she said nothing. The walk through the corridors and stairways was long and slow, like a funeral procession, with her dressed in black in the middle of it all.

Amirra was starting to sweat from the nerves and noticed a single bead trickle down to where she had one of the daggers strapped to her leg. Hilip had provided her with and coached her on how to secure weapons to her body at all times, even in sleep.

The big skirts hid them well but were just as uncomfortable as the corset she wore, restricting her natural movements. She felt like a giant mop, dragging along dust with her while she walked.

The tall doors to the throne room were standing open when they got there, and so the small party marched in, leading the queen to her single throne sitting on the dais. They helped her up and into her seat.

There were a few soldiers around the edges of the room, and she hoped they were all loyal to her, and loyal to both General Daven and General Array.

She hadn't seen much of General Array since he had been trying to keep Lisodanyan troops from entering their borders. The strong, black-skinned man had always had a smile for her and was loyal to her father, but she wasn't sure where he stood when it came to Nikolat being on the throne instead of her. She was glad he was away, so she didn't have to find out. She wanted him on her side and would be heartbroken if he chose Nik.

Hilip and KaLeah stood on both sides of her throne. They were her champions. Hilip had been protecting her and training her to fight, but KaLeah would make sure she wouldn't have to lift a sword. As long as KaLeah survived this duel, at least.

A man called out an introduction from the front of the throne room. "Announcing Prince Nikolat Belarone, son of King Erazus Belarone, may he rest in peace."

Queen Amirra felt as if her heart had stopped, and she realized she was holding her breath. Her brother sauntered in, dressed in his finest sleeveless vest with metal buttons glimmering in the light, and tight, black pants. His muscular arms were shiny and bulging. She was even more glad she wouldn't be the one raising a sword against him.

He held a certain bravado, a careless confidence she resented.

It isn't fair, she thought.

"Sister, general, and dear, sweet KaLeah," he said. "How lovely it is to see you all. It was nice to see my room was in the same condition I had left it in."

Why would we have changed his room, she thought, but she bit her lip. She knew he was just trying to get her fired up.

"Are you ladies ready for me? I see the floor is clear and nobody except for a few of your men are here to watch."

He drew his sword and swung it around, stepping limberly into the center of the room.

KaLeah turned to Amirra, and she almost couldn't look the young woman in the eye.

"On your command, my queen," KaLeah said.

There was a thick lump in Amirra's throat. She said nothing in return but nodded a silent command to begin.

KaLeah bowed, drew her sword, and walked confidently onto the floor to face the first man she had ever kissed.

Amirra slapped her hand to her mouth in realization of what she had done.

KaLeah had once had feelings for her brother and now, she was standing against him in battle to protect Amirra's place.

She was risking her life and fighting someone she might still have feelings for.

Amirra's stomach turned, and she tried to remain composed.

Spirits, please protect her. Please.

↲KaLeah↮

KaLeah stepped onto the ballroom floor. The marble floor glistened, and she heard her footfalls echo across the room. She wondered how hard it would be to clean the blood off the floors afterwards.

But would it be her blood or his? Or both?

Ash wasn't going to save her this time; the dragon spirit had made that clear. KaLeah had to take Nikolat down for good or he would keep coming back and challenge or outright take the throne from Amirra

It was all up to her now.

But after all of her time spent on Denlerack, she hadn't kept up with her practice. She had been pampered in the mansion and allowed to rest for longer than she ever had in her entire life.

She hoped it hadn't made her weaker.

KaLeah held her sword up, trying to ignore the sounds of dragon growls and murmurs that began to fill her mind.

She was so used to the spirit sounds, but whether they were warning her or encouraging her this time, she didn't know. They were just there as a constant reminder that she was different. She was supposed to do something to end their war for them.

"You look so pretty," Nikolat said, smirking. "This is where I first saw you, standing in a red dress, and the first place I kissed you. I still dream of kissing those lips."

Tingles crept up her spine at the memory.

"It will be such a shame to see you fall here," he continued. "You are still so young and still so, so impossibly pretty... especially when you smile."

KaLeah wanted to keep silent and not respond to his attempts to bait her. She wanted to focus on the task at hand and knew that's what she should do.

He whipped his sword to the left and right and slowly walked toward her.

"If you quit now, you can be my bride. Sit beside me. Rule beside me. Baby sister can stay here if she really wants to. I won't marry her off to a stranger like our father had planned. I can make this work for all of us. Let me take care of you. Let me take care of her. We can all be happy here, together."

He lunged at her, and she dodged his blow, his sword slicing by her. He recovered from his miss quickly, dancing on his feet to face her.

"If you are worried about Hilip, I can send him out to replace General Array in the field. I will let you have some alone time with Hilip first, if he is important to you."

His lip curled up, involuntarily, as if he would most definitely *not* be alright with her spending time with Hilip.

"Spirits, you are jealous of him," she said, realizing that maybe she had something to toy with him about in response.

She lunged at him with a smile growing on her face. "You don't understand how I can be attracted to him and how I can choose him over you. Your ego is so big that it is blinding you from reality. Not just about him, but about this fight. You think you rule the world."

She stabbed at him over and over, stepping in closer and closer while he deflected each blow. The smirk had vanished from his face and sweat was starting to show on his forehead.

"I never realized how pretty you look when you're scared," KaLeah said, moving in strong. "You are such a pretty, pretty *boy*."

Anger flashed across his face, and he moved more into an offensive position, striking at KaLeah, and nearly hitting her in the arm.

She pulled back momentarily, giving herself more space to maneuver.

He started grunting louder, yelling as he leapt toward her. It was an eerie sound, especially combined with the dragon growls she was trying to block out from her mind.

"You could have everything," he shouted at her. "You could be my bride, my queen, and live in paradise. You want to visit the other planet? You want to go back to your village? I can make all your dreams come true, Favor. Just say the word."

KaLeah ignored him and kept deflecting and attempting blows. He kept talking in between jabs, and she was starting to pick up on a rhythm.

"Remember when you begged me to stay?" he asked.

An uncomfortable sensation traveled up her spine, remembering that day in the library. It was as if the longing, the desire, the insecurity, and fear all came rushing back to her at once.

She had sought him out, kissed him, and begged to be his wife. She was mortified by the memory.

I am not the person I was, she reminded herself.

She knew she had to forgive herself for making such a terrible decision. She'd had a desperate need to be loved, a desperate need to be seen by someone, and that need had manifested into feelings for this terrible man.

KaLeah also knew this wasn't the time to evaluate and grow from past mistakes. She had to focus or be killed.

Nikolat jabbed with such sudden ferocity, she was momentarily stunned. She was starting to lose concentration from his talking, his yelling, and the memories mixing with conflicting emotions.

I must be present. I must breathe. I must win.

She didn't chance a look, but she knew that Amirra, Hilip, and possibly even Ash, were all watching her. They all needed her to win.

He came at her again. She moved quickly to the side and stabbed him under his ribcage.

Nik grunted angrily and placed a hand over the wound, spinning quick to stab at her but she was able to get in another blow, very close to the second, sending him backward.

"What is this, KaLeah? What are you trying to prove?" he yelled at her. He was clearly less prepared and more distracted, maybe by his own words, than she was. The realization gave her courage.

KaLeah moved in on him, rapidly stabbing and jabbing. He tried to react, but she jumped to the side, and when he dodged her next blow, she spun and kicked him to the ground with her heavy black boot.

He lost balance and fell hard. She stepped on his sword arm and held the tip of her blade at his throat.

"I have nothing to prove," she said, quietly. "I see you now more clearly than I ever have. I felt pity for you because you had lost your mother and because you were second in line for the throne when you clearly wanted to be first. I believed you when you acted interested in me, but you are only interested in yourself. You are incapable of love, and a person who is incapable of love is a monster and does not deserve to be in charge of the lives of others. You will never sit on the Belarone throne. Surrender."

There was a long pause and Nik pursed his lips tightly together. He flared his nostrils, eying her. She could feel him trying to move the sword from beneath her foot.

She started to feel squeamish watching the blood pooling beneath him. As much as she didn't want to admit it, she was still struggling with the idea of killing him. She wanted him to surrender.

"Fine," he finally whispered. "I will surrender."

KaLeah slacked up on her sword, preparing to step back and declare victory.

Nikolat suddenly spun out from beneath her on the marble floor, curling toward the arm she had pinned down. He swept both his legs underneath her feet, taking her down to the ground hard.

She saw the lovely marble floor for a breath of a moment before her head smashed into it. There was a crack and stars flashed across her vision. She could taste blood in her mouth.

The end had come.

KaLeah couldn't feel her fingers well enough to grasp her sword. She wasn't sure if it was still in her hand. She couldn't get her body to move or get up. She waited for his sword to slice through her back and told herself that it would be over quickly.

She would die proud for the life she had lived. She had died protecting her friend, her queen, her sister.

There was a heavy, warm weight on her back. It didn't hurt as badly as she'd expected. There was almost a sense of comfort in the weight.

It's over now, she told herself.

❮Amirra❯

The dagger struck Nikolat's back perfectly, exactly where she had aimed it. The man fell over on top of KaLeah, and Queen Amirra prayed to the spirits he was dead.

General Daven stood frozen beside her, clearly torn between his responsibility to guard her and his concern for KaLeah.

"General, send your men to aid Favor KaLeah," she commanded, helping him out.

"Soldiers loyal to the queen, see to Favor KaLeah," he

called out to the room. His voice was loud but steady, seemingly masking the concern she was certain he felt.

Amirra was worried too. She wanted to see KaLeah stand up and smile at her, victorious. She waited while the soldiers rolled Nikolat off her.

They put smelling salts beneath her nose and Amirra was awash with relief when she saw the woman's head jerk back. They pulled her to her feet, and she looked down at Nik, lying with a dagger in his back.

KaLeah's face was covered in blood and confusion. Her brow was low, and her mouth was open. She looked up at the queen who smiled coyly.

You aren't done here.

There was a voice in her head, but it wasn't hers. Amirra looked to her left and right, as if someone nearby had said something to her in secret.

Claim what you have done here today. Say it loudly.

Amirra took a step forward and raised her hands to address the soldiers in the room.

"I killed my brother," Queen Amirra said, yelling it across the room. She knew even people standing in the hallway would hear her.

"I am your child queen. I am your woman queen. My brother challenged me for my throne, and I have killed him. You are all a witness to this."

Everyone in the room was silent. Amirra saw that KaLeah's sword was back in her hand, though the woman looked as if she was struggling to stand.

The queen felt all eyes on her and knew she had full command of the room. She motioned to her brother's body lying on the floor. "Is this the kind of rage and anger you wish to see in a queen? Is this what you crave in a leader? Do you want her to be as vicious and cunning as the man lying dead before you?"

Amirra looked out and made eye contact with everyone in the room as she spoke. "Or do you want a benevolent queen? Do you want a leader who cares for the people in this castle and the people in this land? That man lying there dead by my blade looked out only for himself. But I will look out for all of you. I promise to always look out for the best interests of Belarone Kingdom or may the spirits strike me down." Then she turned and gave a direct order.

"Soldiers, make sure that man is dead, then burn his body on the lawns. Make an example of his treason and treachery."

Two soldiers stepped forward, turned Nikolat over, and each stabbed him twice. Then four men hauled him out onto the lawns to set him ablaze.

Kings were buried, but lower men were burned. It was a fate she knew her brother would disapprove of.

"General Daven," she whispered. "Take me back to my room."

"Immediately, my queen." He took her arm in his and nodded to KaLeah, who came to join them. She noticed that KaLeah still seemed disoriented, walking wobbly and rubbing her head.

"She may need your arm," Amirra whispered.

Hilip took notice and immediately supported KaLeah once she reached them.

The three of them walked down the hallways. The tapestries all blurred together, and she had no idea how many other soldiers were escorting them this time.

The doors to her rooms were opened and she walked through, then went straight to the nearest couch and collapsed onto it.

She couldn't breathe.

"Get this off of me," she cried out.

KaLeah was behind her, unlacing the back of her dress and loosening her corset. Hilip left the room and closed the doors behind him.

"Is that better? Are you alright?" KaLeah asked.

"Am I alright? Am I alright? I just killed my brother and you almost died, KaLeah. No, I am not alright!"

All of the emotions Amirra had kept bottled up so

tightly began to spill out of her. She was crying, screaming, and hyperventilating. She punched at KaLeah, hugged her tightly, and then threw a pillow across the room.

She kept yelling over and over, while KaLeah stood to the side, just listening, and watching her.

"He was my brother. What did I do?" she asked herself. "That monster deserved to die!" she added, as if responding to her own question.

"Did he hurt you? I saw you fall. I was so scared," she finally said to KaLeah.

KaLeah just stood by, letting the girl scream and punch and yell and cry, clearly not knowing what else to do except just be there.

"What did I do, what did I do, what did I do? You forced me into this position and then you left me. You don't even seem to care about what I am going through!" Amirra waved her hands toward KaLeah, who was still standing frozen.

"Talk to me! Say something!"

KaLeah folded her hands across her heart. "I don't even know what I'm going through, sometimes," KaLeah said softly. "I am a flawed person. It doesn't mean I don't care about you. I just don't know how to show you how deeply I care. I don't know how to show anybody how I care. I was taught how to hunt with a bow, cut a man down with a sword, start a fire, cook, find water, build huts, and hide in the trees. I wasn't taught how to hug or wear dresses or brush my hair."

KaLeah looked around the massive bedroom suite with its lavish decorations in crimson and gold. "Not until I came here. You taught me how to do those things, Amirra. I only cared about one person in my life until I met you."

"You loved my brother," Amirra said, her voice choking on the last word, remembering the knife in his back.

"That wasn't love," KaLeah said, looking down at her hands. "It was infatuation. I was attracted to the idea of him because I thought it would save me, but I ended up having to save both of us *from* him."

"He was a monster," Amirra said, but then her eyes began to overflow again. "And I killed him. How could I have killed my own brother?"

Queen Amirra fell to the floor with her entire back showing now through the unlaced opening of her dress. She was clutching her knees and rocking back and forth. Tears were streaming out of her eyes, and she just stared off into nothing, as if drugged.

Take a deep breath. Everything will be alright.

"Who said that?"

The dragon spirit began to materialize in front of them. She was standing in the middle of the room between the sofas and bed, and she was so big she had to lower her head to keep from touching the ceiling.

Her scales were emerald green, and she had long, translucent wings tucked back behind her.

"Ash," KaLeah said.

"This is the dragon spirit who sent you to Denlerack? The one who sent Nikolat there on the day she floated above me on the balcony?"

"Yes," KaLeah said, walking toward the dragon.

At first, Ash was completely transparent, but she began filling in more and more. KaLeah held her hand out and touched Ash's scales.

"Legends called her Klackire. But her real name is Anissa La Alani. Her mother and her friends call her Ash. Come and meet her."

Queen Amirra stood and took careful steps toward the creature. "I heard you in my head."

Yes.

"And you won't hurt us?" Amirra asked.

Never.

Amirra closed her eyes and leaned into the beast's chest, feeling her warmth through the black dress.

She let out a few more sobs against the dragon before

composing herself, finally.

"He was my brother, but he was a terrible person. I couldn't stand by and watch him kill the only person in this whole world that I truly love."

I understand. You did the right thing. You saved KaLeah.

"KaLeah," she said, as if that name woke her up.

She stood up straight and looked at the young woman who had nearly been killed but was fully focused on her in her time of pain and need.

"I am so sorry, KaLeah," she said. "I haven't been fair to you. I let you put your life in danger for me."

"That was my choice," KaLeah said. "I would do anything for you. There was a time when it was not my choice, but now, it is. I chose to protect you. You are like a sister to me."

"You are more of a sister to me than Nikolat was ever a brother. I'm sorry I haven't treated you better since you returned."

"It seems you've been trying to be strong for an entire kingdom for a long time," KaLeah said, placing a gentle hand on her small shoulder. "I am your sister. Let me be strong for you."

Tears came back quickly to Amirra's eyes. This was her sister; a sister she never knew she always needed.

"Thank you," she said, and she collapsed into KaLeah's arms.

9 MEN

There was a knock at Amirra's door. She sat up quickly and realized she had fallen asleep lying against the dragon's leg. As she blinked away sleep from her eyes, the phantom dragon began to dissipate. She watched in wonder, feeling blessed to have been able to see and hear such a fantastical and spiritual creature.

She heard KaLeah yawn and turned to see her stretching on a chair beside the fireplace. The girls had taken dinner in her chambers after nurses tended to KaLeah's wounds from the fight.

The woman had minor injuries, but they had wrapped bags of ice to her head, where she'd hit the marble floor, and had swapped the bags out throughout the night.

"I will get the door," KaLeah said, standing up. Other than looking sleepy, she seemed back to normal.

After a few moments, General Daven followed KaLeah back into the room. He looked as if he hadn't slept at all. There were dark circles underneath his eyes.

"Your Majesty," he said, bowing. "We have received confirmation early this morning that Lisodanyan troops are in the Belarone woods. They are upon us. They must have received word that Prince Nikolat was killed and no longer a threat to them."

"Well, I am still a threat to them," Amirra said, putting her fists on her hips.

"Yes, however…"

"I am a girl, yes, I know. Nobody on this planet is scared of a little girl queen." Amirra rolled her eyes. She was tired of feeling so small and helpless. It didn't seem to matter that Amirra had training and education. These people were judging her based on her being a young girl.

She knew she was inexperienced, but she was surrounded by advisors. Why wasn't that enough for everybody? She only wanted to keep running her kingdom the way it had always been run. She clenched her fists in frustration.

"We must gather the troops at once and stand our ground to protect the castle and the kingdom from these idiots," she said.

"Yes, but I need you to stay inside, hidden, and preferably in a locked room," Hilip said.

"Not again," Amirra said, throwing her hands up and storming to a window. "I am supposed to be out there with the troops as the leader of this kingdom, like my father was."

"With all due respect, he did not lead any troops until he was much older than you."

"Well, I am not going back into the hidden passageways. It was creepy and lonely and boring in there."

Queen Amirra thought back to the night when she was still a princess, her father and brothers were alive, and the castle was under attack. She had been put into the secret passageway behind her walls for her safety but had grown restless.

Amirra had gone out to see the action and to find KaLeah, only to find an enemy soldier in the castle entrance instead. Luckily, KaLeah had come to her rescue just in time.

She shuddered thinking about the memory. She knew battles were dangerous, but she had trained a lot since then.

She felt like she had grown a lot too.

"They will never see me as their queen if I can't ride out to battle with them," she said, standing firm.

Hilip stepped up closer to her, looking her in the eyes. "You have already gone through so many battles, Queen Amirra. You were kidnapped. You were nearly assassinated twice. You have lost your family, and you had to kill your own brother to save your best friend and keep your throne. They know what you have sacrificed for this kingdom. Let them fight this battle for you."

"Can I at least watch from a balcony or window?" she begged.

"A stray arrow is too big of a risk," he said, shaking his head.

"Dragon's blood," she cursed.

"I will help you setup a comfortable place in the walls. And I can show you how to bar the doors shut from the inside," KaLeah offered.

"Oh, no. You are not leaving me this time," Amirra scolded.

KaLeah's cheeks flushed, and her smile faded. "But I am a fighter. I am supposed to be out there, protecting the castle."

"That is what you said last time, and I was almost killed. *You* were almost killed! You promised to never leave me behind again."

KaLeah took a deep breath and turned to Hilip. "I did promise," she said, reluctantly.

"I will get you wood and nails to secure the doors once I've left," he said. "You must stay in the passageway and make no sounds. Take food and water in case the battle goes on for a long time."

"I understand," KaLeah said.

Amirra watched the two stare at one another for an awkward length of time.

Is there something going on there? she wondered. It was almost like they didn't want to separate.

Hilip finally bowed and left the room, shouting orders for his men to bring wood, nails, and tools so the young women could secure their doors from the inside.

The moment he was gone, Amirra turned to KaLeah.

"Do you like him?" she asked.

"Of course, I like him. He is a good man."

"That is not what I mean, and you know it. I saw the way you two were looking at each other."

KaLeah turned away, but Amirra saw a smile growing on her face.

"I don't mind, you know," Amirra clarified. "You can love whomever you wish; even a general. I am not going to be like my father and brothers. I am not going to try and control the lives of the people around me."

KaLeah turned back toward her. "That's very mature of you," she said.

"They wanted me to go marry a stranger in order to keep the bloodline alive, as if I were nothing more than a breeding draggot. If I am to be the first queen who rules alone, then I will be changing a few other things too."

"So, you never want to marry and have children?"

"I don't know," Amirra said. "And I think it is alright to not know, especially at my age. But at any age, too. It would take a very special person to capture my heart at this point."

"You have been through a lot," KaLeah said. "I have been through a lot too, which is why I think we understand each other so well. I realized with your brother that attraction is not love. You have to trust someone first. When you do know you want a relationship someday, just make sure it is with a good person who has your happiness and safety as their top priority."

"Thank you, KaLeah, for being such a good friend to me, even after the way I treated you for bringing Nik back to Naldash. I understand now that you didn't have a choice. I'm not sure I could have killed him if he hadn't been about to kill you."

"I understand why you were upset with me, Amirra," KaLeah responded, stepping closer to her young friend. "I'm not sure I would have been able to kill him on that floor. You saved my life."

"And you saved mine many times. I hope we don't make a habit of it."

The girls laughed and hugged each other.

Not long after, men were at the door with wood and tools. Dohori brought food and drinks up from the kitchen and let them know the castle was in a frenzy preparing for the invading army.

Inside the passageway, KaLeah hammered nails into boards, blocking the entrance from both hers and Amirra's rooms. It took longer than expected and KaLeah was sweating by the time she reached the last few boards. She grabbed extra swords and the gun she had stashed away.

"Whatever you do," KaLeah told Amirra, "Stay away from this thing."

Amirra admired and feared the strange weapon. But she was glad that KaLeah had it. It only had a few bullets left, and she hoped they wouldn't need to use them.

"No matter what happens, it won't be easy to kick these doors in," KaLeah said. "This gun is the absolute last resort if we are under siege."

Queen Amirra suddenly felt nervous. It was easy to ignore the looming threat, just standing in the room with KaLeah talking about guns and relationships.

But then she heard the horns and shouts from below and knew her reality was much more frightening than marriage to a stranger or being boarded up into a passageway.

She watched KaLeah stalk protectively to the window, looking out cautiously as if a stray arrow could pierce the glass at any moment.

Amirra understood the danger. She knew there were men with weapons coming to take her throne.

She closed her eyes and took a deep breath.

I turned away an army while my father was off at a battle. I challenged my brother for the throne after my father died. The dragon sent my brother to another world. I killed him with a knife.

I am meant to be here. I am meant to be queen. My soldiers will win this battle and KaLeah will keep me safe. Everything will be alright.

She needed to give herself the speech to calm her nerves. "When should we go hide in the passageway?" she asked.

"Let's move in the pillows, blankets, food, and drinks now. Inside with you, I won't be able to keep up with the movements in the field. These windows only provide visibility in one direction, so we don't know where the troops may be. Better to get in the passageway and make ourselves comfortable sooner than later."

Queen Amirra picked up her favorite pillow and hugged it tightly, then started carrying items through the small opening in the wall that was covered by a tapestry of a girl siting peacefully by a pond. She was jealous of the girl in the image, living a carefree life.

The noises were growing louder outside, but it was still quiet inside the dark, narrow hallway behind her walls. She remembered why she was unable to stay there the last time the castle was attacked.

"You can't leave me in here alone again," she said to KaLeah.

KaLeah dropped a handful of blankets on the floor beside her.

"I won't," she said. "And I'm sorry about what happened before. I had never been in a real battle, and it was all I wanted to do. I have seen battles now. I have bled and I have killed. I am the best person to sit beside you and protect you from those men."

"Thank you."

The ladies finished gathering supplies, emptied their bladders, and then closed the door to the secret passageway, locking it behind them.

❧Hilip❧

General Daven rode his golden draggot out onto the cobblestone that covered the courtyard in front of the castle entrance.

He had ridden the steed for many years and knew the animal had a knack for sensing danger. So, he wasn't surprised when the beast immediately stomped his clawed hooves down harder and swat his long tail over his scaly hide with more vigor.

"Easy, Boy," Hilip said, patting the draggot's scaly neck through its furry mane.

"What's the word from the line?" he shouted down to a soldier on the ground. The draggot's back was well over the man's head.

"The enemy is advancing, general."

"Yah," he said, spurring Boy into a gallop.

Hilip knew he should keep his mind on the advancing soldiers and commanding his troops to be ready. He needed strategy, tactics, and numbers.

But his mind kept drifting back to the look on KaLeah's face, her lips, her eyes, and the last time he'd touched her. He wanted nothing more than for this to be over so he could be back with her.

Running into battle meant he could protect her and the queen, but it also meant risking death and thereby risking the chance to ever be with her again.

He grabbed the reins tightly and rode hard to meet up with General Array on the front line by the Belarone forest.

Focus on the task at hand, he reminded himself. *Both young women will be safe locked up in the queen's rooms. I will get back to KaLeah alive.*

The sun was shining, sending a powerful heat over the fields. The queen's men were amassing in long lines, ready for the moment when Lisodanyan soldiers would emerge from the cover of the Belarone forest.

It was not a good position to be in. The enemy had the cover of trees and could easily fire their arrows and take out the front line.

He rode up beside General Zoseff Array, who was sitting tall on a brown draggot. He and the other men were dressed in brown uniforms, Hilip having advised they never go to battle wearing white again.

The man's bare black arms were gleaming in the sunshine, and Hilip found himself jealous of the man's muscles.

He had always admired the general. The man was sharp, cunning, and never kept his thoughts to himself. He was direct and Hilip trusted him completely.

"General Array."

"Ah, young General Daven. Troublesome couple of days we've had here lately."

"Indeed."

"The favor warrior comes back in a flying craft, brings back the lost prince who then challenges Amirra to the throne," Array said, recounting the recent activities. "Amirra kills him and here we are facing an army of men from a kingdom I thought we had reestablished as allies. Just goes to show this place will change as quick as the wind does."

"And the day is yet young," Hilip added.

"Oh no, don't tell me that," General Array said, laughing heartily, and Hilip couldn't help but smile.

"I'm concerned about our visibility here, general," Hilip said.

"I am as well," General Array said looking toward the tree line. "We need to get men in there and at least find out how close the enemy is to us."

"I can take in a handful of men with me," Hilip offered.

"Are you sure? It is risky." Array turned back to look at him.

"It would be riskier to sit here and wait for their arrows to start flying."

"Good point."

General Daven galloped off, ordering men to join him from the front line. He and about ten other men, a few on draggots but most on foot, headed toward the forest.

"Be my ears in there, Boy," he said, patting his draggot's neck again.

Hilip led the way into the woods that surrounded one whole side of the castle. There were trails where village folk routinely hunted or foraged, but it was slow-going.

A few people at a time could make quick work through the forest, as KaLeah and Amirra once had. But he couldn't envision how the entire Lisodanyan army would get their supplies through.

Perhaps, instead of wagons, they wore their supplies and weapons in packs, he speculated. *It would make for a tiresome journey, though.*

He and his men progressed slowly and quietly, fanning out so as to cover as much area as possible. They were looking for signs that Lisodanyan scouts had been there.

They walked for some time in complete silence, except for their footfalls and draggot hooves on rocky ground.

Hilip's golden brown draggot suddenly jerked his head up and stopped. It was the sign Hilip had been anticipating.

He made a whistling sound as close to a juliebee as possible, but with a slight tweak that let the soldiers know it was a warning.

Hilip dismounted and could see a few of the others do the same through the trees. They drew swords and crouched lower, moving forward.

The enemy was there, but he couldn't see them. There was no smoke, and no sounds of a camp, so he couldn't discern if there were only a few scouts up ahead or if it was the entire army.

Either way, he had to be prepared to fight.

He took one more careful step and a man stood up in front of him with his bow extended and an arrow pointed right at his face. Hilip moved fast, ducking, and sliced off the tip of the arrow with his sword.

The man recovered, stepped to the side, and docked another arrow.

Hilip maneuvered again, clipping the arrowhead with his sword. He stepped forward to take out the man's entire bow before he could arm himself. The man tripped over a tree root and fell to the ground.

"How many of you are here?" Hilip asked the soldier, pointing his sword at his throat.

"Enough to take out the few you brought," said another man's voice from behind him.

Hilip swung around and saw a sword pointed to his own neck. He lifted his sword and engaged the soldier, and after that first metal on metal sound, the forest around him came alive.

There were men yelling, shouting orders, blades clanking together and on armored plates, draggots neighing, and bodies slamming against trees and falling to the ground.

Hilip had found the first battle and knew his small band was outnumbered. He tried to look around while he was fighting and realized, thankfully, that the entire Lisodanyan army wasn't there.

The man with the bow stood up and armed himself with a sword, while Hilip was focused on fighting off the man who had come up behind him. He was now against two and hoped that number didn't increase anytime soon.

He could tell the sword was not the first man's specialty and tried to take him out first. Just as he finally got in a hit, a third man came running up to join the fray.

Hilip's heart sunk. He knew there were too many and feared for the men he had brought. Thoughts of what he should have done differently started to play out in his mind, distracting him more.

He needed to get word back to General Array. He needed the others to be warned about how close the Lisodanyan army was. But all he could do was try to stand his own ground against three men for as long as possible, and hope for survival.

"Boy, go! Go!" he yelled to his draggot, hoping he would run back to Array quickly and the riderless draggot would be the warning sign the general would need to prepare for the battle upon them.

One of the Lisodanyan soldiers was distracted by his order, thinking he was speaking to a man and not a draggot. While the man turned his head, Hilip got in another blow.

It wasn't enough, though. His men were falling, and he would be next.

"Liso, retreat!" yelled a man from deeper in the woods.

"All retreat to the castle."

"The castle needs our guard now!"

The calls spread throughout the forest, coming from much deeper than he'd expected. The three men Hilip was battling began to back away, and then they also turned and ran through the woods toward the calls.

Two of Hilip's remaining soldiers ran up to him, panting and sweating.

"Why are they retreating?"

"They had us easily outnumbered."

General Daven shook his head. "I have no idea."

He looked around for Boy, but his draggot had followed his command and was gone.

"I need a draggot. Are there any left?" Hilip asked.

"I believe mine is, sir," offered one of his men.

"Let's go. Soldiers, retreat back to the front line."

The man led him to his black draggot. Hilip mounted and galloped through the woods, back to General Array. He had to keep his head ducked low and still was scratched a time or two by stray branches. The branches didn't hurt the draggot through its scaly hides.

He emerged from the trees and saw the general preparing the front line to advance.

"General Array," he yelled. "The enemy is retreating!"

He rode up beside the general.

"Are you sure?" asked Zoseff Array. "I saw your

draggot come through without you and thought the worst."

"I heard the call for retreat all the way back to their castle. It sounded as though they were being called to protect the castle from something."

"It could be a trick," said General Array. "Nonetheless, I think your instinct is right for us to occupy the woods. I'm sending more men in."

"How many?"

"The entire front line to start."

Hilip nodded his approval. "I need to update the queen," Hilip said.

"She should be here."

"She is just a child," Hilip argued.

"And that is all the men will ever see if she doesn't risk her neck for them."

Hilip considered General Array's words on his ride back to the castle. He dismounted and went in through the front entrance.

Would the men only respect the queen if she were out among them? Would it be worth the risk to her life?

Worry began to build in his mind. He knew wherever the queen went, KaLeah would be by her side.

He wasn't ready to see KaLeah risking her life again.

❧KaLeah❧

Time passed excruciatingly slow for KaLeah and Amirra. KaLeah stared at the candle flames in the lanterns, watching them flicker and dance. She was exhausted, and yet too anxious to rest.

The queen went from pacing, to sitting and tapping her foot, and then back to pacing.

"I wish we could see what was happening," Amirra said for the fifth or sixth time.

"It is best we stay here," KaLeah said, trying to convince herself just as much as Amirra.

"Is that yelling? Did you hear that?" Amirra asked.

From inside the wall, there weren't many sounds that could reach them. But it sounded as if someone was banging on the queen's door and yelling from beyond it.

"Queen Amirra, I have been sent by General Daven."

"He said my name."

"Shh, quiet."

"General Daven is injured and has asked for you to come at once."

KaLeah knew immediately it was a lie. Hilip would never do anything to try and lure them out from the safety of their current hiding place.

"What do you think?" Amirra asked.

"I think it's a trap. We don't know which men are still loyal to your brother."

"But what is the point of killing me now if my brother isn't alive to take the throne?"

"I don't know. Misplaced loyalty, perhaps? Or they would rather choose a general or a member of the favor families to rule this land over a woman—even a royal one."

"Idiot boys," the queen said.

KaLeah agreed.

"So, we stay here?"

KaLeah wasn't sure. If the traitorous soldiers were intent on luring the girls out into the open, then nothing would stop them from trying to get into the queen's chambers while the good soldiers were preoccupied with fighting the Lisodanyan army.

The men knew the queen was here. It might be safer for the queen to be somewhere else just in case they broke through the boarded-up doors.

It was the sound of dragon growls growing in her mind that confirmed it for her. The sound of spirits meant she was indeed in trouble and needed to act.

"I'm afraid they may keep trying to break through," KaLeah said. "They are banging on the door but may be trying to actually break the doors down. If they get through, it'll be harder for me to fight them off from in here."

"So, we leave. Where do we go?" The queen started to bite at her nails and looking down the dark tunnels.

"These passageways will lead to the armory," KaLeah said, knowing the pathways from her sessions with Hilip. "It is a large room with plenty of weapons. We can hide out there and if they find us, either through the passageway or the doors, we can fend them off at either entrance."

They heard another loud bang and a crack.

"We need to move, now," KaLeah said.

The girls gathered their weapons, a thermos of water each, and headed down into the dark hallways with KaLeah holding a lantern to guide them.

It had been a while since KaLeah had ventured through the passageways. Hilip had spent many nights teaching her, showing her patterns of turns, and helping her navigate by memory.

She hoped he was alright and that the soldiers were lying about him being injured.

The pathway came back naturally to her, and she led them through various levels to the armory. KaLeah pushed through the hidden doorway in the wall. She checked to make sure the area was clear. It looked like the men had already taken what they needed to hold off Lisodanya.

"All clear," KaLeah said.

They both walked into the room, which was lit by the windows that ran all along the top near the high ceiling. KaLeah put her back against a large cabinet and used her legs to push it in front of the secret door. It wouldn't stop the men, but she hoped it would slow them down.

The armory was used as a practice room, and so a lot of the floor was covered with gray mats, just soft enough to help break a fall.

There were stacks of mats against the wall and KaLeah had an idea.

"Help me move these mats. Let's build a little fort for us to hide behind in case they follow us here."

The girls went to work pushing and re-stacking mats to

build a fort tall enough for them to crouch behind in the far corner of the room. From the fort, they could watch both the main entrance and the secret entrance. KaLeah grabbed bows, arrows, and throwing knives, and placed them behind the fort.

"Now what?" Amirra asked.

"We get low behind the mats, hold a bow, dock an arrow, and wait. Are you going to be able to shoot and fight in that dress?"

Amirra moved her shoulders and arms in circular motions as if verifying. "I should be alright," she confirmed.

It was not much longer before they heard the men coming.

"Check the armory!"

KaLeah heard the cabinet being pushed out of the way and several pairs of boots stomped into the room.

"We are here to help you, ladies," yelled a man.

"Hey, look over there," said one, more quietly.

"Were those moved?"

"They've never been stacked there before."

"Go check it out."

KaLeah thought she heard at least three different men talking. She got up from a seated position, and into a squat with her bow low but at the ready. She nodded to the queen who took the same position beside her.

They had left small eye-hole openings in the make-shift fort. KaLeah counted two men walking toward them with their swords drawn, and at least two more back at the heavy cabinet.

"Hold," she whispered to Amirra. "Now."

She raised her bow just high enough to fire off an arrow and then ducked back down. Amirra did the same at nearly the same time and both arrows struck the men in their breast plates.

"They are here!"

"Dragon's blood," KaLeah cursed. "Again."

Both girls docked, sat up and fired again, this time higher, aiming for necks or faces.

One man moved out of the way of the arrow and the other knocked it away with his sword.

"That isn't very nice, you murderous little beasts."

KaLeah groaned as she heard more men enter the room. They all had swords, and so she kept firing at them, trying to keep them away from their protected area. She knew it would come to close combat sooner than later.

KaLeah and Amirra kept firing until they ran out of arrows. They managed to take at least four of the men out, but the girls were still outnumbered.

They switched to throwing daggers next.

KaLeah knew she had to come out and face the men before Amirra ran out of daggers. The queen's swordplay was good, but it was KaLeah's job to keep her from having to get that close to the men.

"Stay here, keep throwing, and don't hit me," KaLeah instructed before she jumped out from behind the fort with her sword drawn.

There were at least ten more men standing and coming at her now, all dressed in brown and green uniforms and black boots. Only a few had breast plates on, which was good.

She was surprised and angered by how many men were still loyal to the dead prince and his ideals.

She couldn't believe she ever had feelings for the man and regretted every moment she had wasted thinking about him.

She tried to keep the men in front of her but was aware of a few slowly circling to her back. Luckily, they were putting their backs in front of Amirra, who threw her knives with deadly accuracy.

Bodies thudded to the ground behind her, while she focused on stabbing the men in front of her. They underestimated her, of course, moving slowly and deliberately, while she danced fast, stabbing at every weak opening between their armor.

A tall soldier came at her fast, waving his sword wildly and yelling, trying to rattle her off of her aim. She simply stood still until he was almost upon her. She feinted left and when he missed her, she turned on him fast and drove her sword up under his chin, going through his mouth and into his nose. He screamed and fell back, clutching at his face.

There were only a few men left, but they were determined. They closed in, fighting hard and well, and KaLeah had trouble meeting all three of their swords blow for blow.

She struck one man with her sword but lost track of a man who maneuvered behind her. KaLeah couldn't pull her sword back quickly enough and expected to feel a blade slice into her back.

Instead, the man behind her cried out in pain, dropped his sword, and fell, a dagger sticking out of his back.

"Great throw, Amirra," she yelled.

"That was my last one," the queen warned.

"Stay there," KaLeah instructed even though she didn't think the queen would obey her, especially since there were now only two men left.

Sure enough, Amirra came out from behind the fort with a sword clasped in both hands.

One of the men KaLeah was fighting turned his attention to the queen.

"Hello, baby queenie," he said. He seemed to be twice her height and size.

"You have already lost this silly fight, boys," KaLeah said, trying to taunt their attention back to her.

"That 'baby queenie' killed your weasel of a prince. She has more brain power in her little toe than you two have put together in those big heads of yours."

The man who had spoken had his sights set on the queen and didn't respond to KaLeah's taunts as she'd hoped. He stalked around to Amirra as KaLeah tried to keep the other man from killing her. His blows were well-aimed and strong, and she was starting to feel fatigued.

She wasn't able to watch both men and so her heart began pumping even harder with worry for Amirra. She could hear his sword against hers, pushing her further and further away from KaLeah, back to the fort.

She had to do something. The man she was fighting was clearly good. He was deflecting every blow and even pushing her back slightly.

How could we defeat so many men and yet be struggling with these two? she wondered. It was as if they had saved the best fighters for last. Or maybe these two had been smart enough to wait for the ladies to get tired.

It wasn't fair. It couldn't end here. The gun was tucked underneath her shirt in her waistband. Not knowing how many bullets were left, she had been saving it. But the blows were coming at her so hard and fast, she didn't have a moment to try and pull out the gun.

She heard boots coming through the main entrance to the armory from behind her and she groaned. She hadn't been able to keep an eye on that door.

They had reinforcements, she realized. Her heart sank and the fear of defeat crept into her bones, sending prickles across her skin.

There was no way she could protect her back with this good of a fighter standing in front of her, narrowly missing her with every blow.

"I've got you, go to the queen."

It was Hilip. Her heart soared with happiness as his sword passed in front of her to meet the man's.

She pulled back and ran across the room. Without any hesitation, she pushed her sword straight through the back of the man who had Amirra up against the fort.

He fell over dead.

Amirra wrapped her arms around her, then they turned to see Hilip strike down the last man.

"We did it," KaLeah said. "We're alright."

KaLeah released her and crossed the space again, into

Hilip's arms.

He squeezed her tightly with one arm, the bloody sword hanging from his other hand.

"General Daven, what's going on out there? Why were those men after me? How did you find us?" Amirra fired rapid questions at him while KaLeah just disappeared into him for a peaceful moment. She knew the peace wouldn't last long.

"Do you think more men loyal to my brother will come after me?"

Hilip looked at the bodies lying around the room. "Let's hope these were the last of them," he said. "The Lisodanyan troops were upon us in the woods. We began to engage with the enemy and then they all suddenly retreated. They said something about defending their castle."

KaLeah's eyes grew wider. She stepped out of her comfortable moment of peace next to his chest.

"There is only one thing that would cause an entire army to run back home," she told them. Cold sweat covered KaLeah's body and she shivered.

"The Denlerack ships are here. Naldash is being invaded."

10 MACHINES

Queen Amirra adamantly believed the other kingdoms should be warned about not surrendering to Denlerack.

"If they surrender, then the dictator will enslave us all," she said. "Our only hope is to band together."

Amirra, KaLeah, and Hilip all stood on the balcony above the castle's entrance and looked out over the tops of the forest trees toward Lisodanya. Smoke plumes drifted up from where the castle stood in the distance.

"It may be too late to send word to Lisodanya," KaLeah said. "They may have surrendered already. Their kingdom is being burned to the ground. It doesn't matter if we have one hundred or ten thousand men; Dictator Dayne Keldon's army has flying war ships and guns. He can blow away all of our men by just pressing buttons and pulling levers on the ships." KaLeah remembered flying away from Keldon's compound and seeing how easily the bullets laid waste to the rebels.

"I have been trying to solve this puzzle of how we are supposed to defeat a technologically advanced army since I landed on Denlerack," KaLeah admitted. "We have swords, knives, and arrows. I have dragon spirits that warn me when danger is near. And I have mechanical wings, one ship, and one gun."

"That's right, I forgot about the gun," Amirra said. "We still have the one that killed Bylex too."

"So, we have two guns," KaLeah corrected.

"But what about Ash?" Amirra asked. "The dragon spirit is surely powerful enough to help us?"

"She says she cannot. I asked her to kill them all already and she said that if she knew how, she would have. Her power is only elemental."

Queen Amirra looked out over her land, at her planet, and at the people she knew would face certain hardship if the three of them couldn't come up with a plan to save Naldash from the invasion.

Her mind spun the word 'elemental' around and around, trying to create a solution. She also kept picturing the guns but knew that two alone would not do much against hundreds, or thousands, of guns the invaders would surely have.

"We don't even know how large their numbers are or how many guns they have," Hilip said, almost reading Amirra's concerns.

"Or how many ships," KaLeah added.

The three of them stood quietly for a few moments, listening to the echoes of booms crossing the land between them and Lisodanya.

"I think it is best if you two go deep within the castle and stay hidden until after the invasion is over," Hilip said, moving into the protective planning mode Amirra had seen time and time again.

"I can have soldiers sneak you both out later and you can hide in a mountain village. I am sure the dictator's control won't reach into the villages. You should be safe there for many years."

Amirra ignored him, barely containing her desire to roll her eyes at him, and then she saw KaLeah put her hand on his arm, softly.

"We are not going to hide from this, Hilip," she said.

"This isn't something we can hide from. We have to figure out how to win or we will all go down trying. I met that man—my real father. He won't give up looking for me. He won't quit until he has taken over every piece of this planet."

"Then we fight," Hilip said, seemingly masking his reluctance for their sake.

"Yes," KaLeah agreed.

"But how?" Amirra asked. "I still think we need the other kingdom armies here, fighting with us. We must put up a united front against Denlerack and its ships. Can we use the technology we have to create more? Can we make more guns?" Amirra wondered.

"Maybe if we had started earlier, but it is too late now. Look." KaLeah pointed at the sky and Amirra saw three black orbs coming toward them from the plumes of smoke on the horizon. They watched in frightened silence as the ships approached and landed on the lawn before them.

"What do they want?" Amirra asked.

"It looks like they want to talk. They probably want to discuss the terms of your surrender," Hilip explained.

"But I'm not going to surrender," Amirra said, knowing she had fought too hard for her kingdom to hand it over now.

"Maybe we should discuss whether or not you should, Your Majesty," General Daven advised. "We are facing a situation none of our soldiers have prepared for. This is an unknown enemy with advanced weapons."

"I disagree," KaLeah said. "We know the enemy. I know the enemy very well. I just haven't figured out how to defeat them yet. And we know how their weapons work, at least."

Queen Amirra straightened up in her black dress, smoothing down the sides and wiping off her sweaty palms in the process.

"Let us go see what they have to say," she said, feeling brave. Amira walked slowly and solemnly through the castle, down a grand staircase and out through the front doors.   KaLeah and Hilip followed her across the cobblestone courtyard, through the gates, and out onto the lawn where one man was standing in front of three large black ships.

As she walked toward the man on the lawn, she heard the footfalls of her soldiers quickly lining up behind her. She was afraid that it was a shallow show of force and would do nothing to protect her.

The Denlerackian's face was expressionless. He was tall, lean, with a clean-shaven, dark brown face and dark brown eyes. His uniform was plain, unadorned, and black.

He failed to bow.

"Your Majesty," he said. "I am sent by Lord Keldon of Denlerack. He asks for you to surrender your kingdom to his rule. The kingdoms of Lisodanya and Extelli have already surrendered to us after suffering much death and destruction. Since you are a young lady, we will go easier on you. I also see that his daughter is here with you. He does not wish harm to come to her. It is in your best interest to surrender. No one else on this planet needs to die."

Queen Amirra reminded herself to breathe in and out while listening to his words. He was only a soldier, just like all of her soldiers, and was only here to present an offer.

"And what if I do not surrender?" she asked, feeling a dry lump beginning to build in her throat. She reminded herself to continue breathing.

"If you fail to surrender, then your castle will be destroyed, and your villages and fields burned."

"Keldon wants the fields," KaLeah said. "He will not burn them. He wants the food this planet is capable of producing. He won't fill the sky with smoke, blocking the sun and rain as his family did on Denlerack."

The soldier turned to face KaLeah, and his nostrils flared as he took in a sharp breath.

"I assure you he will burn a few fields to make a point, as well as destroy the castle."

"Then where will he stay?" KaLeah challenged. "If he

were to take a look at the king's chambers, he would want those rooms for his pleasure. He will not destroy this majestic place. He wants to claim it as his own."

The man looked annoyed but said nothing.

The silence made Amirra feel brave. She realized KaLeah was right.

"I will not surrender this land," Queen Amirra said, defiantly.

"Very well," the man responded. He turned quickly on his heel, then returned to one of the ships. All three of the black crafts rose into the sky. She wondered if the rest of the ships were still in Lisodanya but quietly hoped the dictator had only brought a few ships.

There was a single sound like an explosion and projectile flew from one craft toward the castle. She ducked, and Hilip and KaLeah threw themselves over her.

Through their arms she could see one of the castle towers explode, stones flying in every direction.

"Are they leaving?" she asked.

"Yes, looks like it was just a warning shot to scare you," Hilip said. "They seem to be retreating."

"But they will be back with a lot more ships," KaLeah added. "And soon. We don't have much time."

"Come, let's get back inside," Hilip instructed, leading the girls back into the castle. General Array is bringing more men back from the woods, but I'm afraid our resources won't last long against the guns they have on those ships." Hilip looked up in wonder at the damage caused by a single shot. Amirra was too scared to look.

They ran through the entrance together, passing guards and soldiers who were running out to the lawns with weapons.

"You need to get low, down into the corridors that lead to the dungeon," Hilip said.

"But we need to see what is happening," Amirra argued. "I'm not ready to hide yet. We need to watch."

"How about the library?" KaLeah said. "The windows

are small and high in the room, being that the room is somewhat underground. I know how to get to the dungeon through the secret passageways there, if needed."

Hilip took a moment to respond, but nodded, and began leading them in that direction. It wasn't too far from the entrance.

They took a few steps down into the library, closing the big wooden doors behind them. Hilip and KaLeah moved a table underneath one of the windows, so the girls could stand on it and see outside.

There wasn't much to see yet, except for the lawn filling up with more and more of her men, ready to protect the kingdom against impossible odds. She wondered if they would feel better about their sacrifice if a man was on the throne instead of her.

Don't think that way, she told herself.

"I have to go back out there," Hilip said, standing stoically in front of them. He addressed the queen, but she saw how his eyes flitted to KaLeah.

"I'll walk with you," KaLeah said.

Amirra smirked as she turned back to the high windows. *They love each other.*

When KaLeah came back to her side, the woman's cheeks were bright red.

"Did he kiss you?" Amirra asked.

KaLeah laughed, embarrassed, and nodded.

"At least there is one good thing happening right now," Amirra said.

They watched out the windows until the black ships came back. There were so many of them she lost count. They hovered over the forest and fields, then came to the lawns.

The soldiers fired arrows, yelled, and raised their swords.

"I can't watch this," KaLeah said.

"Where is the dragon? Why can't she help us?" Amirra asked.

The spirit began to materialize in the library as if she'd been there the entire time. Amirra leaned back to look up at her, even though standing on the table made her at least as high as the creature's knees now.

Ash's emerald scales glimmered in the sunlight streaming in from the windows. She was magnificent.

But she was useless.

"Can't you send the ships away or blow them out of the sky or something?" Amirra asked, her voice squeaking desperately.

I cannot. If I send them away, they will only return in a few days' time.

"That is fine. It will buy us time!" Amirra said.

"To die another day?" KaLeah asked. "No matter how often they come back, we can't defeat their weapons with our own."

"Then send away their weapons—their guns, bullets, whatever it is they are firing at us," Amirra said, feeling brilliant. "Send those away."

Ash began to dissipate in front of them. Amirra turned to the window alongside KaLeah. "Can she do that?" she asked.

"I don't know," KaLeah said.

They couldn't see Ash, but they saw blue flames appearing and disappearing all throughout the sky. It was little pops of blue color, exploding and then flittering away.

The sounds of bullets stopped. Amirra's soldiers stopped falling to the ground.

"I think she did it," Amirra exclaimed.

"I can't believe it," said KaLeah.

"She did it! She sent away their weapons!"

Amirra started to dance on the table, her arms high up in the air. She felt weightless and euphoric. "We are even now. They have to come out and face us like men."

"But what if they just go back to their planet for more ammunition?" KaLeah leaned closer to the window.

Amirra hoped they wouldn't, that some sense of pride

would cause them to do something other than flee.

She watched as the ships continued to levitate. The men on the ground had stopped wasting their arrows.

"They are staying," Amirra said. "They have to come out of their ships and fight now, right?"

Instead of fleeing, a few of the ships began to dip down, crashing into the Belarone soldiers standing on the field, smashing into them, and flinging or flattening them into the dirt.

Some ships turned toward the castle and began pummeling the stone towers and walls. The sound of stone smashing and falling filled the air.

Amirra screamed and backed away from the window as it shattered, falling backward off the table. KaLeah jumped down, grabbed her, and they ran for the passageway deep in the library stacks.

The queen could hear the castle crumbling all around her as they ran.

❮Elektra❯

Elektra woke up on the cold, hard floor. She sat up and rubbed the deep pains out of her neck and the back of her head.

"We made it to morning," she said, looking up at Colt, who was already pacing the small cell.

Rustin was crouched in a corner with his head leaning against the wall, snoring lightly.

"How are we supposed to get out of here?" Colt asked. "The ships have taken off. We should be back at headquarters making plans to destroy the compound while the dictator is gone. This is not good, Elektra."

She could tell that he was still upset with her, so she said nothing as he continued.

"And what will they do to us? Will we be stuck here until we die, will they feed us, or will there be some sort of trial and punishment? I can't stop wondering what we are going to do now."

"Clearly," Elektra said, getting to her feet. "We need to remain calm and take each challenge as it comes."

"Like you took the challenge of going down the hall and getting us caught? Look at Rustin. He's just a kid, Elektra."

Guilt flowed through her. She had never heard Colt talk this way. He was still angry and frustrated.

Scared, she realized. *He is scared for us.*

She took a deep breath and tried to keep her thoughts to herself. She knew he was still processing his anger and she didn't want to say anything that would upset him further.

A guard brought them one meal and one glass of water each sometime during the middle of the day. Colt peppered the man with questions, but he said nothing except for them to eat and shut up.

"So, how can we get out of here?" Rustin asked, after quickly eating his portion of food.

"We don't," Colt said. "I have scoured every section and there is no weakness. There is no way to escape. Even if we took out a guard, we'd have to find our way back down to the tunnels and to the ship. They probably already took the ship back to the compound, so we'd have to figure out another way out. If we make it out of here, we will have to cross the desert on foot. We are going to die one way or another."

Elektra raised her eyebrow at the man and realized that she couldn't keep quiet any longer.

"Wow, I am impressed with your lack of hope," she said. "Hasn't anyone ever told you about the power of positive thinking?"

Elektra began doing stretches, reaching her right arm over her shoulder, and pushing it back by pressing her left hand into her elbow.

"I have to believe we will get out of here, somehow," she said. "There is a solution; I just haven't found it yet."

She repeated the stretch on the opposite side.

Colt guffawed.

"You are going to magically will us a key and an escape plan, huh? Or are you planning on using those muscles to scale the side of the tower without being seen? I'll just use my elbow to break this glass so you can get started."

Elektra resisted the urge to roll her eyes.

She wasn't used to people she cared about being angry with her. Her mother was the only person she had ever truly cared about. When her mother was afraid or angry, it was different. There was always a level of guilt, like her mother was ashamed that she'd let Elektra down, even when it was Elektra who had failed to bring home money or food.

Zatia had been a frustrating woman to have as a mother, and on days where Elektra was almost gunned down running from another deal gone wrong, she didn't expect her mother to thank or praise her for risking her life again for their survival.

She had always felt like an equal, even at a young age. Zatia was more like an older sister who wasn't very good at that job either. Elektra could see trouble a few blocks away, where Zatia would skip right into it with a smile on her face.

It was ironic that Colt was now accusing her of the same kind of flippancy. He didn't know her. He didn't know how she had grown up having to scrounge, lie, beg, steal, and outsmart thugs in order to survive the Sarda slums. She had only been a child, but she was all she had. Her mother, as sweet as she was, had been useless. Without Elektra, they would be dead.

She let her arms fall forward and leaned over, letting her body fall heavily above her toes. Tension she had been holding onto for days slowly released. She pictured it running like water out of her fingertips, cascading over her feet and into the stone floor. The pain in her neck began to lessen.

Another day and another night passed.

They were provided limited food and water, and no answers to what they could expect to happen to them.

"I can't take this," Colt said.

Elektra had stopped responding to his fear-based rantings. It was how he needed to cope with the situation. She was coping by intermittently relaxing and exercising. She pictured the guards coming back to get them and played out her plan for overtaking them. She would be ready to break free when the time came.

The time finally came that night.

There was a thud in the hall and footsteps.

A dark brown woman with straight, black hair unlocked and opened the gate to their cell.

"Mom, is that you?" Elektra asked.

"Only a woman from the Sarda slums would be dumb enough to try and break her daughter out of jail," Zatia said.

"Mom!" Elektra ran into her mother's skinny arms.

"I think you mean 'brave' enough, ma'am," Rustin said, smiling from ear-to-ear.

"Mom, this is Rustin and Colt, my friends."

"Nice to meet you, but we need to go. Now," said Zatia, ushering them through the unlocked door.

"We need to get to the lower levels and out through the underground tunnels. We still have some supplies there and a ship in the yard, if they haven't taken it," Elektra said in a whisper, carefully stepping over the unconscious guard.

"Follow me," Zatia said. "I know the way. Don't make a sound."

The four of them crept around doorways and down corridors and stairs. In the dark, Elektra was completely turned around. The district was quiet and any lights they came across had been dimmed to simulate the nighttime outside.

She was surprised by her mother's heroics. The woman had never lifted a finger to support Elektra.

"Why did you come for us?" Elektra whispered.

Zatia sighed. "Because you left me," she answered.

They kept walking and Elektra was impressed that Zatia seemed to know exactly where to lead them.

"When you didn't come back for days, I knew it was all my fault. I could have tried to talk to you. I should have asked if you were happy in here. With everything we've been through together, you never abandoned me. I know that you could have. You could have gone off on your own to make your own way at any time. But you decided to leave me after we got into a veritable paradise. We finally have an easy life, everything we need to survive, and you couldn't handle it."

The group slowed down to cautiously go around a corner before proceeding.

"I am your mother," Zatia continued. "I should have known that you weren't happy. You should have been able to tell me you wanted to leave."

Elektra considered her words. "My leaving had nothing to do with you, mother."

"Then why didn't you tell me? Why didn't you talk to me?" Zatia shot her arm out protectively, stopping the small group in its tracks.

They froze, listening.

Up ahead of them, two men passed each other in the dark. Guards were changing shifts.

The woman waved her hand, motioning for them to continue moving. She slid into a corridor and opened a door to another staircase.

They silently entered, gently closing the door behind them, and were greeted by the thickest black she had ever experienced, feeling momentarily blinded.

"One step down at a time," Zatia instructed. It was the most motherly statement Elektra had ever heard her utter.

"How did you know I was here?" Elektra whispered to her mother, who was leading them down the dark stairs.

"Word gets around, although, nobody knew who you were or that you are my daughter. I just had a feeling that the brown girl and boys from the slums were somehow connected to you. And if it hadn't been you, I was hoping whoever I found in that cell would tell me if they had seen you. I have been worried."

"I'm sorry I made you worry, mother. I didn't leave because of you. You need to know that. I left because I don't belong in a diamond district. I don't belong around people who ignore the suffering of others. I had to find my tribe and I found them. We are working together to take this world back from the dictator."

"Well, that is much worse than I imagined, then," Zatia said. Her nervous chuckles drifted through the hollow space. "Are you at least being safe out there? Are you alright? Getting enough food? You look skinny."

"Mom, I'm fine. I'm much tougher than you know."

"I know."

"How's my baby brother?" Elektra asked, picturing him only as the fetus in the fishtank.

They reached the end of the stairs and there was finally a little bit of light again. Elektra felt like they were much deeper in the center tower now, and close to their way out.

"He's almost fully cooked and ready to come out of the bubble," Zatia said. Both women laughed and the boys looked at each other, confused.

"That doorway at the end of the hall will lead you to the exit. You all need to go, quickly. But I hope I can see you again. I hope you can meet your brother someday."

Elektra hugged her petite mother tightly. "How did you know how to get us out of here?"

"Denny has a framed copy of the district blueprints on his wall. Ever since you left, I've been staring at them. I thought I had been drawn to them because I wanted to escape this place. It is too safe, too secure, and my life seems almost too easy now. But I guess my intuition just knew I'd have to help you someday. I'm glad I could finally help you, Elektra, after all the times you helped us survive. Now go."

The three rebels ran back down the hallway and through the door they had first come through. They were relieved to see the weapons and ammunition that they'd gathered was all still piled at the bottom of the ladder.

"Grab as much as you can," Elektra said. "We have to try to make as few trips as possible. I don't know how much darkness we have left up there."

Elektra started to collect weapons and ammunition and noticed Colt standing there with his arms crossed.

"What?" she asked.

"We make one trip," he stated, firmly.

"But we almost died for all of this," Elektra protested. "We need it all to win this thing."

"Then we can come back for it later," Colt stated, firmly. "I am not risking us getting caught again. We got lucky with your mother. She won't get another chance to get us out of that cell if we get thrown back in. We carry what we can in one trip and then we leave. I just hope that the ship is still there."

"It'll be there," she said, confidently.

"How do you know? More wishful thinking?"

Elektra rolled her eyes, not holding back in the dim light. She was loading up her pack and arms, shuffling things so she could still climb up a ladder, and didn't have the patience for him at the moment.

"Nobody patrols around the perimeter of the district," she said. "You can't see outside from the inside, and the only guards they send outside stand at the gates all day. It'll be there."

Elektra was really just hoping, but she needed to believe it and sound convincing.

They climbed up, crawled out of the manhole, deposited their loot onto the ground, and then Elektra started to walk through the darkness.

"Ship, open the door."

Lights began to flicker, and she heard the mechanical sound of a ship coming to life.

"Thank the spirits," she said. "Let's move."

They loaded the weapons and Elektra commanded the ship to take off, to leave its lights out, and make way to the rebel headquarters building.

Elektra stared at the nine towers of the district as they lifted off, its lights twinkling like they said stars were supposed to.

It was a painfully long, slow, and quiet voyage. Rustin passed out in one of the captain's chairs, and Colt went down below the deck. She assumed he was purposefully avoiding her.

Alone with her thoughts, her heart started to ache with guilt. She knew she had put them in danger and jeopardized their mission. It was a dumb mistake.

She wanted to believe that she could be a leader, lead the rebels, lead a battle, and yet, she had needlessly risked the lives of people she loved by being careless.

The black night passed by. Building after building, and then out over the open dry lands. Aside from a distant campfire in the mud lands, she saw no other light. The world was bleak and desolate, and she wanted to save it.

But she was starting to realize she may need to step back once in a while and let someone else lead. Let someone else help her. Tonight, her mother had helped them escape. Her mother had never helped her in any meaningful way. If her mother could grow and step outside of her comfort zone, then Elektra owed it to herself and to her friends to try and do the same.

It wouldn't be easy or natural for a loner who had been in charge of every move she had ever made in her life to set aside that control.

Elektra rolled the tension out of her neck, pulled back her shoulders, then swung her arms to the left and right, twisting and untwisting her mid-section.

"I flew across Denlerack. I saved an alien woman. I snuck into the dictator's compound. I can let go of my pride for a little bit."

She smiled at her own statements and let out a small laugh. Rustin breathed heavily and shifted in the captain's chair but didn't wake up.

He was such a sweet kid.

I would do anything for these people. Letting Colt lead and not jumping so quickly into danger will be worth it.

She sat down in another chair, leaned back, and closed her eyes.

A little bit later she awoke to the ship telling them they were coming in for a landing.

Elektra got up and peered through the window. She saw the rebel's dilapidated building and the ruins of the first diamond district.

They landed in front of the building and made their way across the overgrown exterior with as much of their loot as they could carry in one trip. They came into the building through an overgrown courtyard, pried open a metal door, then slinked through hallways and stairwells, traveling down into the basements of the building that seemed unhabitable from above ground.

Elektra began to feel anxious anticipating the anger that would come at her from the others once they found out she had taken them to the diamond district and been captured.

She knew Colt was still angry, because he hadn't said a word to her throughout the flight, loading up the gear, or walking through the building. The longer his silence stretched out, the bigger the pain in her chest grew.

They came to a metal door that led down into the basement. Colt pressed a button on a box that was hidden to the side of it.

"Colt, Rustin, and…" he paused, then looked over to her, finally. Without any emotion he added, "Elektra."

The way he said her name was like a knife to the heart. Anger, disdain, hate, disgust. All of those thoughts filled her mind and she had to stop herself from turning around and leaving.

You don't need these people. You don't need him. Just go take Keldon out yourself. You'll be saving them from him and from you.

She tried to change the narrative of her own voice in her head.

I will do better. I will be a better friend. I will listen and not try to take charge of every situation. I can do this. He has every right to be angry.

The door unlocked and they walked through, listening to it automatically lock again behind them. They were in the main part of the hideout now on a balcony overlooking the living area. She had to force herself to keep putting one foot in front of the other.

She hung back while Colt and Rustin walked down the staircase. Their friends stood up expressing a mix of shock and relief, but those looks quickly turned to frustration. There were others in the rooms, tribe leaders and members, who didn't stand, but looked confused.

"We brought back weapons and ammunition," Colt said, emotionless.

"You went without us. We thought you were dead," Alister said, glaring.

"You said you were coming back here after talking with the professor," Zuri said.

"We were so scared," Lina and Lainie said in unison.

Their voices increased in volume as they expressed their concerns, fears, and disappointment. Colt reached the bottom of the staircase and deposited his armload of ammunition onto the nearest table.

"How could you go without us, Colt?" Alister pressed.

Elektra quickly realized by not taking responsibility for the decision, he would appear weak to the rebels who looked up to him. He had not been in charge, and that put everyone in jeopardy. She had to own up to the mistake without making him look weak.

"It was all my fault!" she yelled out. Everyone stopped talking and turned to her, still standing on the staircase.

Rustin had stepped away and set down his bag and a box he'd been carrying. Elektra emptied her gear right there on the stairs.

"Colt and Rustin didn't know I'd directed the ship to the diamond district until we were there. I left the ship, and they were forced to come after me. I was trying to get more weapons for us, and I disobeyed a direct order. They were forced to save me. I am so sorry."

She let her words fall across them all, but she turned to look at Colt. Elektra wasn't an emotional person, but she hoped that her expression was conveying the deep regret and shame she felt at that moment. She needed Colt to forgive her.

She took a few hesitant steps down the stairs toward him.

"Please forgive me?" she asked him. "I'll defer to your leadership, your guidance. I know you listen to me. I want to prove that I can listen to you too."

Before Colt could respond, Rustin suddenly yelled out, "Everyone look!"

All heads turned to where he was pointing. In the middle of the living room, there was a flash of blue flames. And then another. And then another.

A flash would come and when it vanished, it left guns and ammunition behind.

And not just handguns. There were long guns that looked like they'd been snatched off of spaceships.

Elektra started to giggle and then laughed loudly.

"The dragon spirit. She has sent us more weapons. We can attack the compound now. We can attack them tonight."

"No, Elektra." Colt's voice was stern.

When she turned to look at him, she noticed he had come a few steps closer to her.

"We are not going to attack the compound without the tribespeople who have gone back out to the desert."

Every muscle in Elektra's body twitched to step into him with her own, "no." Her nostrils flared and her eyes widened in the way she was used to responding. She wanted to take the two ships, all the weapons, and go pulverize that compound without a moment's hesitation.

Instead, she took a deep breath.

These are my people. This is my man. He is the leader here. He has been leading them for years. My rash actions have gotten people killed and imprisoned. He was too inactive. But if we work together, listen to, and support each other, then we are unstoppable. We can win but only together.

"You are right." The words were almost painful to say. "Can we take the ships to go alert them and bring them back here? I think we should strike as soon as we can, while the dictator and most of his army is invading Naldash."

The energy in the room shifted and the few members of the tribes nodded their agreement. Colt seemed to loosen up a bit also.

"I agree that we shouldn't wait long," he said, "but let's see who we can get back from the desert tribes. Let's take stock of what the dragon spirit has sent us. And let's devise a strong plan. Together."

He's meeting me halfway, she realized with relief. Elektra smiled and nodded.

"Come down here and let's all talk about the plan," Colt said, extending his hand to her. She walked to him, feeling relieved, and took his hand.

The rebels sat with the tribespeople and created their plans together.

After a short amount of time discussing strategies, ships were flown back and forth to find and bring back whoever was still willing to come and fight. Many more had stayed close to their hideout than she'd expected. They still had a substantial army of people available to fight.

Everyone packed supplies and weaponry, then those with mechanical wings put theirs on. It only took them another full day to prepare for the next invasion, but she knew that Colt probably would have preferred to wait another few days.

"Do we need to wait for Ludwig?" she asked Colt.

He looked at her and she thought she saw a return to tenderness in his eyes.

"No," he said. "Ludwig and the others can catch up.

We have enough here now to begin the journey."

Elektra couldn't contain her excitement as she spread the word of the attack throughout the tribes. They all came together, packed, and prepared to walk across the land to the compound. Some people walked, some flew, and a few climbed into the two ships.

Elektra stood at the controls of a ship, with her wings behind her, feeling like a commander, a defender, and a warrior. An exhilaration filled her bones when she finally saw the compound in the distance. It took every ounce of discipline to wait for her foot soldiers to catch up.

A mansion, barracks, nearly empty spaceship yards, and factories stood protected behind a thick, tall, stone wall. Elektra knew they would win this time. There were barely any guards and soldiers left to stand in their way.

When everyone finally reached the compound, she ordered the ship to smash through the gates and walls, letting her and Colt's army into the fortress.

This world would either be saved by her and her friends, or they would all die out from pollution and starvation in a few short years. It was now or never.

The rebels who were on foot walked into the compound, firing at any of Keldon's soldiers who were brave enough to stand their ground.

Elektra fired on the walls and fired at the mansion in the middle, the home of the dictator. She shot down any men who tried to run toward the remaining ships in the shipyard. And then she gave command of her ship over to one of the tribesmen.

"The factories need to be destroyed next," she said. "I'll get the slaves out. Wait for my signal." She flew through the open ramp and toward the factories, with the two commandeered ships in her wake.

She flew ahead to make sure there were no slaves or servants working late or sleeping in barracks nearby. She landed and ran into one of the factories, calling out for people. There were not many, but she did see some workers as she flew from factory building to building, yelling, and warning people to leave.

"Run," she called out to them. "Escape this place."

She watched a few men, women, and even some children dressed in brown rags evacuate the factories.

The two ships were floating nearby, waiting for her signal. Once it was all clear, she motioned to them to fire at the factories and shoot down their towers. The sounds of their long guns shook her nearly out of the sky. The air filled quickly with smoke and fire and Elektra started coughing.

I should have grabbed us masks for this, she told herself.

The smoke made flying a challenge, so she stayed low to the ground, navigating her way out of the maze of buildings. She was so focused on trying to breathe and escape the smoke and falling debris from the destroyed building, that she wasn't paying attention to her surroundings.

Bullets whizzed by her ear, and she ducked.

"Surrender," said a man's voice.

She saw one of Keldon's soldiers standing a hundred feet or so in front of her. He was wearing a mask.

"Why are you still fighting?" she asked, coughing, and squinting through the dirt and smoke. "Do you even know what you are fighting for?"

"Lord Keldon runs our planet and pays me well," he said.

"He is running this planet into the ground," Elektra yelled down at the man. "You deserve air you can breathe."

"You are the ones making the air worse right now," he said, motioning toward the burning factories.

The soldier was a handsome young man with ashy blond hair. She wondered about his life and his story. She didn't want to shoot these men who were so brainwashed by a dictator who had destroyed their world. It wasn't his fault he was on the wrong side.

He had his reasons, as he'd said. He was being paid and

it was so much easier to work for someone who pays you than to struggle to provide for yourself. She understood him and pitied him.

"Look around you," she said. "You can kill me, but you can't kill all of the rebels. You can't rebuild these factories. You can't bring back all of the slaves. But you can go build yourself a home, dig for water, and try to farm. You can try to help make this planet better than it was before."

"I can't believe you are ready to die for that idea," he said, cocking and aiming his gun at her.

In that moment, she realized she was ready. Everything she had done had been to try and make the world a better place for her mother and for her new friends.

She was ready to die for this idea and was at peace with the thought. She was proud of what she had accomplished and what she had survived so far.

You have done well.

She heard the words as if placed inside her head.

The soldier dropped his gun and ran away faster than she'd ever seen a man run before.

Elektra turned around and saw a giant, emerald-green dragon floating in the air behind her.

"It's you," she said.

I am Ash.

"Ash, you saved us."

Ash began to disappear as quickly as she had appeared.

"Elektra, where are you?"

"I'm over here," she yelled back.

Colt came flying at her from out of the smoky sky. He wrapped his arms around her with such ferocity, she thought they'd both fall to the ground.

"I thought I'd lost you," he said. "I'm sorry I didn't believe in you. I'm sorry I was so angry."

Elektra smiled, collapsing entirely into him as they slowly drifted to the ground together.

"I understand why you were upset," she said. "And it's nothing because I love you."

As their feet touched the ground, he pulled her in closer and kissed her passionately while the world burned down around them.

She didn't know how long they stood there, but it didn't seem long enough.

"We need to get out of this smoke," he said, seeming to come to his senses. "It is done. The compound, the mansion, the factories are all burning."

"I'll follow your lead," she said, and she meant it in every single way.

They ran back toward the compound entrance together, hand-in-hand, running into other rebels along the way.

Elektra stopped, looking at the field littered with spaceships the dictator hadn't taken with him.

There were hundreds of dragon spirits standing around the ships like a thick fog. They were drawing her attention to the ships. They wanted her to do something.

"We aren't done yet," she called out to the rebels.

11 MONSTERS

The dragon spirits had been a constant nuisance in KaLeah's head since before the first ship had arrived.

They continually blasted her with the guttural moans of angry growls mixed in with whispers of words she tried to ignore.

Come out, fight, save our world. Don't hide, coward. Just a girl. Weak. Go for blood. Kill. Fight.

KaLeah tried to ignore them as she covered the queen with her body from inside a hallway. There were more loud bangs and crashes of castle stones falling around them. She worried the young women would end up getting buried alive.

Coward. Little babies. Why don't you fight?

"If you want us to win so badly, then help us, you stupid dragon spirits!" KaLeah yelled at the voices.

"Ash did help by sending their guns away," Amirra said, defending the only spirit she was aware of.

KaLeah was sick of being haunted by all of the others. "I can hear more than just Ash," she said. "The others are useless nuisances that bark orders in my head without offering any help. It's getting old."

The girls were silent for a moment, but KaLeah didn't dare move them, yet. She looked ahead to see if she could determine the nearest path to a staircase that would take them deeper into the castle and to safety.

"Listen," Amirra said.

"I don't hear anything."

"Exactly. The crashing stopped. Do you think they stopped ramming the castle?"

KaLeah looked back toward the entryway and then the library. "We can try to look, but we need to be careful."

They shoved open the door that led back into the library. Books had fallen in front of it, and shelves were knocked down all throughout. They stepped over piles of books and toppled shelves, making their way to the broken window.

KaLeah climbed up onto the table and carefully peered out.

Black ships still hovered in the sky, but a few had landed on the lawns. Belarone soldiers with swords drawn kept their distance, not knowing for sure whether the Denlerack men still had guns.

There was suddenly a voice blasting through the air like some god commanding them.

"I can't believe you won't surrender after all of this!" said the voice.

KaLeah recognized the voice. It was her father, the dictator.

"I don't want to destroy the entire castle the way I destroyed the others. You should know by now I am not going to negotiate. I am taking over this entire world. It is time for you silly little girls to surrender."

"Father?" KaLeah said, surprised to see Clegg out on the castle lawn amongst the soldiers.

"The man speaking is your father? The dictator?" Amirra asked.

"Yes, but the man who raised me is also here." Clegg Trapper was walking across the field toward a ship. His pace was firm and fast, as if he was angry.

"What's he doing?" Amirra asked. The girl had climbed up beside her, not able to resist looking outside.

"It looks like he's yelling at the ship, but I can't hear anything from here."

The door to one of the ships began to open and KaLeah could see her biological father, Keldon, standing there.

She couldn't stand her own curiosity. She pushed back from the window, climbed down off the table, and marched through the rubble and bookshelves toward the door.

"Where are you going?" Amirra asked, fear lacing her voice.

"I have to know what is happening out there!" KaLeah yelled, unable to resist. Both of her fathers, her real one and the one who raised her, were coming face-to-face in the middle of a war.

"But it's dangerous, and you're supposed to protect me by getting me to safety!"

Guilt rippled through KaLeah. "Ash sent all of their guns away. They all only have hands and swords to fight with now."

"What about the ships running us over?"

"They can't hit us all at the same time. Keldon just said that he doesn't want to destroy this place. He won't do any more damage. Come along or stay here."

She heard Amirra scrambling to follow her. KaLeah knew she probably should have taken the queen deeper into the safety of the castle. There probably wasn't anything that KaLeah could do against her father that the other men couldn't do except… she had a gun on her.

She may be the only one left in the kingdom with a gun.

KaLeah walked through the castle entrance, across the cobblestone, and past the gates, gaining confidence with every step.

With everything her biological father had put her through, she hadn't had the chance to tell him how much she hated him. She was glad he hadn't been the one to raise her. Her feet touched the grass, and she froze to take a deep breath. There were ships on the ground, ships floating in the air, and her two fathers were about to meet eye-to-eye.

Surrounding the entire area, for as far as she could see, was what looked like a thick, moving fog. But it was like no fog she had ever seen.

She saw heads, talons, wings, scales, and teeth. Dragon spirits surrounded the battlefield from the woods to the spaceships that had landed on the ground, and even drifted beneath the crafts still hovering in the sky.

Amirra came up beside her.

"Do you see them?" KaLeah asked.

"Spirits," Amirra said, gasping. "They are everywhere. Are they going to help us or hurt us?"

"I think they are Nala dragon spirits, the ones from this planet. I don't know if they can do anything other than stand there and creep us out."

"Are we the only ones who can see them?" Amirra asked.

KaLeah did a scan and it seemed like all soldiers were focused only on the enemies. "It looks like it," she said.

Yells drew her attention back to the ships.

"I'm going to go closer, but I think you need to stay with the guards at the gate for your own protection. You shouldn't be out in the open or too close to the enemy."

Amirra sighed. KaLeah knew the girl wanted to argue and go with her, but surprisingly, she nodded and held back. Guards and soldiers, realizing who she was, began to surround the queen for her protection.

As KaLeah ran toward the ships on the field, she realized she didn't see Hilip anywhere.

Had he been crushed by a ship? Was he injured somewhere? Worry filled her mind, but she tried to focus.

"There she is," said Keldon, mischievously. "Are you the one responsible for our guns magically disappearing, dear daughter?"

"She's not your daughter," Clegg snapped back.

The dictator turned his glare to Clegg.

"She's not your daughter, either," the dictator responded.

"I raised her to be the woman she is today," Clegg said.

"Women are not supposed to be this strong," the man who was dressed in a crisp brown suit waved his hand at her like he was motioning to an exhibit. "Just look at what happened to Huntra. A woman with too much fire in her bones does nothing but burn herself out."

He turned his cold eyes to KaLeah. "Come with me, child, and let me temper your flames."

"You need to leave this place," KaLeah ordered. "Take your ships and fly back to Denlerack. Let the people of Naldash live their lives in peace."

"Peace? It looked to me like your peaceful inhabitants were fighting again. Apparently, the other kingdoms realized how weak Belarone would be with a little girl on the throne. I really don't blame them and must admit that we have been watching all of the drama for quite some time. Although, finding you on Denlerack and never knowing you were here was quite a surprise. Clegg was very good at hiding Huntra's little secret."

KaLeah felt so uncomfortable with both of her fathers standing before her, the Denlerack dictator speaking about her and Huntra as if he knew them both so well.

Both men felt like strangers. The one who raised her had always been emotionally unavailable, and yet he had trained her to fight, how to hunt, and how to survive. KaLeah knew nothing about Clegg, however, because he had never shared anything that would have helped her know him better.

She didn't know his thoughts or his emotions, other than when she made a mistake or didn't hit a target.

Then there was her real father, from whom she'd been stolen before her birth. She had to believe her mother, Huntra, had a good reason for taking her from him. After spending time with Dayne Keldon in his mansion, in the middle of his compound on Denlerack, she knew he wasn't a good man.

She felt so little emotional attachment to either, their arguing seemed nothing more than a waste of time.

Back on Denlerack, she hadn't been able to kill Keldon, even after he'd slain one of her friends. She knew he was bad, but she still didn't think she could kill her own flesh and blood.

She fingered her sword at her side and the daggers in her belt. The gun was tucked behind her back, but she wasn't confident in her ability to shoot it straight at Keldon under pressure from this distance. Even if she could pull the trigger, she wasn't close enough.

"Enough of this," Keldon shouted. "Tell the queen to surrender her kingdom to us and we will spare her castle. She can keep living in it with me as her king. You can both be my little princesses. Doesn't that sound lovely? You can finally have the father you deserve."

Clegg moved up the ramp so fast, it shocked KaLeah. He flew at Keldon, throwing a punch that landed hard against the dictator's nose and cheek, smacking loudly. The man screamed and Clegg punched him again, but lower in the side as Keldon recoiled from the first hit.

Keldon's men came from behind and pulled Clegg off, locking both of his arms behind his back and putting him into a choke hold.

Blood spilled from Keldon's nose and mouth. The dictator spat the blood out onto the ship's ramp.

KaLeah noticed the Belarone soldiers had been slowly creeping closer to the ships during the altercation. They had their swords drawn and shields up, but they had no idea whether or not the invaders would pull out guns at any moment.

"Tell your child queen I am running out of patience," Keldon said. "You may have magicked away my ammunition, but I will send these ships into all of the towers. I can bring more ships with guns and ammunition at any time."

KaLeah stepped forward. "If you keep coming, then Ash will just keep sending your guns back. She will send your ships back. She will send your men back again and again and again until you are all so exhausted from coming here, you'll give up."

She kept walking forward slowly as she spoke. "You may as well quit now. You can't go against a magical dragon."

KaLeah's fingers tingled.

Grab a dagger and throw it, she told herself. *Shoot the gun.*

She could see the soldiers and dragon spirits all closing in like a fog in her peripheral vision.

She could hear Clegg choking, struggling to breathe, and fighting against the soldiers holding him. She knew she could throw a dagger at the soldiers restraining Clegg. And she could throw one at Keldon's neck, but she felt paralyzed.

"Why won't you bring all your men out to fight?" KaLeah called to Keldon.

"You stole their weapons, child," he said.

"I am not a child and without your deadly machines, they are just men and should face our soldiers as men."

"You all have swords, and we have ships," Keldon said, haughtily. "Ships beat swords, dear. We will chase and pummel your men into the ground like nails."

He snapped his fingers at his guards, who tossed Clegg off of the ramp. They all went back into the ship and the ramp closed behind them.

KaLeah ran to help Clegg up to his feet.

"I'm sorry I didn't act quickly enough," she said.

"And do what?" he asked, rubbing the tender spots on his neck.

"Throw my knives at him," she said, not wanting to mention the gun.

"I can understand your hesitation when it comes to him. And you could have hit me if you'd aimed for his men." He said it very matter-of-factly.

"Are the dragons here?" he asked.

"You mean the spirits?"

"Yes. Are they here with you?"

KaLeah looked around the edges of the battleground. Soldiers were still creeping closer, even though the ships had returned to the skies.

Dragon spirits still surrounded them like a thick fog. "They are in the fog," she whispered, as if not wanting to trigger them.

Clegg looked around, squinting his eyes. "They are the fog," he said.

"Can you see them?" she asked, suddenly feeling optimistic.

"I can see the fog, but not the dragons. You can see them though, can't you?" he asked.

"Queen Amirra and I can, yes. But I don't know why. It doesn't help us. Ash, the one who has spoken to us, says she can't help us. If she sends them away, they will only return. She is the one who took their weapons, though."

"We need to move," Clegg said, looking skyward. "They will resume ramming soldiers with their ships again."

"Our men can hide in the woods," KaLeah offered.

"The invaders will just take out everything they can until the queen surrenders."

"She won't surrender," KaLeah said.

"And neither will Keldon," Clegg said.

Clegg started to head back past the line of soldiers and toward the woods. KaLeah followed him for a few paces and then heard the whir of a ship behind her. She watched the soldiers in front of her drop down and immediately dropped to the ground, flattening herself against the cool grass, without pausing to look back.

The dictator's ship flew right over her. It was so close she could feel the heat on her back as it passed.

The smell of grass and dirt flooded her senses, and she lifted her head up as soon as the ship was gone. She watched as some men tried to attack the machine with their swords.

They were helpless against the ships. If the men did not come out, there was no way for this to ever end. She remembered the machines needed some sort of fuel supply, and her hopes sparked.

If the queen's men did not surrender by the time the ships ran out of fuel, then the dictator's fleet would be grounded. They would have no weapons and they would be stuck on Naldash.

"Ash, where are you?" she yelled out to the sky. "Push them back, over and over and over until they run out of fuel!" *All we have to do is wait them out,* she said to herself.

She jumped up and started to look for Amirra and Hilip. She needed to tell them what she'd realized.

She saw Amirra across the lawn, but the stubborn queen had come too far out into the open. One of the ships was careening toward her.

"Amirra, get down!" KaLeah yelled. She ran as fast as she could toward her friend and hoped the guards surrounding her would lay their lives on the line in order to protect the queen. She worried that some of the soldiers could still be loyal to Prince Nikolat.

"Ash, where are you? Why aren't you helping us?" she cried out as she ran.

Finally, the dragon materialized above the queen, floating in the face of the oncoming ship, with her green scales glistening in the sun and her transparent wings spread wide.

The look on the dragon's face was fierce, blue flames coming out of her nostrils. She looked like a mother protecting her baby.

KaLeah felt so grateful and relieved but didn't stop running. She wouldn't stop until the queen was safely by her side.

"Amirra!"

The ship had stopped, apparently mesmerized by or

cautious about the monster floating in front of them.

The queen had huddled low to the ground, and a few men were standing over her with their swords drawn.

"Get lower than that. All the way to the ground," KaLeah shouted as she ran.

The queen curled up her lip, apparently disgusted by the idea.

"Just do it!"

Hearing KaLeah, the queen finally laid down flat on the ground. KaLeah reached her and hovered over her, watching Ash thwart the ship.

"What if it tries to land on me?" Amirra asked, her voice squeaking.

"We need to run you out of here. We can try to get back into the castle or to the woods."

Ash began to fire off blue flames, engulfing the ship above them and transporting it back toward the mountains.

KaLeah helped Amirra to her feet as the dragon kept firing off blue shots, transporting ship after ship so far away they looked like pebbles.

She knew they would keep coming back, but as long as Ash could keep moving them away, they at least had more time.

If the ships ran out of fuel, Keldon's men would be forced to come out and face them all on foot. They would have no weapons left at that point. She finally started to feel hopeful.

That is when the sound of atmospheric booms began popping up above them.

"What is that sound?" Amirra asked.

KaLeah didn't want to believe it as she looked up to the sky. More black ships burned through the atmosphere, speeding toward them.

We are doomed, she realized. "Get ready to run."

"What is happening?" Amirra screamed.

"It looks like Denlerack has sent reinforcements. Keldon has ships with guns and ammunition again," she told the queen, her heart sinking. Her original plan of waiting them out wouldn't work if they could resume shooting down Belarone soldiers with ease.

She saw they were closer to the castle than to the forest, but her gut was telling her that hiding among the tall trees would be safer.

"We are running to the forest," KaLeah ordered.

The queen's slippers were covered in mud and debris, but the queen looked resolute. Taking her hand, KaLeah ran them across the fields toward the protection of the forest.

She tried to stay focused on the goal, while the sounds of guns, explosions, crashes, and men yelling out seemed to surround her. They might lose the castle, the kingdom, and even the entire planet of Naldash, but KaLeah would not let them take the queen.

The girls ran into the forest, jumping over fallen logs, and zig zagging along paths between the foliage.

Being in the woods again after so long reminded her of the first day she had set off in search of her father. She had stumbled upon and killed three bandits, not knowing they had a kidnapped princess in their possession.

She felt like a thousand lifetimes had passed since that day.

"Here, let's stop here. Down behind that log." KaLeah pulled Amirra down to her knees in the mud beside her, and they both peered through the trees toward the battleground.

She hoped that Ash would continue zapping away ships and weapons but wasn't sure how long that would go on and whether or not more ships would just keep coming for them.

"This dress is ruined," Amirra said with a whimper.

"Why are you wearing a dress during an invasion, anyway?"

"I honestly don't know." Amirra let out a laugh and KaLeah shook her head, smiling.

They laid there and listened to the carnage. It was so

much louder than before, and the ground below them shook over and over.

"What is happening out there?" Amirra asked.

KaLeah didn't know. She pictured the worst and tried to keep her mind in the present moment. She needed to stay alert in case the dictator sent his men into the woods to find them.

And then she heard it.

Men's heavy boots were running toward them. There was no time to escape. She sat up into a crouched position and drew her sword.

❞Elektra❝

Elektra had never felt more alive.

"Is that supposed to happen?" Rustin asked her as they entered the Naldashian atmosphere.

Flames covered the front window, the ship rattled, and it sounded as if they were in a raging storm.

"From what I remember reading about spaceships, the extreme heat and sound is normal," Colt said, looking mesmerized.

Once the view cleared again, the scene before them was even more magical than traveling through space had been. Elektra had never seen so much green. There were white-capped mountains, lakes, and beyond the mountains, a large body of water that seemed to curve around the edge of the planet.

"Is that snow?" Rustin asked, pointing to the mountain range.

"Look at those trees," Colt marveled.

There were dense forests and farmlands.

"No wonder Keldon wanted this land so badly," Elektra said. "There is so much richness here. So much life."

As they traveled closer to the surface, Elektra could see a castle. It was similar to Keldon's mansion, but more ornate. Its white walls seemed to glimmer in the sunlight.

"It's all so beautiful," Rustin said.

"Well, it won't be for much longer if Keldon takes control," Elektra said. "Let's find that monster."

They headed toward the castle. The black ships were the first objects they could see clearly, and then soldiers started to come into focus.

Elektra pressed a button that allowed her to speak to all of the other ships. They had brought at least twenty and armed rebels and tribe folk were loaded into each of them.

"Fire on the ships, rebels," Elektra ordered. "Take them all out."

They unleashed a firestorm down upon the ships that were on the castle lawns and the ones that were hovering below them.

Caught off-guard, the ships that had been floating, suddenly tried to turn and fire back upward at Elektra and her friends. But the bullets didn't come. Instead, the ships came at them at ramming speed.

"Why aren't they firing back at us?" Elektra asked.

"Ash took all their weapons, remember?" Colt said with a smile.

"Dragon spirits, that's right." realization dawning on Elektra. "Ash sent us everything. They can only crash into us."

She pressed the communication button again.

"Their ships have no more guns or ammunition. They will try to ram us. Take evasive measures and blow them out of the sky."

She watched as the ships they shot fell out of the sky like massive raindrops.

"Look out below!" she yelled, smiling to herself.

"You are really enjoying yourself," Colt mused.

"Spirits, yes I am!" She laughed, telling the ship to fire again on another of the dictator's ships.

She had no idea what to expect when she had decided to talk the rebels into taking all of the ships that were left at the dictator's compound.

It had been exhilarating taking off, leaving Denlerack behind, and flying across the stars to Naldash. Seeing the endless speckled night was a spiritual experience

"I guess that after everything we've gone through, I was expecting more of a battle," she told Colt, who was standing beside her. He hadn't left her side since finding her in the smoke and rubble from the burning factories. She was so thankful that he wasn't angry with her anymore.

Danger puts your relationships into a different perspective, she figured.

"It would have been very different if Ash hadn't sent their weapons to us," Colt said. "We owe a lot to her."

"Spirits bless that dragon," she said.

They flew until they had shot down every last ship and made sure the ones that were already on the ground were fully inoperable.

"Let's pull back away from the rubble," Elektra commanded over the communication system. She led the way in her ship, landing it on the castle grounds beyond the crashed and destroyed ships that were sending plumes of smoke and fire into the air.

"Aren't we landing kind of far away?" Rustin asked.

"We don't want the queen and her soldiers to think we are also here to invade and conquer," Elektra said. "We have to make sure we approach peacefully and let them know we are their friends."

"I guess that makes sense," Rustin said.

The trio exited their craft, followed by rebels and tribe folk from their ship and others. They all walked across the fields together, heading closer to the castle, with Elektra, Colt, and Rustin at the lead. She felt like a general, guiding her army to accept their accolades for saving the world.

Elektra saw soldiers in brown uniforms who were armed with swords pulling men dressed in black, the Denlerack soldiers, from their burning ships, and chaining their hands behind their backs if they were able to stand.

It was a glorious spectacle. She couldn't believe everything had worked out so well.

Elektra got closer to the fray but didn't see KaLeah anywhere. She was worried, not seeing the woman running among the soldiers.

"Halt, who are you?" asked a large, black skinned man dressed in a brown uniform. He was riding on top of an ancient black draggot.

Elektra and the rebels stood in amazement at the creature. Its body was covered in scales, it had clawed hooves, and sharp teeth poking out from its long muzzle. Draggots had been extinct on Denlerack for so long they had never seen one.

"We are friends of KaLeah and friends to the queen," Colt shouted, coming to his senses before Elektra. His voice woke her out of her excitement and adoration at seeing the draggot.

"We brought reinforcements from Denlerack to help you win this war," she added.

"We shot the bad guys out of the sky," Rustin said, to simplify the message and fill the awkward silence.

The man looked them over, seemingly perplexed by the differences in style. Then he let out a raucous laugh.

"Well, isn't this a pleasant surprise. I guess that young favor didn't waste her time on the dead planet after all. I am General Array, and you are all most welcome here. My men are locking up the invaders now. I would take you to the queen, but I believe she and KaLeah ran off to hide. I sent General Daven and some men into the woods to bring them back safely now that your troop shot them all out of the sky."

Elektra felt relief and excitement about seeing her friend again. They started to all walk toward the castle, and she saw that although it was damaged, it was still mostly intact.

She imagined a grand celebration in the palace or out on the lawns and looked forward to everyone finally being able to relax. She took in a deep breath, feeling stunned, and amazed by the fresh air and vibrant surroundings.

The grass below her feet was a bright green and she could see fields of crops growing further out. There were tall trees comprising a thick forest, and treetops reaching high into a bright blue sky where the sun was shining. Behind the white castle towers was a massive mountain range. Her own ugly, dark planet hung in the sky like an enemy.

"I see why Keldon wanted this planet so badly," she said. "Everything is gorgeous. Are those flowers?"

She pointed to lush gardens growing just outside the castle gates.

"It really is beautiful," Colt said. "Especially if you look past all of the broken ships we just destroyed."

She laughed with him, feeling so happy and proud to have him beside her through the most important battle of her life.

"We must see everything as soon as we know KaLeah, and the queen are safe."

Colt turned to her and took her hands, giving them a squeeze. "I'd love to walk with you through the gardens and explore that forest with you," he said, sweetly.

Her heart warmed at his words but something behind him stole away her romantic attention.

"Spirits, is that Keldon?" Elektra asked, gasping. She held onto one of Colt's hands and spun him around to see what she was seeing.

A man was being pulled out of a black ship. His gray hair was matted to his balding head with blood, and his uniform was tattered.

They broke away from the general who was escorting them toward the castle and headed instead to the dictator.

The man looked completely flustered and wobbled while the queen's soldiers attempted to bind his hands together.

"Keldon," Elektra said, walking up to him.

"Who in bloody spirit's name are you?" he asked.

"I am Elektra Dean, and I am the reason you will not be taking over Naldash and destroying it like you did Denlerack."

"Elektra!"

She turned, hearing her name, and saw KaLeah running toward her, towing a blonde-haired girl in a muddy black dress behind her.

Elektra was relieved to see her friend, and who she assumed to be the child queen, alive.

The two women embraced in a quick but firm hug.

"What are you doing here? How did you get here?" KaLeah asked.

"We came to save your butts," Elektra said with a smile. "We destroyed the dictator's compound on Denlerack and saw some ships just sitting there. Ash also helped out by sending us this fool's guns."

"You know Ash too?" asked the small blonde one.

"I do," Elektra said proudly. "And you must be the queen."

"Yes, I am Queen Amirra Belarone, and you are most welcome in my kingdom as my honored guest."

"It seems to be more of a queendom," Elektra said, both words sounding so strange to her, having lived under a dictatorship with diamond districts and slum cities for years. Kingdom and queendom sounded so much classier and more elite.

"Girls," said Keldon, spitting onto the ground. The word was laced with hatred and disdain. "Girls and women have caused me nothing but trouble my entire life. You three are the worst I have ever known. You don't know who I am, where I have come from, and what I can do to each of you to make your lives miserable. You are nothing. You are weaker than me, dumber than me, and serve no purpose other than to birth children."

Elektra, KaLeah, and Amirra all turned toward the decrepit man, with blood streaming from an open head wound.

"I think you hit your head a bit too hard there, old man," Elektra said.

"These two women could kill you with their bare hands," Amirra said.

"I am ashamed I once thought you could be worth redeeming," KaLeah said, shaking her head. "You are the most worthless excuse of a man I have ever known. I understand why my mother wanted to leave you so badly she ended up leaving an entire planet behind. Anything less wouldn't have been far enough."

"Your mother was a hussy and a liar!" Keldon yelled.

Elektra took a step closer to the dictator. Blood and anger boiled in her veins. She had been so angry with men for as long as she could remember.

A man had abandoned her and her mother. Men threatened their survival every day in the Sarda slums growing up. She'd rescued KaLeah from men many times, and they'd both been shot out of the sky by men.

But all of it led back to this one man—this creator of evil and pain.

"Weak men cannot handle strong women," Elektra stated. "All they have are insults. You are not special. Evil men have been trying to keep down strong women from the beginning of time."

Elektra knew how far she had come from hatred, control, anger, and fear. It wasn't that men were evil; it was just that she hadn't met the good ones. She was finally learning how to trust others, including men.

She realized that she had only been wronged by insecure men. The only men who were threatened by women and girls were weak men who didn't deserve them.

"Luckily for us, we have good, strong men in our lives who help lift us up," she continued. "Compared to these men, you are no man at all. You are a weak, shallow, insignificant speck of dust on their shoes. You are nothing but a fearful and insecure, evil man. You are pitiful. And you are a loser. Nothing you say to us will ever make up for the fact that you lost. You were out-witted, out-smarted, and frankly, out-manned by three strong, lovely *women*."

KaLeah and Amirra stood beside her as she berated this man. "I don't even want to kill you right now. I want you to sit in a cell and think about these words for the rest of your miserable life. I want you to see the three of us standing in front of you, mocking you over your largest defeat, that just happened to come at the hands of three women you were unable to command or destroy."

Elektra felt so proud standing there after her speech. She didn't really know what the queen would do to the man, but she didn't care. After years of wanting to destroy him, she saw he was finally at his lowest point. He could not hurt anyone else.

Colt and Rustin were standing behind her. Colt placed his hand on her shoulder, and she was so glad to finally know such wonderful men. There were other men who had gathered behind the three women, too.

She saw an older man with shaggy brown hair and a big beard walk up behind KaLeah. A handsome young man in a brown uniform and blond hair stepped up behind KaLeah and Amirra. General Array sat nearby watching from his draggot.

She smiled. They were all supported and protected, and both of their worlds would now be better and safer.

They had all the support they needed.

12 SISTERS

Queen Amirra stood with her friends on the battlefield, looking down on the dictator who was on his knees, hands tied together behind his back. Her fingers ached to grab a dagger and jam it into the man's heart.

The dictator had nearly destroyed her home with his selfishness. He commanded an entire planet and that still wasn't enough for him. KaLeah and Elektra may want to stick him in a prison cell, but she wanted to stick him in the throat with a pointy object.

"What are your orders?" General Daven asked her.

She looked up at everyone's faces.

There was KaLeah, her sister, and a warrior. There were the new warriors from Denlerack. And there was General Daven alongside General Array, men who commanded armies who also protected her. They all looked to her expectantly, but all she wanted to do was scream at the dictator and tell him where to go, while the soldiers executed him right then and there.

A vision of throwing the knife across the throne room and into Nikolat's back flashed through her mind. They were both bad men and she felt no guilt for wanting them to get what they deserved.

But Keldon wasn't about to kill anyone. He looked like a pathetic, old, pale-skinned, balding man who had fallen to his knees during battle, too weak to get back up.

She didn't pity him; but she couldn't just kill a man who was clearly no longer a threat.

She was torn.

"Throw him in the dungeon, for now," Queen Amirra commanded. "And then round up his soldiers. Bring them all before me."

"Yes, Your Majesty," General Daven said. He turned on his heel to give the order to his men.

"What do you have in mind?" KaLeah asked, her voice low.

"Escort me to the balcony while I think about it."

KaLeah, Elektra, Colt, and Rustin all walked with the queen, flanked by a few of her soldiers, across the courtyard and into the castle.

The three alien visitors were stunned by the ornate details and dragon carvings throughout their walk, commenting on the beauty and wonder of the place.

They followed the queen up a flight of stairs and onto the balcony that looked over the courtyard. The soldiers from both planets were beginning to assemble there.

The Denlerack soldiers looked disgruntled, grumpy, and defeated. They had no weapons and were led like a herd of wuvats across the cobblestone.

"Where is the dragon, Ash?" the girl Elektra asked KaLeah.

"She really only appears when she is needed," KaLeah responded.

Queen Amirra stood up tall, feeling proud, knowing she wouldn't need the dragon spirit for this. She combed her fingers through her hair and then straightened out the fabric of her dress, feeling as if she'd just been tossed around in a windstorm.

This is my kingdom. These are my people. This is my kingdom.

She repeated the mantra to calm her nerves and to keep herself from jumping up and down on the balcony screaming, *I won the war, I won the war!*

She waited until the courtyard was nearly full of soldiers, both Naldashians and Denlerackians. She raised her arms and the chatter stopped. It seemed as if nobody even dared to breath. She held their fate in her hands.

"Visitors from Denlerack," she began. "Although you came with the intent to claim Naldash as yours, let me still be the first to officially and cordially *welcome* you to Belarone Kingdom."

Queen Amirra leaned forward, looking down on everyone as she continued. "Very seldom in this life are we provided the luxury to choose the leader that we serve. We are placed like pawns in front of them on a game board as they play with our lives."

She closed her eyes and shook her head, thinking about her words. "I have seen two types of leaders in my short life, so far. One has learned from every mistake he has made. He realizes that life is rare and precious. He makes decisions to save lives. He gets to know the people around him, no matter their rank or stature. This type of leader does not conquer others out of desire to be first or best or rich. This type of leader only goes to battle when the alternative would risk lives."

Amirra wanted to be this type of leader. She knew in her heart. She had seen her own anger, her own struggles and fears, a knife fly from her hand and into her brother's back. She knew she could be either good or evil, but she wanted to be good.

"The other type of leader is selfish and is the type I have put down with my own two hands," Amirra continued. "The other type of leader cares only to be the first, the best, and the richest. He goes to war to conquer others only for his own benefit, tossing lives aside as expendable collateral."

Amirra looked toward where Keldon was being

restrained. "Dictator Dayne Keldon is this type of man. He does not care about you or your lives. He did not attempt to take Naldash for the good of the Denlerackian people. And I think you all know this to be true. I am the first type of leader, and I will prove it to you all today. But first, I want you to imagine Keldon in your minds. If he were the man standing on this balcony right now, speaking to you, enemies who had just invaded his land, tell me honestly, would he give you mercy?"

She stood quietly then, looking out among their faces. There were looks of confusion, furrowed brows, and a few of them looked to one another as if cheating on a test.

"Tell me," she said, louder. "Would Keldon give you mercy if you were his enemies?"

And then she heard it—a small murmur through the crowd that spread from a whisper and grew.

"No."

"No."

"No."

Over and over until the answer was clear. She repeated it back to them. "No. The second type of leader would never grant his enemies mercy. There would be no safe path back home. There would be no option to stay and live freely on the new planet. With one wave of my hand, I would have my phantom dragon dispose of you in flames."

For theatrics, Amirra raised her arms up into the air. The men watched with worried expressions and looked around for the dragon spirit.

Ash didn't appear.

"Remember I said I am the first type of leader," she said, slowly lowering her arms to her side. "I do not wish to see death. Every life is precious, and we are all just trying to do the best we can with what we have. We all want to survive. Some of us wish to thrive. Some of us wish to fly."

She raised an eyebrow and looked back at her friends on the balcony.

"So, now I ask you if you want to live?"

The men broke out into raucous cheers, claps, and yells.

After the noise died down, Amirra continued. "Then I will show you *mercy*. You all have two options. First, you may return to your home on Denlerack, the dead planet. You may go back and try to help that world become better. You will be returning without your previous leader and taking the stories of my mercy and of our phantom dragon with you. You will refer to our sister planet as a peaceful ally." Amirra paused to give them time to consider this option.

"Or you may stay here on this lush, life-giving planet, with us. You may stay in my kingdom and be a soldier for me as we work to ensure that life is protected on this planet. Who knows, maybe we use these ships and make sure life is protected on every planet we can reach."

KaLeah stepped up beside her then and whispered in her ear. The queen smiled.

"My dear sister has just offered me a third option. Anyone who wishes to join the dictator in his cell is invited to choose that option as well. I dare say only the most loyal truly qualify for that option."

And then she heard the men laughing. It was the most wonderful sound she had ever heard.

"Go now and clean the mess you have made of my beautiful kingdom. Clear the bodies, the broken ships, and rubble. Work with my soldiers to rebuild the damage that you have done under the guidance of a terrible leader. Once you have completed the restoration of our home, then I will let you decide if you want to return to yours or make this place your new home." Amirra made a sweeping gesture.

"We will feed you. We will let you rest. And then we will let you live. Never forget that Queen Amirra Belarone of Naldash let you live."

The men cheered so loudly she thought she felt the balcony shaking. She smiled and KaLeah patted her lightly on the back. Elektra and Colt commented on the success of her speech and her generosity.

Amirra felt happy knowing nobody else had to die. Well, almost nobody.

☣

Many days passed.

Amirra's soldiers and the Denlerack invaders, who had completely surrendered, spent the days cleaning and rebuilding.

Hilip kept her updated on the percentages of men who wanted to return compared to how many wanted to stay. It turned out that more of the Denlerackian men wanted to stay here, with them, under a female leader, than return to their desolate, lonely wasteland of a planet.

Even though Amirra hadn't had time to plan her speech to them, she understood they had all been under the command of one man and hadn't destroyed her home on their own. She also didn't want to punish her own men by having them do the clean-up and rebuilding alone. Everything was working out as she'd hoped.

She watched the activity from her window. Her chambers hadn't been damaged, so she was able to sleep comfortably in her own bed. But the walk through the hallways to her room had been at first blocked by stone, and then bits of glass and debris. It was cleaned first, so she could rest comfortably and help the staff plan the celebration dinner.

She would host the event after she released the Denlerack soldiers who wanted to return home. However, they may not be as enthusiastic about their mode of transportation. Amirra planned to keep all of the remaining ships on Naldash. The Denlerackian soldiers would have to return to their planet by way of blue dragon fire. She smiled to herself thinking about how scared they would be.

The night of their departure, and of the celebration festivities, had come.

By the smiles on the soldier's faces, they didn't seem to

mind leaving their dictator behind. They shook hands with the Belarone soldiers and slapped each other's backs as they bid their farewells.

Working so closely together cleaning up and rebuilding the castle seemed to have helped them all bond. They'd had time to discuss their differences, realizing that their troubles were really all the same.

They had friends, family, wives, or girlfriends to support, and even children. They felt misunderstood and an enormous pressure to be men in a world that would never allow them to achieve the position of top man because Keldon held that role.

General Daven shared stories with her and KaLeah about how the men had forged new friendships, reaching points of understanding and camaraderie that even he had not expected.

The young queen had expected it, to a degree. Just because they were men did not mean they did not have struggles and emotions. They needed to feel heard and understood, just like anyone else. They needed a chance.

And she had given them that chance.

Keldon was heavily guarded in the bottom of the castle, deep in the dank dungeons. But she was still nervous about him being alive. Her brother had been freed from the dungeons by men loyal to him, and she didn't know how many men loyal to either of them were still lurking around, pretending to cooperate. She hoped that it was very few but even a few could do a lot of harm.

Amirra paced her suite the night of the celebration dinner, considering various options for ensuring the dictator could never hurt anyone again. She had already killed her brother and had watched KaLeah kill men intent on hurting her. She felt as if it should be an easy decision, especially for a queen.

He was a bad man. He was a monster. And he deserved to die.

She could order Keldon to be put to death for his

crimes against her planet. She could hand him over to the Lisodanyan king to deal with if he was still alive. She hadn't heard anything from the other kingdoms since she'd defeated the alien army.

She could just keep him locked up and stop feeding him.

It was frustrating how difficult of a decision it was for her. She had already killed her brother, a prince, to save her friend, so it didn't matter what the people in her kingdom thought of her. There was no going back to being a sweet and innocent princess.

She was now a fierce leader. She, Ash, KaLeah, and Elektra had all stopped an interstellar invasion, but she knew this wouldn't be enough.

The kings and people of Lisodanya and Extelli would see her as weak and come for her if she didn't take firm action against the invader. Her own father had Lamone killed for his treachery.

A shiver ran down her spine.

She was expected to bid the Denlerackian soldiers farewell, entertain favors and soldiers during the celebrations, and make a decision regarding the fate of Keldon that evening.

She knew that her father would not hesitate to execute Keldon. "I don't want to do things just because my father did them," she said to her empty room, needing to hear her own voice. "I don't want to make decisions out of fear or hatred. I don't want to be like the men before me."

She was suddenly very tired and sat down on her sofa, sinking into the cushions.

Amirra drifted off into a light nap until a tapping at the door woke her up. Dohori arrived to say that the soldiers were nearly done cleaning up and the ballroom was set up to host the celebration.

"They will need you dressed and on the balcony to pardon and release the Denlerackian soldiers," Dohori said, passing along instructions from the general. "Once they are gone, you'll welcome the favor families, generals, and soldiers to the ballroom for the festivities. Of course, some of the men will stay behind to guard the castle."

Dohori explained the protocols and then the nurse helped her wash and dress in an elegant black gown.

"I think I am done mourning, Dohori," she said, looking herself over in the tall mirror. "I think it is time to wear something other than black. How about the pink ballgown with the white sash?"

"Right away, Your Highness." Dohori scampered off to the retrieve the gown from the closet.

Once the queen was dressed, she took a deep breath, feeling a sense of relief. She felt lighter, somehow. She knew there was still a lot for her to deal with, but she wanted to do it on her own terms and as a young woman moving forward.

Two soldiers escorted her from her room and across the castle to the balcony above the entrance. It was the same balcony where the dragon spirit had protected her and sealed her fate as the queen.

She walked out onto the balcony as the sun was setting. She was greeted by cheers and applause that warmed her as much as the fading sun on her cheeks.

Favor KaLeah, General Daven, and the Denlerack friends Elektra and Colt were already waiting there for her. General Array was also there, and he gave her a smile and a wink.

"My kingdom," she said, extending her arms to welcome her people. "Although we suffered casualties, we did not suffer a defeat. We have come out of this victorious thanks to our soldiers, our generals, our friends from Denlerack, and the dragon spirits. Belarone is an old and fierce kingdom, built on tradition and loyalty to its people. We have not shown mercy to our enemies of past. We have not extended peace to those who would do us harm." She paused to take a deep breath.

"But I do not come to you today as a man king. I do

not come to you as a traditionalist. I am here before you as your queen and vow to always lead by my heart. To look down upon women because they make decisions based on their heart or their emotions is as silly as assuming that men do not also have these things. The men around me are the strongest men I have ever known, and they make decisions on logic, strategy, and heart. Their hearts are the strongest because they belong to warriors.

"As you learn to embrace me as your queen, do not think that ruling by the heart means that I do not rule by the mind. Do not think I am any different from the good, strong, male rulers who have come before me. I promise to be even better. I promise to help you all see things in ways that you never have before.

"The Denlerackian men who stand among you did not come to attack us of their own free will. Their leader sits and awaits your judgement in our dungeons. But these men have helped restore our castle and restore the damage they have done.

"Some of these men have sworn to leave and only to return in peace, if they should return at all. I will show them mercy and allow them to return home."

There were cheers from the crowd, and she watched as Belarone soldiers shook hands and patted the backs of their new Denlerackian friends.

"Some of these men have found a home among us here and will choose to stay, joining our army to ensure continued peace for Belarone."

Again, more cheers rose up, even louder than the first.

"For those who are returning to Denlerack, our dragon spirit, Anissa La Alani, awaits you in the gardens. Join her and she will transport you home. Take word of our mercy so it may buy us favor and help us all avoid this situation again."

Amirra stood and waited, KaLeah and Hilip standing close behind her, while the soldiers turned to one another, puzzled and slightly frightened.

"Do not fear our dragon spirit," Amirra called out. "She has transported my friend in the same way, and you will make it home safely, I swear."

The men slowly began to leave the courtyard and head toward the gardens. Amirra saw Ash appear there, sitting near a fountain. One by one, the dragon blew blue flames over the men, and they disappeared as the sun was setting.

"How do you feel?" KaLeah asked.

"I feel good," Amirra said. "In a way, I feel like a hero."

"You are," Hilip said, smiling.

"But what if another leader rises that wants to invade Naldash again?" Amirra asked, too exhausted to do all of this again.

This time, Elektra and Colt stepped forward. They both bowed to her like soldiers.

"We will create a regime of rebels and ensure that doesn't happen," Elektra said. "It will become our mission now that we have rid the world of Keldon."

Amirra's heart sank. "But Keldon is still here. Alive. We haven't really rid the worlds of him."

She saw KaLeah and Elektra exchange looks.

"What do you normally do with war prisoners?" Elektra asked.

"Her father, King Erazus Belarone, rest his soul, would sentence some to death for treason against the crown and kingdom," General Daven said.

They all turned their eyes to the queen, and her nostrils flared as she took in a deep breath. She absolutely wanted to sentence the man to death, but she didn't think she could make the decision alone.

"KaLeah," she said, turning to the woman who was like a sister to her. "He is your father. I cannot take any action against him without your involvement."

KaLeah turned and looked off toward the Belarone forest and then up at the dark orb of Denlerack.

"I had many chances to kill him in his own home," KaLeah said. "I held our friend Felisha as she bled out from a wound he had given her. I saw the death and destruction he caused here and know he would have killed me if I had gotten in his way. And yet, I don't know if I can agree to kill him, even now. It feels as if I am agreeing to have a piece of me killed."

Hilip placed a hand on her shoulder, and she continued.

"I know the right thing, the traditional thing, would be to have him put to death. I know that. And still, I cannot support it."

Amirra nodded, understanding. "I wouldn't have been able to kill my brother if he hadn't been about to kill you. I only threw that dagger out of fear of losing you."

"Nikolat was the type of person who could kill his own family. You are nothing like him," KaLeah said, reassuringly.

"I know," Amirra said, nodding. "So, we leave him to rot in the dungeon, then?"

Everyone on the balcony was quiet, looking around as if someone else could make this decision.

"Maybe not," KaLeah said. "Maybe Ash can find another planet to send him to. One that has no technology. One that has no people for him to command and manipulate. A planet with just enough food and water for him to survive on."

"There are other planets?" Amirra asked, looking up into the sky again.

"There may be countless ones, Your Majesty," Elektra said, smiling.

Countless planets? Amirra couldn't imagine such a wonder.

"Your Majesty, the ballroom is filling up with guests," said a soldier, stepping onto the balcony and bowing.

"Right," Amirra said. "Let's go celebrate our victory, my friends. We can talk more about this later."

KaLeah and Hilip escorted her through the back entrance of the ballroom, while the others went in through the main entrance.

Amirra sat on her throne and looked out among the crowd. The room was alive with music, dancing, laughing, and the smells of food and drink.

Amirra could feel her dark mood lifting. Lights were hung low, strung across the ballroom. Everyone was dressed in their best. Her cheeks started to burn from smiling so much.

Her friends went off to enjoy themselves, while favors and soldiers came up to bow, curtsy, and say their thanks for her leadership.

A petite girl came up with long, red hair, and a deep blue dress.

She curtsied and Amirra smiled at her. The girl had freckles splattered across her cheeks.

"Hello Queen Amirra, I am Tasis, daughter of Favor Aris Ardatu."

"I know you," the queen said, remembering the girl from the dining hall. "I thought you were a servant here."

"My father does have me work here, yes. Since my mother has been gone for many years, and I have no younger siblings to care for, it is better for my family if I work in the castle from time to time."

"I see. You look to be the same age as me."

"I was born the same year, yes," Tasis said.

"My father used to say I was born on the day the sun didn't rise." Amirra felt a nostalgic sadness begin to creep in, remembering her father who should be here celebrating with them.

"I have heard that. It was because of the loss of your mother," Tasis said, a respectfully sad tone to her voice.

"Yes. I suppose we have that in common." Both girls of the same age, both growing up without mothers.

"My father never found another woman, and so he has raised me alone," Tasis said. "I know how to sword fight and swim and even ride draggots, even though we only have one very old one."

Queen Amirra sat up a little straighter.

"You sword fight and ride draggots? But that is unheard of for a girl."

"Yes, I know, I'm sorry," Tasis said, her cheeks turning red. "I wasn't supposed to tell anyone."

A man with bushy red hair and a red beard came up beside Tasis, bowing to the queen.

"Your Highness, I apologize for my daughter. I am sure she has worn out her welcome and thanked you for your leadership. We will take our leave."

"No, wait," Amirra said. "You have taught her to fight with a sword, ride draggots, and I assume read books?"

The man's cheeks flushed as he cast a sharp look at his daughter. The girl looked embarrassed, but he looked fearful.

"I do apologize," he said, bowing low. "I did not know how to raise a girl. I have made terrible mistakes."

"Not at all," the queen said. "I find it refreshing that you allow her to do these things. My father also allowed me to learn these things. If he had not, I'm not sure I would be sitting on this throne today. I would love for you to bring her to the castle so we may read and spar and even ride draggots together. I believe Tasis and I could be great friends."

The man stood up straight and his jaw dropped. Tasis beamed.

"Father," she said, nudging him out of his shock.

"Yes, of course. Yes, I would be honored to bring my daughter to the castle as your friend. We would be honored."

He bowed again, very low.

"I shall see you both soon then, Favors Aris and Tasis Ardatu." She nodded a dismissal for them, and they scampered away hand-in-hand.

I am going to have a friend, she realized, feeling elated.

Her eyes found KaLeah and Hilip, laughing together on the dance floor. Looking at them made her feel lonely because she knew she was losing them to each other. So, the idea of having a real friend her age to spend time with, made her feel excited with anticipation.

KaLeah was not quite a sister and yet, more than just a friend. She wanted the young woman to be happy, but knew she had her own life to live outside of the castle. Amirra couldn't keep KaLeah around forever.

Elektra and Colt seemed to be a couple also, she realized, watching them walk up to KaLeah and Hilip. She was jealous for a moment, not being a part of their conversation. But then she spotted Tasis across the floor and smiled.

She had made a new friend.

❧KaLeah❦

"You don't need me for that," KaLeah said, arguing with Elektra. Colt and Hilip stood beside each of them, listening.

"But I think we do," Elektra said. "If we go back without Keldon, then another rich man is going to try to stand in for him and setup the same factories, the same problems. If you come back with us, as Keldon's only child and heir, you inherit his fortune and can do *real* good with that money. We have blueprints for more diamond districts. We can make sure every person gets a chance to live in a self-sustaining community. Every child will have food and clean water."

Elektra grabbed KaLeah's shoulders and looked her directly in the eyes, her passion for saving her planet intense. "For people who are doubtful or pushback, they will be more accepting if it is Keldon's daughter telling them to embrace the change."

KaLeah looked at Hilip's sweet face and light blue eyes. She wasn't ready to leave him behind and yet, she knew what Elektra was saying made sense. If she arrived on Denlerack as Keldon's heir, inherited his fortune and lands, she could help make that world a better place.

"This is the only home I've ever known," KaLeah said. She loved Naldash. She loved the trees and mountains, the air that was actually breathable, and Amirra and Hilip were here.

"But you can come back to visit anytime," Elektra said. "You will own and command all of the ships."

"What about the queen?" KaLeah asked.

Elektra and Colt exchanged glances while KaLeah looked over at Amirra sitting alone on her throne. The girl looked so small, and KaLeah already felt guilty about leaving her the first time she went to Denlerack.

"Why don't you two go back and take over Keldon's fortune?" she asked them.

"Because we are rebels," Elektra explained. "The people will only ever see us as thieves. You are his daughter. And because you have never had the same desire for riches, you won't become corrupted by it. You'll do the right thing. You'll be the richest woman in the world. In both worlds."

KaLeah felt uncomfortable about the idea and had the sudden urge to talk to Clegg, the man who had raised her as his daughter. She looked around, wondering if he was at the celebration, but then took her attention back to the queen.

"She will be so sad if I leave her again," KaLeah said.

"Let's go talk to her about it," Elektra suggested.

A warrior, a soldier, a runaway, and a rebel, headed to the far end of the ballroom to see the queen. Amirra was sitting in a pink dress on the dragon carved wooden throne. The young girl sat up straighter when she saw them approaching.

They bowed and curtsied together.

"My friend," KaLeah started. She got right to the point. "I have inherited my father's fortune. They wish me to return with them to Denlerack to use his money to help rebuild their communities."

Amirra was quiet while she looked them all over.

"I understand," she said. "You have been like a sister

to me from the day you rescued me in the woods, but I know you have a greater calling than to be my bodyguard. I think the worst is behind us now."

"Your Majesty," General Daven said, taking a step forward to stand slightly in front of KaLeah. "With your permission, I would like to take some of my men and go with her. I think it would be wise to learn more about this planet, for you to have a presence and a voice in what goes on there, and..."

He turned to look at KaLeah and she felt a lump in her throat. "I desire to be by KaLeah's side, always. I can't stand to watch her leave again."

KaLeah's cheeks burned as this hero among men stood before her and professed his love.

Had she really ever seen him? She had been so blinded by feigned love she couldn't believe how close she'd come to almost missing the real thing.

She became dumbly aware of the painful smile on her face and Hilip's own smile as he stared at her and waited for both ladies to respond.

A nervous laughter burst from her lips and soon Hilip and Amirra were laughing too.

Hilip took KaLeah's hands in his. "KaLeah, I've wanted to know you since the moment I first saw you. And somewhere between the lessons, battles, kidnappings, dragons, and invasions, I fell in love with you."

KaLeah felt completely stunned hearing the words that she didn't have to beg for. This man just loved her without her having to chase him or try. And she admired him beyond words.

"Please allow me to escort you to Denlerack and anywhere else you may travel to for the rest of your days. I need to be your man, your partner, in all things, forever. If you'll have me."

All she could do was smile and nod at him, while tears stung the corners of her eyes. It was a strange new feeling for her. Luckily, he leaned in and kissed her before the tears had a chance to fall.

When they pulled apart, she saw that Amirra's small hand was over her mouth. She swallowed and took a deep breath, removing her hand to speak.

"As much as I don't want to see either one of you leave, it looks like that's what is happening. A broken-hearted general will be no good to me here," Amirra said. "I will miss you both so, so much."

She stood up and ran to them, wrapping her arms around their waists as they pulled her in and hugged her back.

"I don't want you to go," Amirra said to them, "but I love and support you in going. You will always have my love and support."

❧Amirra❧

"Are you sure that you can do this alone?" KaLeah asked.

Queen Amirra was standing in a blood red dress on the bright green castle lawns late afternoon on the following day. The new day had brought with it a maturity she had never known. After everything she'd been through, she was now ready to be a queen.

"I am ready," she told KaLeah.

The girls were holding hands, standing in front of a black spaceship. Hilip and KaLeah had packed their things onto the ship, and Elektra, Colt, and Rustin had already fired up the engines. A few of their friends had already headed back to Denlerack in the flying crafts or been transported through Ash's flames.

"I am really proud of you," KaLeah said, squeezing her hands. "I'll never forget the day I pulled you out of that sack in the woods. Or when I met your father for the first time! He was so scary."

Both girls laughed together, sharing memories.

"I thought you were so peculiar and yet so remarkably untamed. I wanted to be just like you," Amirra admitted.

"Well, you have turned out even better and so much stronger," KaLeah said.

"Will we see each other again, sister?" Amirra asked, feeling her eyes begin to fill with tears.

"I promise that once we are settled on Denlerack, I will come back and visit. We are family, after all."

Amirra nodded. "We are family."

KaLeah pulled Amirra into a hug, squeezing her tightly and kissing the top of her head. After a few long moments, she released her and backed away toward the ship.

"I love you, little sister," KaLeah said before she turned and climbed up the ramp.

Amirra knew she would always love her too. The woman had saved her in so many ways.

"We should step back, Your Majesty," advised General Array, the man who would become her new closest guardian.

The ship fired up its engines and began to lift off.

She let the general walk her back toward the courtyard, turning around just in time to watch the ship head off toward the clouds.

"Dragon's speed, sister. And may Anissi La Alani keep you safe."

"We have the prisoner, and the dragon is waiting," General Array informed her.

"Good. Take me inside. I'm ready."

The general escorted her into the castle, up the main staircase, and out onto the balcony. She walked to the edge and placed her delicate pale fingers on the balcony railing.

"Where are you taking me?" Keldon yelled out, his voice echoing across the courtyard.

Soldiers drug Keldon from the castle, across the cobblestone, and stood him right below the balcony before the queen. General Array stood behind her with his hand on his sword. With Hilip leaving, the fierce General Zoseff

Array had promised to never leave her side, except for when she was safe in her chambers.

The dark-skinned, loud, and giant of a man had always felt like a second father or uncle to her, so she was happy to have him looking out for her safety from now on.

"Oh, hello child princess," Keldon said, looking up and noticing her.

The sun was setting, and the balcony was already lit up with candles.

"Dayne Keldon of Denlerack. You are found guilty of launching an invasion against our beloved lands. You have lost and now you must suffer the fate you deserve."

"So, it's to be death then? I can handle that." The man who was held back by soldiers tried to puff out his chest defiantly.

Ash materialized in front of him, using her wings to slowly float down to the ground.

His eyes went wide, and he took a step back from her, looking her over from head to tail.

"What is this? What kind of magic is this?" he yelled.

Ash opened her jaws and blew bright blue flames over Keldon. His entire body was covered and began to disappear.

Amirra had decided that instead of killing him, she would have Ash send him to a far off and uninhabited world.

Having no one to control would be the worst fate for a man like that, Amirra presumed. She smiled as she watched him vanish into nothing.

EPILOGUE: SPIRITS

❧Elektra❧

"I dedicate this district to the people of Sarda. May you never again know hunger or thirst. May your families thrive."

Elektra smiled wide and she cut the red ribbon at the entrance. The crowd cheered and slowly began to move into the completed diamond district, carrying their few possessions with them.

She watched Rustin and Lina ushering them forward, giving directions and instructions. Food was already growing, and water was flowing, but the people needed lessons on how to maintain their new home.

"Congratulations, Elektra," Colt said, leaning in and kissing her on the cheek.

"Congratulations to you," she said. "I still can't believe how quickly we were able to accomplish this build."

"Well, it was clever of you to reduce the size for a smaller community. Once we have this one up and running, the others will come together just as quickly. People can see how successful this one is and begin replicating the builds across the planet."

"One more of these and we can house all of Sarda," she said, looking over at the Morbel diamond district where her mother lived.

"She didn't come," she said, disappointed.

Colt pulled her in close, wrapping his arms around her.

"I'm sure she just got busy."

"Elektra!"

"Mom?"

Elektra pulled away from Colt and saw her mother walking across the dirt, wearing a thick mask to protect her from the polluted air. She was lovely; petite with her light brown skin and dark brown curls bouncing with every step. It made her so happy to see her mother's hair look natural like hers again.

She ran to her and hugged her tight.

"You came!"

"I'm sorry, I had to wait for Denny to get back from work. I didn't want to bring your brother out into this air."

"I understand," Elektra said, rubbing her mom's soft arms with her hands. Although her mother hadn't ever protected her to the extent she had her brother, Elektra was comfortable with who she had turned out to be.

Most of Denlerack saw Elektra as a hero now. She had brought back the rightful heir, destroyed the factories that polluted their air, and convinced KaLeah to spend her father's money on making the entire world livable again.

"Elektra, this is just magnificent," Zatia said, looking at the new mini-district.

"I can't believe you and your friends did this. I am so proud of you. I hear stories about you now and it's as if I am hearing about a legend and not my daughter."

Elektra smiled, soaking in the praise.

"And to think, it never would have happened if you hadn't come and let us out of jail!" Colt said, reminding them all.

The three of them burst into laughter and they hugged again while they admired the new community building.

"If you two aren't busy, I'd love to have you up to the apartment for dinner."

Colt took Elektra's hand in his and smiled at her, warmly.

"We would love to, mother," Elektra said.

❧Amirra❨

The queen was in a crisp white riding outfit with pink ruffles at the sleeves and neck. Her pants were so wide they looked like a long skirt when she stood up but parted easily so she could sit properly on her white draggot.

Tasis was dressed similarly, except her outfit was a baby blue and she rode on a golden brown draggot.

The air smelled like spring, with floral blooms sending fragrances across the fields and lawns.

"I win," Amirra said, teasingly.

"Well, I wasn't racing. I was just enjoying the ride and fresh air."

"Tasis, everything is a race. You must at least try to beat me sometimes."

"You mean you want me to try and poke you with a sword during practice when General Array is watching? I think not."

The girls laughed.

"Let's have a picnic," Amirra suggested.

"Here? But we haven't brought food."

As if on cue, two men came riding up with their draggots carrying baskets. They laid out a large blanket and set food, drinks, plates, and utensils out for the girls. Then, the men helped the young girls dismount from their tall draggots.

"Have you always lived so lavishly?" Tasis asked.

"Not always. There was a time when I slept in the forest, drank water from a canteen, and ate the forest creatures that KaLeah killed for me. Of course, that only lasted for a few days before I was back home again."

"Wow," said Tasis, her mouth hanging open. She shook her head. "I forget that you aren't just a girl. I forget you have had so much hardship already. I have only had one loss and yet you have suffered so many."

The queen sat down, crossed her legs, and lifted a glass to her lips. A sweet, light pink wine lifted her spirits.

"I think we have a choice. We can either be defined by the hard things that have happened to us or we can define how we choose to see ourselves afterwards. I was sad and scared for a very long time. But now, with a new friend, a castle, a home, and a responsibility to be a good leader to my people, I have found happiness and purpose."

"I have helped you find purpose?" Tasis asked.

Amirra admired the girl's red hair and freckles. Her eyes were always so pleasantly attentive and curious, and she genuinely cared about her.

"I don't think it is good for anyone to go through life alone. Here, as the only young woman in a world of men, I felt very alone without a companion who was like me. You know me and understand me, and so, that gives me purpose. You give me a reason to be seen as a person and not just as a queen."

Tasis reached across the picnic blanket and took Amirra's hand.

"You are more than a queen. You are my very, very dear friend and I love you."

Tears stung Amirra's eyes.

"Thank you for being my friend. I love you too."

❧KaLeah❧

She watched Clegg Trapper command men at her newly acquired compound. Seeing him in his element made everything come together for her.

The man who raised her was not a bad man; he had just

not been a good father. He wasn't meant to be a father.

Clegg was a soldier, and now, he was the general to her new army. He listened to her, as the new ruler of Denlerack, and as the richest woman in two worlds. He led the soldiers through a massive cleanup and began organizing humanitarian trips to the underground villages and through the city slums.

KaLeah ensured the money was used to provide food, water, and resources people needed to start creating their own grow operations or expand existing operations, housing, and water collection and treatment centers.

Elektra, Colt, and their friends were leading the mission to build more diamond districts, and having the gates and guards removed from existing structures.

There was resistance, at first. Nobody in the districts wanted to share their resources with anyone from the dirty slums. Elektra was able to build relationships on both sides, showing people how much more prosperous we could all be if we helped one another.

Having money for even more resource construction didn't hurt either.

"There you are," Hilip said, walking toward her. She was standing in the foyer of the mansion, and he had just come in from the dust.

"You should be wearing a mask if you are heading out there," he said.

"So should you," she said back at him.

"I know. I guess neither one of us has gotten used to them yet," he admitted.

"Hopefully when those trees we planted start to grow bigger, the air quality will start to improve."

"It would be nice to breathe fresh air by the time our children are born," Hilip said, winking.

KaLeah's cheeks turned red.

"Our children?" she asked, eyebrows rising on her forehead.

He smiled and laughed, pulling her in close.

"Eventually, I hope."

"Eventually," she agreed. "We have a lot of work to do, first."

"Work, work, work," he said, teasingly. "Let's go play a little while everyone else is out saving the world."

He pulled her in close and kissed her deeply, wordlessly promising more. Taking her hand, he walked her back into her mansion.

KaLeah was ready to love him. She was ready to trust him. He was the hero she didn't even know she needed in a world where it was acceptable for her to be a hero too.

❧Anissa La Alani (Ash)☙

Ash had never felt more fulfilled than when she was watching the three young women make their way in the worlds they had saved. They were finding themselves and they were finding love.

They found purpose and happiness, and Ash beamed with pride.

She flew often between the worlds. Lifting off unseen from Naldash, soaring out across the stars, and then through the thick, dusty clouds of Denlerack.

She watched Elektra and Colt building homes. She watched KaLeah organizing out-reach excursions to ensure no one was starving on the planet she had inherited.

But she didn't like seeing them roaming around without masks. Every time they coughed from the pollution, she worried about what it was doing to their bodies.

Inside the diamond districts and inside the mansion on the compound, the girls could breathe the cleaner air that was recycled and filtered through pipes. It was engineering she didn't fully understand. But outside the protection of those areas, her young friends were susceptible to pollutants on Denlerack.

She saw the differences in the planets very clearly. Naldash was lush and beautiful while Denlerack was starving and dying. In some small way, she felt like it was her fault. She had been the one who split the planets and sent them on their individual trajectories.

Ash beat her transparent wings, kicking up dirt and dust all around her. She was sad about the condition of Denlerack and wondered how many years it would take for KaLeah and Elektra to make a real difference.

Is it too late, she wondered? *Will the planet ever really recover from the damage?*

You can do it.

She heard the words as if placed inside her mind, but the voice was unfamiliar. She had seen and heard dragon spirits before, but normally it was during a battle of some sort, and it was the angry ones sending messages of blood and war.

This was a very new experience.

I can do what? she asked the mysterious voice.

Save the world.

Ash spun around in the air, looking all around her for someone possibly playing a trick on her.

She had already done so much to help support the humans in saving their worlds, she didn't see how she could possibly do anything more. It was all up to them at this point.

It's time for magic. It's time for sleep. It's time for you to show them who you really are, Ash.

She dropped down to the ground, landing hard on Denlerack's surface.

It was her mother's voice. She knew it. She recognized the way her nickname sounded.

Sleep. What did that mean? Did she have the magic?

As if in response, there was a tingle in her feet as her energy connected to something deep below the ground.

Was it water? Was it something trying to grow?

She looked into the sky and realized her magic was elemental, and that this planet was missing vital elements.

Ash suddenly understood she had the power to send all

of the pollution, all of the smoke, smog, and dirt away. But more than that; she had the power to help the world grow again.

She could create water sources, grow trees and grass, grow fields of food, and restore the entire planet.

But it would cost her.

It would cost her the immortal existence she had known since the day she had first split the worlds apart.

And she also knew she was ready. She was ready to finally sleep. It was time for all of the dragon spirits to sleep.

Ash took a deep breath and dug her talons into the dirt. She pushed her blue flames up into the sky, grabbing all the thick clouds and transporting them out into space. Then, she sent her energy deep into the ground, letting it spread wildly and freely through every speck of dirt and rock.

She thought that giving her life to the planet would be painful. She expected her bones and veins to ache. But instead, there was a warmth underneath her scales that became more and more comfortably warm, lulling her into a calm state.

Her life force, her magic, all flooded into the world around her, and she felt euphoric. The green faded from her scales, and she watched as green grass and trees began to sprout up all around her. She watched her blue flames burn off the clouds blocking the sky and sun. And then the blue transferred into a bright blue sky when the sun hit it, sending rays of sparkling heat across her scales.

As she faded away and into the world around her, everything became more and more beautiful. She saw springs of water pop up from underground and turn into rivers and streams, pooling into lakes.

She had never felt more pride and happiness than in that moment.

This is what I was meant to do.

She watched as the fog of dragon spirits dissipated. All except for one.

A single dragon stood on the land in front of her, as if

she had been waiting for a very long time.

Ash.

Mother.

The sun's rays reached the ground of Denlerack, and everything was immediately brighter. The sound of flowing water from underground springs filled the land.

Ash and her mother drifted up into the sky. From a distance she could see Elektra holding her baby brother in her arms near her mother's apartment window.

Elektra gasped.

"Look," she said. "Everyone, come look! You can see the sky. The clouds are gone. The skies are clear."

Ash saw KaLeah in her bedroom in the mansion. She and Hilip stood near the window, together.

Tears filled KaLeah's eyes as she looked out and into the sky.

"The skies have cleared," Hilip said, amazed.

"And look, we can see Naldash. We can see our home."

Ash followed her mother's spirit into the black space between the two planets.

Is it almost time, mother? she asked.

Almost, my love. One last goodbye and then we become one with the stars.

Ash saw the queen then, having a picnic on the castle lawns with her new friend Tasis. The young redhead pointed up to the sky.

"Look," she said. "Does Denlerack look different to you?"

Amirra saw what Ash could see. The dark planet was coming alive. There were now greens and blues replacing the dark brown colors of the planet.

Amirra smiled.

"They figured out a way to save it," Amirra exclaimed, breathlessly.

"Who?" Tasis asked.

"My sisters," Amirra said, looking up at the dead planet as it came back to life.

And then Ash and her mother joined the other dragon spirits, turning into stars.

ABOUT THE AUTHOR

Tiffany Nicole Terry (TNT to her friends) is a corporate communications manager by day, a novelist by night, and a mother to daughters and dogs every moment in between. A bit of a bohemian nomad, she has lived in every time zone in the continental United States but prefers to live where she can see mountains on the horizon. She is passionate about equality, diversity, and inclusion and believes the world can be a kinder and more sustainable place. Her books are full of positive empowerment messaging for girls, especially those raised through trauma, neglect, and abuse.

FROM THE AUTHOR

I wasn't ready to tell my story at 15, at 22, at 26 or 35. It wasn't until I'd left an abusive marriage, was a single mom working full time, had lost my dream of having a fairytale life, and was journaling 100,000 words a year while I tried to make sense of it all at 38, that things clicked for me. I tried writing my story so many times but failed because I didn't understand why I needed to write it.

I now know I need to reach young girls and young women, so they don't repeat generational patterns of abuse. Instead of creating stories where the girls fall for bullies and abusers (like their fathers or through lack of good father figures), I'm determined to show young readers how to choose themselves and how to reject toxic people. We can be heroes in our own lives.

If you enjoyed this book, please leave a review, and spread the word. Help me reach more people who need this message. Thank you!

Love, TNT

9 789898 649502 6